GATES
OF HELL

ISBN-13: 978-1-63696-278-8

ISBN-10: 1-63696-278-5

Cover design by: Damonza

Printed in the United States of America

www.righthouse.com

www.instagram.com/righthousebooks

www.facebook.com/righthousebooks

twitter.com/righthousebooks

USA TODAY **BESTSELLING** AUTHORS

BLAKE BANNER DAVID ARCHER

GATES OF HELL

A **ROGUE** THRILLER

R

RIGHTHOUSE

ONE

I opened my eyes. First I saw the ocean at the end of South 4th Place: blue and still. Then I saw the windshield, right up close, and the steering wheel and the dash. Then I saw the dry blood on my hands. That was when I realized I didn't know who I was.

I opened the door of the truck and stumbled out. I saw it was a white Dodge RAM 1500 and walked unsteadily to the sidewalk, leaning on the hood. In front of me was a building, the side of a house, painted an ugly blue-gray. Looking at that blue-gray wall, I felt a sense of panic, wild, thrashing adrenaline burning in my gut. I turned and walked to the corner of the street. The entrance to the ugly, blue house was on Ocean Boulevard. You went up five steps situated on a small patch of lawn and there was the white front door. I stared at it and saw that it was open, just an inch.

I can't say it was a decision I made. It was more like something inside of me, something I wasn't conscious of, that was driving me forward. I moved down the short path across the patch of lawn, climbed the five steps, and pushed open the door.

The morning light behind me moved across the dark entrance hall, framing my shadow. There was a beige carpet on the floor that led down a hall on the left, where there were two doors. On the right, a staircase rose to the upper floor. There were four bloody footprints on the carpet, and on the steps I noticed bloodstains, drips, and partial prints.

I stepped inside and eased the front door closed with my heel, and when I heard it click, I moved to the first door on my left. I pulled a blood-stained handkerchief from my jeans pocket, turned the handle, and let the door swing open. It was a living room that ran the length of the house, from the front window to the glass doors that led out to the back yard. The floor was tiled and strewn with a couple of rugs. There was an old sofa beside the door with a long coffee table and a huge TV opposite. The TV was still on. At the far end, in front of the glass doors, there was a dining table with four chairs.

On the sofa there was a guy with his belly split open from side to side. His upper body was lying across the cushions, but his lower body and legs were hanging at a grotesque angle down toward the floor. The sofa was saturated from end to end with his blood. Protruding from the left side of his chest was a wakizashi, the shorter version of the Japanese katana. At the foot of the sofa, there was also a large pool of partly congealed blood.

I took a few steps around the coffee table, toward the TV, so that I could see more clearly into the dining area. A couple of the chairs had been knocked to the floor, and the table was slightly displaced. It had that look like there had been a struggle. Lying across the rug between the overturned chairs was another man. His head had been split in half down to his collarbone. It made each side of his head and each eye gaze bizarrely in a different direction. The blood from the wound had sprayed up to the ceiling and onto the walls before he died. Beside him there was an axe, the kind you might use to go camping in the mountains.

The numbness I felt inside had become almost like a pain in itself. I backed away, out into the hall, but instead of leaving the house and getting away from that place, I climbed the stairs, going deeper into the nightmare. There were three bedrooms up there and a bathroom. I found the third body in the first bedroom. He was lying in the bed, undressed, and had a full katana driven through his solar plexus. I knew what that meant. If it had been driven through his heart, he would have died almost instantly. Driven through his solar plexus, it would split his diaphragm and make it impossible to breathe. He would not only have suffered severe agony, but death would have been through suffocation.

Somehow I knew where the next body would be. It was in the bathroom, in the bathtub. He had obviously been showering, though the shower had been turned off. The shower curtain had been pulled down. The pole was across the floor. The curtain was wrapped around him and had been tied tightly around his throat, and both his arms had been broken to stop him removing it.

A voice in my head, a voice that was calm and rational, said, "This was rage. Whoever killed these men hated them with a real passion."

That was when I turned and ran down the stairs three at

a time. I stepped out into the California sun, slammed the door behind me, and walked back to the truck. There I stood leaning against the tailgate and saw that it had Nevada plates. I looked again at the blood on my hands. Was I from Vegas, Sin City? I tried to penetrate the blackness in my mind and found only more blackness.

I climbed behind the wheel and searched the cab for some clue to who I was. There was none. I fired up the truck, spun the wheel into a U-turn, and eased out onto East Ocean Boulevard headed west. I crossed the river and at San Pedro and turned north on I-110. It was only then, as I moved from Wilmington into Carson, that I realized I knew where I was going. Though that wasn't quite right. Because if you had asked me, I would not have been able to tell you. It was almost like the truck, or my hands and feet, knew where we were going, and I was going to find out.

After about ten minutes or a little more, at Figueroa, I came off onto Martin Luther King West. I followed that east, going slowly, trying to remember, trying to see if I would remember, aware that in some dark part of my mind I knew this route. I followed it right to the end, to Hooper Avenue, where I turned left and then right and then left. There I came to a halt at the corner of Compton and East 32nd.

It was the kind of desolation you only get in Los Angeles: wide open sunny spaces where there is no soul because every living thing has been concreted over, even the people. On my left was the Emanuel Church of God in Christ. Ahead of me, the road continued straight and broad and dusty through empty industrial lots, and on my right was East 32nd Street, where the giant primary school was just another soulless industrial lot in which the raw material of humanity was shaped, conditioned, and packaged to generate revenue for the state.

On the corner there was a house. It had two floors and was painted a dirty beige under a brown gabled roof. The ground floor was faced in mock stone, and an exterior wooden staircase led to the top floor. I parked outside the house, killed the engine, and swung down. I felt in my jeans pockets and found a cell that I knew was a burner and a set of keys on a ring. I stared at them a moment, then stared up at the door at the top of the steps. I felt rather than knew that this was my house, and they were my keys.

I pushed through the gate in the rusting iron fence, passed the overflowing trashcans, and climbed the wooden steps. At the top, I stopped and looked around. Nobody was looking back. The street was empty. The whole damned neighborhood seemed to be empty.

I put the key in the lock and turned it, and the door swung open easily. I stepped inside and closed the door behind me. I was in an all-in-one living room, kitchen, and dining room. There was a sofa and a TV over by the window overlooking Compton Avenue. Directly opposite the door was the kitchen with the breakfast bar, and just below that was the small dining table with a couple of chairs. There were no books. There were no vases of flowers or photographs, and that punched a hole in my gut. I had to fight back the tears.

On my right was a short passage with a bathroom on the left and a single bedroom straight ahead. I moved down and through the bedroom door. Dusty light was leaning through a window in the right hand wall. The bed was made. The room was neat and clean. There was a built-in wardrobe and beside it a chest of drawers. At the foot of the bed, against the wall, allowing a narrow passage, was a small desk.

The chest of drawers revealed only jeans, shirts, underwear, and socks. The closet had a couple of jackets, one black leather and one linen, a good suit, boots and shoes, and a large box containing two revolvers and a semi-automatic, each in its own holster. Beneath them was a suppressor. I knew what the guns were before I examined them. The revolvers were classic Smith and Wessons. The smaller one was a .357 chambered for a magnum cartridge. The larger, a full foot in length, was the 29 with a 6.5" barrel, chambered for the .44 magnum.

The thought passed through my mind as I took the weapons from the box that revolvers were useful weapons. They were simple, reliable, and accurate. They required a minimum of maintenance, and they didn't leave shells behind. It was true they had almost a third of the magazine capacity of some semis, but—and I found myself smiling at the thought—all you had to do was not miss, and six rounds would usually do the job.

The semi-automatic was the BUL SAS II Ultralight 4.25". Twenty-seven ounces and eighteen 9 mm rounds in the magazine. I liked the super-light trigger and the efficient speed of the weapon. It was one of the most underrated guns on the market. There were a couple of boxes of rounds too. I closed the box and slid it back into the wardrobe and eased myself into a sitting position on the floor with my legs crossed.

I knew all this about guns. I had blood on my hands. Had I killed those men? The balance of probabilities said I had, but they had been rage killings, killings of hatred. When

I had looked at their faces—all but one—I had felt nothing but nausea. I had not felt hatred or triumph.

I turned where I sat and looked around the room. It told me nothing, but under the bed, I saw two sports bags. I moved over, reached under, and pulled them out. They were dense and heavy. When I unzipped them, I saw why. They were stuffed full of used bills. There must have been several hundred thousand bucks in cash in each one.

I said, "Sweet Jesus" and heard my own voice for the first time. It was a shock and made my skin run cold.

I stood and moved to the bathroom. I looked at myself in the mirror. The room seemed to rock. I stared at myself, and it was like staring at a stranger. I didn't know who I was, but I knew I killed people—and I knew I had hundreds of thousands of dollars in stolen cash under my bed.

Who the hell was I?

TWO

I MADE COFFEE AND SAT FOR A WHILE THINKING. Eventually I pulled out my cell and searched for private eyes in Los Angeles. I took my time over it. I didn't want some big agency that was hidebound by rules, but neither did I want some ex bent cop who was going to take my money, cut all the corners, and give me shit in return. Eventually I settled on The Dave Marshall Agency, a one-man show on Washington Boulevard. The guy's CV said he'd worked for the Feds for ten years, and his reviews all seemed to say the right things. So I called. The woman who answered sounded like she was smiling, wanted to mean it but didn't. I told her, "I need to see Mr. Marshall urgently."

She was still smiling when she said, "I can give you an appointment foooor..."

I cut her short. "It has to be today, this afternoon. I'm willing to pay over the odds in cash. Like I said, it's urgent."

"Oh, I see." The smile had faded. "Please hold." The line went quiet for a couple of minutes, and she came back. "Mr.

Marshall can see you at one p.m., but he can only see you for half an hour. We usually require at least—"

"I'll be there at one."

I hung up, took five grand in cash, slipped the BUL in my waistband behind my back, and stepped out into the street.

Before I climbed in the truck, I took a walk around the block. I was curious to see where I lived, but I was also half-hoping somebody would greet me with a "Hey, John!" or "Joe, how ya' doin'?" but nothing like that happened. The streets were practically empty, and the few people there were kept their eyes on the ground.

The neighborhood was a strange mix, part industrial units and part small residential pockets made up of houses dating back before the '30s. Most of them were boarded or dilapidated and uninhabited. I counted three hair salons you wouldn't want to go into unarmed, two bars—The Suspiritos de Sinaloa and the Coca Cabaña—which looked even more dangerous than the hair salons, and one liquor store. There were no grocery stores or shopping malls or any place you'd want to take your family. If you had one.

I got back to my truck after forty-five minutes and headed west on I-10 toward Marina del Rey. At Inglewood Boulevard, I turned south toward Washington Boulevard and parked outside a clothing store across the road from the Marshall detective agency. I sat and studied it for a while. If you saw the website, you'd expect it to be on the top floor of a steel and glass tower in the Financial District, but it was a two-story house with a Spanish tiled roof and oxblood walls. Downstairs was a laundry on one side and an insurance broker on the other. The Dave

Marshall Agency took up the whole top floor, and the way you got there was up an outdoor stairway from the parking lot.

I got out, crossed at the lights, and climbed the stairs to the agency.

The woman behind the reception desk was attractive, in her late thirties or early forties. She had a face that said she was intelligent. It also said she knew who I was and had made up her mind she didn't like me.

I told her, "I have an appointment to see Mr. Marshall at one."

She raised her eyebrows higher than seemed natural, pinched her mouth, and said, "Name?"

"I didn't leave a name."

"Ah, yes," she said. "You must be the gentleman who hung up before I could ask."

"It's one o'clock."

She gave me the once-over and picked up an old-fashioned telephone from her desk.

"Mr. Marshall, your one o'clock is here. Shall I send him in?" She listened to an answer I couldn't hear, then hung up and pointed to a door across the waiting room. "He'll see you now. Through there."

The office was bigger than it looked, but it was crowded with overflowing bookcases, filing cabinets, and files stacked on all available surfaces. It had one window that overlooked Washington Boulevard, and his laden desk was beside that window. Halfway down the room, there were a couple of well-used armchairs, a sofa, and a coffee table.

He stood as I came in, chewing and wiping his mouth. He was lean. He looked healthy. He held out his hand, and we shook. We sat as he swallowed, and he said, "Mr. one o'clock," and laughed. "Betty couldn't get your name."

I nodded. "That's the problem. I don't know my name. I don't know who I am."

He pushed his food to one side and sat blinking at me. "You don't know who you are? You'll need to explain that to me."

"I woke up this morning with no idea who I was. There is nothing in my house or in my car that can give me a clue, except my license plates. I don't know what I am doing in LA, where I am originally from, or anything else relevant to my identity. I need you to find out."

He narrowed his eyes, like he was calibrating me. "That sounds like a job better suited to a doctor than a private investigator."

"I'm not crazy. I just need the facts about who I am."

He spread his hands and gazed at the wall behind me, shaking his head, not in the negative but like a man putting together a random list in his head.

"Um, driver's license, credit cards, debit cards, rental contract, insurance card, car registration, tax returns, gas bill, electricity..."

He trailed off. I said, "I already told you. All I have is my license plate." I took a pen from my pocket, pulled over a jotting pad, made a note of the plate number, and pushed it across his desk. "Your website says you're ex FBI. Can you trace the plates or not?"

His eyes had narrowed still further, and he was watching me closely. When I was done, he nodded. "Yeah, I can trace your plates. Where were you when you woke up?" Before I could answer, he said, "You want a coffee? Something else?"

"Yeah, coffee would be good."

"How do you take it?"

"I don't know." I shrugged. "Black. No sugar."

He picked up the phone. "Betty, bring us some coffee, would you, honey? One for me and one black no sugar." He hung up. "You want to talk me through it?"

I thought about it. "There are things I can't tell you. I'll tell you what I can."

"You can't tell me why?"

I did something that came close to a smile. It felt odd. "I can't tell you."

He sighed. "Okay, tell me what you can."

"I woke up on South 4th Place, off Ocean Boulevard. I was in a white Dodge RAM 1500, and I had no idea who I was, what I was doing there, or how I got there. I drove home by muscle memory and found nothing in my house to show who I am. No photographs, no bills, no documents of any kind. All I have are my license plates."

He was making notes. The door opened behind me, and Betty came in carrying a tray of coffee with two cups, cream and sugar. She set it on the desk and left.

"I don't remember who I am, Mr. Marshall, but I do know that if you are going to trace my plates, you don't need to know where or when my amnesia kicked in."

He nodded a few times and dropped his pen on his pad, then sat back and crossed his arms.

"I have a reputation, a pretty good one. You know how I got it?"

"If I did, I don't remember."

He gave a snort of a laugh. "Looks like you had a sense of humor, anyway. I got my reputation for going the extra mile to protect my clients' interests. That's what I do. Now if you'll bear with me, let's put these pieces together: You're driving a truck with Nevada plates in California. There are no documents of any sort in your truck. You are living in a place where there are no clues as to who you are, no bills, no contracts, nothing, and you have come here willing, and presumably able, to pay cash. What are the chances, would you say, that this truck is yours? And what are the chances that it ain't?"

I didn't answer. It was obvious, and I had been too close to it to see it.

He went on, "I'd say that the chances of the truck being stolen are pretty high. Did you steal it? I don't know, and I don't care. But what I do care about is what you are hiring me to do. So you need to decide, are you hiring me to trace these plates, or are you hiring me to find out who you are?"

He poured coffee and slid my cup across the desk. I picked it up and sipped while he stirred sugar and cream into his. I took a second sip and set down the cup.

"Initially," I said, "I want you to trace the plates. Depending on what you find, we'll take it from there."

He nodded for a bit, drinking and watching me.

"Go to a hospital. There are treatments for amnesia. They can help you. I can get information. They can cure you."

"No. Right now I don't want to be cured. Right now I want information. How much do I need to pay you?"

He spread his hands. "Pay me a grand and I'll trace the plates. Then we'll talk."

"How long do you need?"

"I'll call you tomorrow..." He closed his eyes and shook

his head. "You haven't got a cell, have you? If you had, you wouldn't be here talking to me."

"I have a burner."

I gave him the number. When he'd finished writing it down, he gestured at it on the pad and said, "Can you see what I am getting at?"

I gave a single nod. "Are you going to pass this information to the Feds or the LAPD?"

"And tell them what? I have a guy who lost his memory and lives like Jack Reacher? If we keep heading for dystopia, there will probably come a time soon where it's illegal not to own a cell phone with a contract and a computer and be connected to the great hive in various other ways, but as of today, as far as I know, you haven't committed a crime."

"I'm just the kind of guy who could have."

He shrugged. "If you say so. All I am saying is that knowledge of who you are might not be at the other end of these plates."

I reached in my wallet and handed him a grand. I drained my coffee and stood.

"If I haven't heard from you before, I'll call you in twenty-four hours."

I stepped out of his office and stopped at the reception desk on my way out. I looked down at Betty. She looked up at me and raised her eyebrows.

"May I help you?"

"Mr. Marshall said he thought perhaps I had a sense of humor. Do you think he was right?"

Her cheeks colored, and she blinked furiously for a couple of seconds. "I am sure I have absolutely no idea!"

I smiled, turned, and left. On the way down the stairs

into the parking lot, I kept smiling. Maybe he was right after all. Maybe I had had a sense of humor.

I TOOK the RAM and drove down toward the beach. It was warm and sunny, and I was hungry. My body was asking for a steak sandwich and a cold beer. I came to Santa Monica and found a parking lot on Hollister Avenue, then strolled along the beach till I found a café that called itself Masons, where I could sit and look at the ocean. I took my seat at a table on the patio, and a kid came out with floppy hair and arms you could put a Bolognese sauce on.

He recited, "Hi, how are you today? My name is Alex and I'll be your server today?" He was one of those kids who make statements like they're asking questions. He went on, "Will you be eating or just having a drink on this beautiful afternoon?"

I watched him and waited till he'd finished. When he was done, I said, "Bring me a steak sandwich and a beer."

He shifted from one hip to the other and lifted his chin. "Will that be rye, whole-wheat, mixed grain—"

"Bread."

"Yes but—"

"Bread."

"Fine, bread. And your beer, would you like mimosa, strawberry, elderberry, hard kombucha…"

He trailed off. I narrowed my eyes. "Just beer. Beer doesn't taste of fruit."

He wriggled a little where he stood. "What *does* it taste of then?"

"Beer."

"Steak sandwich on bread and beer that tastes of beer."

"That's what I want."

"Then that is what you shall have."

He spun on his heel and left. I sat looking out at the vast ocean thinking maybe I didn't have a sense of humor after all.

There was a misty haze that obscured the horizon, so the sea and the sky seemed to merge and become one. Somehow the little performance with the skinny waiter brought the question back into my mind: Who am I? Was that me? Bread and beer.

Somewhere I had read that ninety percent of our mind is unconscious. Our conscious mind is just a small ten percent poking above the surface. Did I, in that vast, dark, ninety percent, know who I was?

Something crept into my memory about a guy running through a house with hundreds of rooms, and he was frantically opening one door after another searching for himself—and he never realized he was the one searching.

I smiled out at the ocean. Who was I? I gave a small laugh. I was the one asking the question. I sat a while, enjoying that feeling. I didn't remember what had happened to me over the last thirty-odd years, but I knew who I was.

The waiter returned with his noodle-arms and set a pint of beer and a steak sandwich in front of me. He told me to enjoy it and left. I bit into the sandwich, and it was good, and I knew this was something I had always enjoyed. As I chewed, I thought about Dave Marshall. He thought I was a crook. Was I? I had to agree with him that I gave the impression of being outside the law. But when I thought about it, I didn't feel like a crook.

I pulled off half my beer and knew that was something I had always enjoyed too. I leaned back in my chair and listened to the waves thud and sigh. At that moment, a strange knowledge came into my mind—into my conscious mind. If I had killed those men, and I did not know that I had, but if I had, it had not been a crime.

I tried to follow the thought, but like the horizon between the ocean and the sky, it became hazy.

I finished my steak sandwich and drained my beer and made my way back to the RAM. Behind the wheel again, I made my way steadily back up I-10 toward Nevin and Compton Avenue. In my mind, I kept seeing the two bars I had passed that morning, the Suspiritos de Sinaloa and the Coca Cabaña. I wondered briefly if I used drugs but knew that I didn't. Yet there was an impulse in me, a drive, a drive to be in that environment where dealers hung out. And I knew beyond any doubt that I had to go and visit one of those bars that night. It didn't matter which one; it was just something I had to do. I had to go through those dark doors and see what was on the other side.

THREE

I TOOK A HALF HOUR OVER SHOWERING AND shaving. I changed into clean clothes, put the .357 under my left arm, and pulled the black leather jacket over the top. It was as I was about to step out the door that something made me turn back and go to the bed. I removed the pillow and found there a long, sleek black knife. It had a double-edged blade that tapered into a sharp point, and the handle was ridged steel. It was a dagger, a fighting knife. A Fairbairn and Sykes fighting knife.

As if by muscle memory, out of the force of what I assumed was a habit, I tucked it into my boot and strapped it to my right calf, under my jeans. Then I walked out the door and down the steps into the night.

The Coca Cabaña was only a couple of minutes' walk down the road, on Adam's Boulevard, but I took the RAM anyway. There was nothing to be gained by letting people know you lived nearby. I parked beside the door and swung down. The name was illuminated in strip lighting over the door, and as it flashed on and off, it reflected on the black-top, making it look wet and oily.

I pushed through the door and was struck by the smell of tobacco and weed. It was full and noisy, with thumping music and voices and shrill female laughter. It was dark and bigger than it looked from the outside, so that the corners were lost in gloom. The bar was on the left, on the right there were tables and chairs, all occupied, and at the back, it made a dogleg where there were nooks, couches, and big armchairs. Behind the bar there were TVs on the walls showing sports. A couple of cute waitresses were serving tables, and there were a couple of guys behind the bar.

I took that in in a second. I also took in that nobody looked at me, nobody recognized me or greeted me. I pushed my way through the groups of talking, laughing people and crossed the room, where I found a table in the corner. There I sat and ordered a beer from one of the cute waitresses. She didn't ask me if I wanted raspberry or strawberry flavor. She asked me if I wanted a hamburger, and I told her I did.

At the far end of the dogleg, they had made a kind of nook with a sofa, a big, low round table, four armchairs, and dim lamps. There was a group there who caught my eye. At the center of the sofa was a man in what looked like an expensive Italian suit. He had a paunch, olive skin, and very black hair. I put him in his fifties. He had a hooker on either side, one under each arm. Like him, they looked Mexican, or at least Latina. Unlike him, they didn't look real happy. They were trying, but they weren't making it.

There were three other men there, sitting in the armchairs. One of them was in his thirties. He had on a beige linen jacket that must have cost a thousand bucks, jeans, and

Spanish riding boots. He was slim, excessively well groomed, and had a trimmed moustache that was probably real popular in Mexico.

The other two guys looked like they belonged in LA. They were both in their thirties. One of them had a blue shirt with parrots on it, Bermuda shorts, and Havaiana sandals. He was smoking and had a glass with a complicated drink in it. The guy I had decided was his pal had a crew cut above a face like a slab of concrete. He was wearing a brown leather jacket, jeans, and the kind of leather boots you lace up. He didn't laugh much. When the others laughed, he watched them. He had that look like he was ex-special ops, maybe Russian.

When I'd finished the burger and the beer, I told the waitress to bring me a large whiskey. When she asked me which whiskey, I didn't know. My mouth said, "Bushmills" like it knew what it was talking about. "No ice."

She smiled. "The way a man drinks it, right?"

I tried a smile of my own. "Right."

As she walked away, I shifted my attention back to the group. They were drug traffickers. I had decided that, though I wasn't sure how or why. The two well-dressed guys were here from Mexico. The other two were distributors. They were closing a deal. It was all information that came into my conscious mind ready made, like somebody had emailed it into my brain. And at the same time, as I realized I knew all that, I became aware of two other things: I had come here tonight to find these people, or people like them, and I wanted to kill them.

The waitress came over with my whiskey. She gave me a wink as she set down the glass and walked away. I barely noticed. A strange feeling had come over me. The only way I could describe it was as a burning coldness. A hatred so deep it brought with it a strange kind of peace born of certainty. I realized that I knew that I was going to kill these men, one at a time, and that brought me peace. Though I had no idea why, I didn't care. All I knew was that they had to die.

It was one o'clock a.m. when they got up and started moving noisily for the door. I paid my waitress and left her a good tip, then I went out into the night and took my time getting behind the wheel of the Dodge. The gang were standing laughing, talking loudly, and shaking hands. Then the two well-dressed guys climbed into a Mercedes sedan with the two hookers, who still didn't look happy. The other two guys waved them off and got into a dark BMW. The crew cut got behind the wheel, the guy in Bermudas got in the passenger side, and as the Merc's red taillights receded west along Adams Boulevard, the BMW rumbled into life and pulled out onto the road.

He didn't drive fast. This wasn't the kind of guy who was going to draw the attention of the cops. He drove at a steady pace, playing it safe. I let him get ahead and pulled out after them.

At Hoover Street, they turned right and took the ramp onto I-10. I followed but kept a minimum of hundred yards between us. There was little traffic at that time, and no chance of losing them. I followed them all the way down to Santa Monica, and at the 11th Street overpass they came off, slowed and turned onto Lincoln Boulevard. There, nice and slow, they took a couple of bends and turns and pulled up outside a house on 9th Street. It was a nice bungalow set back from the road with a big oak tree and a palm.

I pulled up outside some kind of storehouse on the corner, sixty or seventy yards back. I killed the engine and the lights and watched them while I decided what to do.

The passenger door of the BMW opened, and Bermuda shorts got out. He was stoned and drunk and making a lot of noise, laughing. He closed the door and waved as the BMW accelerated away.

Should I follow?

No.

I watched him enter the front yard through a small gate and head toward the front door. I swung down from the RAM and covered the distance to the bungalow at a quick walk. By the time I got there, he had disappeared, but the lights were on in the house. I crossed the lawn along the crazy paving, rang the bell, and then knocked. After thirty seconds, I heard a voice. "Who is it? Whaddya want? Pete, is that you? You know what *time* it is?"

Without thinking, I said, "It's me. You left your endyha in the car."

It was a meaningless murmured noise. The kind of word it's easy to think you'd misheard something else. There was a moment's silence, then, "My *what?*"

"Come on, open up. I want to get home."

The door opened, and there was Bermuda shorts squinting at me through his THC and alcohol haze.

He said, "I left my *what?* Who the hell are you?"

I smashed him in the nose with my right fist, and as he staggered back, I stepped in and closed the door. He was bleeding profusely over his chin and his mouth, holding his nose with both hands and saying, "Oh, oh, oh..."

I pulled the .357, cocked the hammer, and put the barrel in his face.

"Are you alone? Can we talk?"

He nodded. "Who are you? I didn't do nothin'. Why...?"

"Are there any women or children in the house?"

The question surprised even me. He looked confused and shook his head. I could see in his eyes he was holding on to my question, could we talk. If we were talking, that meant he was still alive.

And if I cared about women and children, maybe he had a chance. His eyes turned pleading.

"Why'd you hit me, man? You didn't need to hit me. You didn't need to do that."

I jerked my head. "Living room."

He backed up and stumbled into a sparsely furnished room with a huge TV, a sofa, a coffee table, and more remote controls for computer games than you'd think any one person could use. There were empty beer cans and pizza boxes, and the room smelt of stale air and sweat. He was still holding his nose, and there was blood oozing through his fingers.

"Let me get some Kleenex for my nose, man." He pointed to a box of tissues on his coffee table. I nodded, and as he stuffed paper into his nostrils, I sat on the sofa and said, "Get on your knees."

He froze. "You gonna kill me?" His voice was nasal and ridiculous because of the paper. "I ain't done nothin'. I don't even know who you are, man. You don't need to kill me."

"Get on your knees. That's the second time I've told you. Don't make me tell you again."

He got on his knees. His expression was pathetic. Terror had turned him a waxy yellow color.

"Tonight you live or die. It's up to you. You cooperate, I walk away, and you never see me again. Obstruct me, lie to me, try to mislead me, hesitate too long over an answer, and I will not kill you until you beg me to. Do you understand what I am telling you? Do I need to prove I am serious?"

He was shaking his head like he'd been switched to quick motion.

"No, no," he said. "No, no, no, I will! I won't hesitate. I will cooperate. For sure, man. I ain't no hero. Just don't hurt me anymore. I'll cooperate. You have my word."

"Your word isn't worth shit."

"No, that's true. You're right. But I promise, man. I said I ain't no hero. I don't want to upset you. Whatever you want, man, that's cool."

"Who were the men at the Coca Cabaña?"

"They are heavy dudes, man. They are bad men. Very bad men. They will cut me open, do bad things—"

"Don't make me ask you twice."

"No, I am tellin' you, man! That's Don Jesus Sanchez. He was the guy in the suit. He's from the Sinaloa Cartel. He's like third in command. He controls the area of Los Mochis, in the north. He is a very powerful man. He is a real dangerous man."

"What's he doing here talking to a punk like you?"

"He is reporting direct to Zambada. You know what I'm sayin'? El Mayo. You don't wanna cross those guys."

"This is a .357 magnum. The next time you don't answer a question I am going to put a slug through your ankle, and you will lose your foot. What was he talking to you about?"

"The guys who were running distribution in LA were slacking. They were using the dope. They were no good. He wanted better distribution. So they talked to Pete. He's a real together guy, you know? Makes things happen."

"That's the guy driving the BMW?"

He nodded. "Pete called me coz he knows he can rely on me. I'm good, you know? He always calls me. And we made them an offer. We got Los Angeles. That's a lot of dough, man. *A lot* of dough. You want in? We can talk, man. I can introduce you. I can help you. I'm good."

"Pete what?"

He swallowed hard. "Pete Barta."

"You have merchandise in the house?"

He shook his head. "No."

"Are you lying?"

"No, man. No. I ain't lyin'. I swear!"

"If there is no merchandise, there must be money. You either have merchandise or you have cash. Which is it?"

"Cash. I got cash. But man, you take that cash and they will kill me, man. They will make it bad. They don't fuck around." His face was twisting, like he was going to start crying. "You don't want them to kill me, man. I ain't done nothin' to you."

"You should have stayed at school and become a doctor, like your mom told you." I grinned. He looked like he was going to be sick. I said, "I'll let you keep ten grand. Run tonight. Go east. Disappear and start a new life."

He looked at me like I was talking ancient Greek. I said, "Where is it?"

He looked over at the wall, behind the TV. "There used to be a fireplace there. There's a panel. It opens and I keep the stash, the money, everything, I keep it in there. In the safe."

"How much?"

"Five hundred?" He said it like he was asking me. "But you know more than half of that is supposed to be for buyin' more stuff. They'll punish me."

"Open it."

He got to his feet, moved the TV, and opened a panel in the wall that was practically invisible. Behind it there was a large safe set in the wall. He hesitated a moment, looking back at me. Then he turned back, entered the combination, and the safe swung open. Inside there was a sports bag which he pulled out and showed to me. There was easily half a million dollars there.

"This is peanuts," I said. "If you start working directly with Jesus Sanchez, you'll be dealing in millions. You'll be looking into money laundering and off-shore accounts."

For a moment, there was a glimmer of hope in his face. He tried to smile around the tissue in his nose. "Right?" he said.

"What's Pete's address?"

"He's got a big house on Corona del Mar, out at Palisades Park." He told me a number.

I looked into his eyes for a long moment. "What's your name?"

"Steve...?"

"Are you asking me or telling me?"

"Steve."

"Steve, how many of your customers have you watched

as they waste away, as their bodies become sick and emaciated, as their souls die and their minds shrivel?"

"Oh, God..."

"How many, Steve?"

"I don't know. I don't...you said if I cooperated. I cooperated, didn't I?"

"How many times have you lied to your customers, Steve, as you cut their heroin with talc or bicarbonate? How many lives have you destroyed, and how many lies have you told?"

"Please..."

"Do you think you deserve to continue living in this world?"

"Please..."

"Let me tell you something, Steve. Whatever thought you have in your mind when you die, the Buddhists believe that will define how you are reborn. Now here is what I would like you to do. I would like you to think back over your life, over all the really bad choices you have made, that have brought you to where you are right now, in this moment. And think, fervently, that next time, in your next life, you are going to make better choices and *give* a damn about your fellow man."

I gave him a second. He screwed his eyes shut and clenched his fists, and then I shot him in the head. His two round, startled eyes made a perfect triangle with the hole in the center of his head while his brains sprayed out the back.

For a moment I felt sorry for him, and I hoped the Buddhists were right.

I holstered my piece under my arm, took the bag of money, and left by the front door. As I walked down the still, quiet street, the only sounds were the soft tread of my boots and a single bird making a complicated song under the amber light of a street lamp. I put the money on the back seat of the truck, thinking about the other bags of money I had back at the house. You didn't need to be a genius to realize I had done this before. I wanted to ask why, but my mind shied away from the question. It was like some part of me didn't want to know why.

I climbed up behind the wheel and fired up the big engine, then did a U-turn and made my way back up I-10 toward Nevin and my dark, silent house.

FOUR

Dave Marshall sat with his elbows on his desk on either side of his morning coffee. His right fist was cupped in his left hand, and he held it before his mouth like he was praying. His eyes were fixed on the printout in the file in front of him. He did not look happy. He took a deep breath, which seemed to help him make up his mind. He picked up his cell from his blotter, scrolled through his contacts, and finally called a number. It rang a couple of times before a voice like resonant gravel said, "Dave, my man, you missin' me already? It's only been two years."

The man's laugh was like a handsaw cutting through a tree trunk.

"Elroy. You know how it is, man. I missed your ugly face so much I couldn't bear the thought of seeing you in person again."

This time the laugh was louder, more like distant, ironic thunder.

"How you doin', you son of a bitch? I hear good things

about you. You doin' all right in the field. We miss your brains around here."

"Elroy, I'm self-employed. That means I make three times as much as when I was at the Bureau, lose most of it in taxes, and I work three times harder. I think I'm still married, but I haven't seen my wife or my kids since Christmas, so I'm not sure."

"Yeah, that's the down side, man, though I think you forget how much overtime we do here. Anyhow, I hope it pays off in the long term. Now I just know you didn't call to pass the time of day. So how can I help you?"

Dave scratched his head and leaned back in his chair. "This is going to sound pretty weird, Elroy, but bear with me because as I go along, it's going to get even weirder. I had a guy come in yesterday morning. He looked rough, like he'd been through the mill. He told me he'd woken up that morning with absolutely no idea who he was. He wanted me to find out."

"Shit. You serious?"

"Deadly. Deadly being the operative word. Because he told me there was nothing in his house or in his car—a white Dodge RAM 1500 with Nevada plates—that gave the slightest clue to who he was. Zero documents—"

"Nothing?"

"Zip. You can run through the list. I did, all the way from credit cards and driver's license to rental contracts and utility bills. Nada. So the only thing he has—"

"Are the Nevada plates on the truck. But I'm guessing if he has come to you instead of some guy in Vegas, that house you mentioned which has no rental contract—or any other documents attached to it—is not in Nevada."

"You're quick, Elroy. He didn't give me his address, but I'm pretty sure it's in the LA area. So he gave me his license plate number, and I traced it."

"Right, and you're going to tell me it was stolen in Vegas. How long ago? A week?"

"Three days. But that's not all, Elroy. It gets weirder. When he came to see me, he said he'd woken up *in* the truck, and he returned to his house by a kind of muscle memory while he was driving."

"This is leading somewhere, isn't it? Okay, so hit me. Where'd he wake up?"

Dave took a deep breath and sighed. "South 4th Place, off South Ocean Boulevard. Yesterday morning."

"Shit."

"The four bodies who were found there, Elroy, is that case with the Long Beach Police Department, or has it been passed to you?"

"It hasn't come to the Bureau—yet. At the moment, it's a Long Beach homicide, but we're looking at it. Those boys were from out of town, and they all had links to Jesus Sanchez and the Sinaloa Cartel."

"Yeah, I figured as much. There may be no connection, Elroy, but the loss of memory, waking up right there on that street, in a stolen truck..." He trailed off.

"What kind of a man is he?"

"That's just it. He's tough. Not gym tough, real tough. This guy's not auditioning for a Rambo remake, but he'll give you ten K without breaking a sweat and then go six rounds with Tyson Fury."

"I hear you, but it's not a lot to go on."

"I know. That's what I thought. So I gave him coffee. I

think I've kept the cup somewhere. I might have put it in a plastic evidence bag. I'm not sure. If I have it, would you like it? You never know, you might get a hit on IAFIS or CODIS."

"Son of a bitch. Yeah, I'd like it. What do you want in return, Dave?"

"He employed me to find out who he is." He gave a small shrug. "Also, I want to satisfy my curiosity. *I* want to know who he is. It's the weirdest case I ever had."

"Okay. Just keep tabs on him while we find out, will you? Don't let him get away. When you seeing him next?"

"He's going to call today, and I'm going to ask him to come in. You want to come talk to him?"

"No, not yet. But keep me posted. What about this cup?"

"I'll courier it to you now."

"We'll run it, see if he's in the system. He may not be. We may draw a blank."

"Sure, but it's worth a try. Give me a call if you get a hit."

"Sure. Hang loose, Dave."

He hung up and sat staring at the file for a moment. Then he stood, picked up a small parcel he had by his side, and took it out to reception, where Betty looked up at him in mild surprise.

"You emerged from your den. It must be serious."

"Yes, sweetheart. I needed to see you. It's been too long. Also, have this sent to Special Agent Elroy Jones at the FBI offices on Wilshire Boulevard, will you? It's urgent."

She arched an eyebrow at him and took the parcel, then glanced at him along her eyes. "I saw you wrapping it. It's the cup that awful man drank from yesterday, isn't it?"

"Yes. It's a long shot, but he might be on one of their databases."

"I don't like him. Call it a woman's intuition, but that man is dangerous. The way he came in here, the way he refused to give his name..." She shuddered.

Dave smiled. "Well, to be fair, he doesn't *know* his name."

"All the same"—she shook her head—"he had the reek of death about him."

He looked away, out the window, thrust his hands in his pockets, and went up on his toes. "He did that," he said absently, but in the back of his mind, he couldn't shake the fact that the dead men in the house on Ocean Boulevard were all known dealers and killers on the FBI's most wanted list.

So what did that make this guy? A vigilante, some kind of rogue. But what kind of rogue?

————

AT THE ROOFTOP bar of the Intercontinental, Don Jesus Sanchez stood beside his table with his hands in his pockets looking out over Los Angeles. He was very high up. So high up he felt he was looking down on the mountains. It was a position he liked to be in. Occasionally he grunted as his mind examined his problem from one angle and then another.

Mateo Guzman, who was a guest at the hotel, sat sipping his glass of the Macallan and watching his boss. Eventually his boss turned and looked down at him and sighed.

"Who?"

Mateo shrugged. "Nobody knows."

"Somebody knows. First Felipe, Nestor, Oliver, and Eulogio. Then Steve last night. You know what this means?"

Mateo gave his head a small shake. "It looks like we have a contract. But that is impossible. Nobody is that crazy."

Jesus gave a small shrug with his left shoulder. "I don't know. A contract? Maybe. Maybe a grudge. But more important—" He took his right hand out of his pocket to shake his finger at Mateo. "More important, it means that he was there last night."

Mateo frowned. "Who?"

Jesus grunted. "Come on, Mateo! Think! Steve was killed at his house fifteen or twenty minutes after Peter left him there, after they left the bar. This son of a bitch followed them in his car from the Coca Cabaña. Which means he was there, at the bar.

"He follows them, and when Peter leaves, he goes into Steve's house. You read it in the paper: The lock was not forced. They were in the living room. Nobody heard nothing, nobody seen nothing. This guy he comes up, he rings the bell, that asshole Steve lets him in, and bang. He kills him."

"And you think that means he was at the bar?"

Jesus spread his hands. "Otherwise, he was waiting for him at his house. But you gotta ask, how does he know Steve is not there? What, he just goes to his house on the possible chance he is or is not there? No." He shook his head, pulled out his chair, and sat. "No, this guy is good, he is methodical, he is professional." He shrugged. "He is a hunter. He stalks, he follows, and at the right moment, *pam!* He kills. He was in the bar."

"You want me to go talk to the owner?"

"Agustin?" He thought about it. "No, tell Peter. Agustin is not stupid. He runs that bar with Sinaloa money. Things will be bad for him if he does something stupid. He doesn't know nothing. Tell Peter to go talk to Agustin and the waitresses. They serve somebody last night who killed the asshole Steve."

Mateo nodded and pulled his cell from his pocket. As it rang, he glanced around. They were alone on the terrace, but even so, he stood and walked to the far corner where he could not be overheard.

"Yeah." It was not so much a question as a statement.

"Don Jesus thinks whoever visited Steve last night followed you from the bar."

Pete was quiet for a long time before he answered, "How could he know we were going to be at the bar? On my side, only me and Steve knew."

"We'll make whatever enquiries we need to make on our end. You go to the bar, talk to Agustin and the waitress. Agustin has friends in Sinaloa. Don Jesus does not suspect him, so be polite. Treat him with respect. Talk also to the waitresses. Maybe they noticed somebody new, somebody different."

"You giving me orders now, Mateo? I don't work for you. I distribute your merchandise."

"I can send somebody else. But my advice? Is better to have Sinaloa grateful than pissed."

"Okay, I'll do you this favor and let you know. Then you owe me."

He hung up. Mateo turned and retraced his steps to where Don Jesus was sitting staring at the table top. As

Mateo took his seat, Don Jesus spoke, as though to the table.

"There was a book I read, Mateo, when I was learning English." Now he blinked and looked at Mateo. "It was science fiction, by some English guy, Frank Russell? Eric Franc Russell. It was call *The Wasp—La Avispa*—and I remember a scene where there is a guy in a car, and there is an avispa in the car with him, flying in his face, stinging his neck—you know? And the guy is driving and trying to kill the fockin' avispa at the same time. You know what happens?"

Mateo shrugged. "He killed the wasp?"

"No." Don Jesus shook his head. "The car crashed, the guy was burned to death in the crash, and the fokin' wasp flew away. I got a bad feeling, Mateo. I want this guy found and I want him dead before he makes us crash and burn."

"We'll find him, jefe, and we'll kill him. You got my word."

Don Jesus regarded his man with dead eyes. "You better, Mateo. If you don't kill him, he's gonna kill you."

———

JUST FIFTEEN MILES due west as the crow flies, Peter was sitting in his back yard with his cell in his hand, staring at the slow turquoise ripples in his pool. He hadn't liked Steve. Steve had been useful, but he was not the kind of guy you could like. He stood and slipped his cell in the back pocket of his jeans. Still looking at the water in his pool, he said, aloud, "But that ain't the point."

The point was they had not respected him. When you

have been raised by a whore, with one dad after another who beats you and tells you that you are good for nothing. When your teachers at school tell you you are good for nothing— when the whole godddamned world is telling you you are good for nothing—you have no family, you have no friends, you have nobody walking by your side, the only goddamned thing you *have* in the world is the respect you earn. And if somebody disrespects you, you have to hurt them and hurt them bad. So everybody else knows that disrespecting you has consequences, and they should not make the same mistake.

He went inside the house and took the keys from the fruit bowl beside the carport door and went out. He remembered the guy in the big white RAM who came out at the same time they did, and he remembered the waitress who had been flirting with him.

FIVE

I GOT UP THE NEXT MORNING AND SPENT A COUPLE of minutes staring at my face in the mirror. I remembered everything that had happened the day before. I had killed a guy and stolen half a million bucks from him. I didn't feel anything about that. More than anything, I was interested by the fact that I had done it efficiently. Like I had done it before. Like I knew how to do it, and I was good at it.

I showered, shaved, and dressed. I put the BUL in a pancake under my leather jacket and went out to the truck. I wanted to buy some food, but I also wanted to expand my wardrobe. I didn't know why exactly, but it was something I wanted to do. Just like I didn't know where I was going exactly, but I knew the truck would take me there.

It took me to the big shopping mall at Figueroa Street, downtown. I left the truck in the underground parking garage and made my way up to the mall in the elevator. There I spent half an hour buying things I didn't need but thought I might. It was oddly interesting and kind of weird buying things when I didn't know what I liked and what I didn't. Eventually, I bought a lot of steaks, almonds, and beer.

After that, I wandered around the mall until I found a small bookstore called Paper Books that Smell of Books. That made me smile, and I went inside. There was a lot of wood and soft amber lighting, and the few people inside were quiet, standing at the shelves or sitting on sofas and chairs, examining books. It felt good, and I wandered, staring at the shelves and wondering if I read a lot. I thought I might. Some of the authors' names looked familiar.

Then I saw a set of shelves in a corner with a sign that said *Self-Help Books*. I went there and started working through the shelves systematically but taking my time, looking for any reference to memory loss or amnesia. I found lots that promised I could achieve everything I wanted in life by visualizing it. Others said I had to remind myself every day that I was unique and precious to the Universe (with a capitalized U) and a spark of the Divine Flame. Others promised to help me find myself, though most said I had to kill or destroy my ego in order to do so.

I must have been making noises of disgust because by the time I had reached the end of the second shelf, I heard some quiet feminine laughter beside me. I glanced and saw a very attractive, well-dressed woman holding a book and smiling at me. I held up the book I was looking at.

"Half of them tell you you have to find yourself, the other half tell you to destroy your ego. Ego is I in Latin, so who is doing the searching and who is doing the destroying? I, right? So once I has found I and/or destroyed I, depending which of these fools you listen to, what do you do with the I that did the finding and/or the killing?"

Her eyebrows were about as high on her forehead as they could get without being lost in her hair, and she had a big smile on her face. That made me smile too, and it felt good. It felt like I hadn't done it for a long time.

"Well," she said, "I'd say that was a pretty good question."

"It's a rhetorical one." I put the book back. "You can't do anything to I because I is always the one doing it."

"Wow." I looked at her again, surprised at the tone in her voice. She said, "Were you looking for something in particular? Not yourself, obviously. You seem to have found that."

I gave a small sigh. "Yeah. My memory." I smiled at her again. "I lost it."

"You lost your memory? You have amnesia?"

"Total."

Her eyebrows went up again. "You have total amnesia? That is very rare. Do you have a support network?"

It was hard to suppress the desire to laugh. "A what?"

She gave her head a shake that for a moment looked bewildered. "Well, family, your doctor, you must be seeing a psychiatrist..."

I think it was the look on my face that made her trail off. When she started to frown, I said, "No. I don't know who my family are, or is. If I have one, I don't know where they are. I don't know who I am. I only know that I am."

She narrowed her eyes and shook her head. "You're pulling my leg." She gestured at my clothes. "You're well dressed. You're looking at books. So you have money and somewhere to live. Therefore you have an income, a debit card at the very least, a house or an apartment..." She trailed off again, closed her eyes, and held up her hands. "I am sorry. That was completely unacceptable. I apologize."

I picked up another book, glanced at the back cover, and said, "Everything you said makes sense. But the circumstances are unusual." I put the book back and smiled at her. I realized it was something I enjoyed doing. "But I can't work it out because I don't have the necessary data." I tapped my head. "It's locked in here. And don't apologize. It's actually good to talk about it."

Her frown was deepening. "How long have you had this amnesia? I mean—"

"Since yesterday morning."

"Good lord! There are various ways of tackling amnesia. You need to see a specialist." She gestured at the books. "They won't help. You need to talk to a psychiatrist. Hypnotherapy could help."

"You sound like you know what you're talking about."

"Well..." She gestured at the shelves in front of her. They were next to the self-help books and headed *Psychology*. I said, "You're a psychologist."

"I'm a psychiatrist."

"Don't you have your own specialist bookstores?"

She eyed me cautiously, nodding. "I am looking for a book on child psychology for my sister who just got pregnant. Something for the laywoman."

"Can you help me?"

"Good lord! This is very irregular. I don't normally get my clients in book stores!" She said it half-laughing but not very amused. I said, "How do you normally get your clients?"

"Well, usually they are referred to me by a doctor, or they make an appointment with my receptionist."

When I answered, it was with more feeling than I expected, and I surprised myself. "Not everybody fits in with the hive, Doctor. Often the people who need the most help are the very ones that have fallen outside of the system. The system takes care of itself, but who takes care of the loners, the lost and the strays? Who takes care of the rogues?"

She had gone very serious. "I am not accustomed to being lectured to by strangers."

"I wasn't lecturing you, Doctor. I was asking you a question. But like my previous one, it was rhetorical. Nobody takes care of the strays or the rogues. We have to take care of ourselves. Have you got a card?"

She gaped a moment and blinked. "After what you just said to me, you want to make an appointment?"

"I like talking to you. I think you might be able to help me."

She took a deep breath and sagged a little as she sighed. She reached in her purse and pulled out a card. It was embossed and said she was Dr. Elizabeth Grant and had her office at 901 Flower Street.

"Call my receptionist and make an appointment, Mr. ..." She trailed off with an ironic smile. I returned the smile and said, "Rogue. Call me Mr. Rogue."

I left the shop and made my way out to the street. There I called Dave Marshall. He answered on the first ring.

"Hey, where are you? You want to come in?"

"I'm downtown. You got something?"

"Yes and no. It's not that simple."

I stared absently over to my left. The sparkling vastness

of the Intercontinental Hotel stared down at me, towering into the sky over the shopping mall. "Why am I not surprised?" I said half to myself. It was clearly a day for rhetorical questions. "Sure, I'll come down."

A little over half an hour later, I stepped through the door into Dave Marshall's office. I paused at reception to smile down at Betty behind her desk.

"Black, real strong, no sugar."

She didn't answer but watched me cross to Marshall's door like she was visualizing slapping my face, not once but several times. I went through without knocking. He looked up, then stood and held out his hand. As I took it, he said, "It's nice if you knock."

I pulled out the chair and sat. "I guess I forgot my manners along with everything else. Why is this not simple?"

He gave a small sigh as he sat, then, "Okay, so, cutting to the chase, the truck was stolen in Vegas. The presumption will be that you stole it."

"Do you presume that?"

"I presume what you pay me to presume. But unless you're going to tell me you just remembered that you happen to pull a lot of weight in judicial and law enforcement circles, that is what the law is going to presume if they track you down."

"Okay, so I do not own that truck, but I probably stole it. Who'd I steal it from?"

"If you stole it, you stole it from the parking lot at Caesar's Palace." He tossed me a piece of paper. "That's the owner, Rick Henson. That's his address and telephone number. If you return it, that shows you didn't intend permanently to deprive the owner of it. So it's not theft."

"Right. You couldn't tell me this on the phone?"

"There's more." He paused with his eyes narrowed, like he was trying to see inside me. "Do you watch the news, read the papers?"

"I don't know. Not since yesterday. Why?"

"Where you woke up, in your stolen truck, right next to that place there is a house. You might have noticed it. It's all blue."

I went very still and cold inside. "What about it?"

"Well, it must have been only a short time after you woke up, anything from a few minutes to a couple of hours, that the cops found four men in that house. They were very dead. Time of death is practically impossible to establish unless you have something like a broken clock. But the blood—and there was plenty of that—the blood was not dry even though the house was warm, and there was no decay in the bodies, so they hadn't been dead for days. More like hours than days."

"Are you saying you think I killed them?"

"I am not saying I think you killed them. But I am saying that you ought to be aware that there appears to be a connection."

I grunted. "Do you know anything about the victims?"

"Yeah. The Bureau was looking for them. They had ties to the Sinaloa Cartel. Felipe Ochoa, wanted in Mexico and the US for murder and drug trafficking. He was cut in half with a samurai sword. Nestor Gavilan, Felipe's cousin, wanted on the same charges. His head had been split open with an axe. That was downstairs. Upstairs in his bedroom was Oliver Peralta, also Mexican, wanted back home and here for murder, drug trafficking, and extortion. He'd had a

Samurai sword driven through his solar plexus. It had split his diaphragm so his death would have been slow, very painful suffocation. And Eulogio Borja, also Mexican, also wanted back in Mexico and here for drug trafficking and armed robbery. He had had both his arms broken to stop him removing the shower curtain that had been tied around his head. Cause of death suffocation."

"Am I supposed to feel sorry for these guys?"

He gave a small shrug. "You know what? They probably had it coming and deserved what they got." Then he added, with some emphasis, "The killer certainly seemed to feel that way." He paused a moment. "They were all from out of town."

"Where from?"

"New York. The New York Feds had been watching them. Suddenly they went off the radar and showed up..." He trailed off, watching me. I said, "In Vegas." He nodded. I turned and stared out of the window and spoke half to myself. "So what made them come here from Vegas?"

"Really? That's your question?"

I turned back to look at him. "Have you shopped me? Have you told the cops about me?"

He leaned back in his chair, frowning, curious. "If I had, what would you do? Cut me in half, split my head open, shoot me in the eye...?"

I thought about it. It was a reasonable question. Finally, I shook my head. "No, Dave. I'd leave. As far as I am aware, you don't sell drugs or hurt kids or innocent people."

"Are you telling me you did this?"

"Honestly, I don't know. I don't remember anything before yesterday morning. But something I do know, even if

I *am* able to hurt a son of a bitch who works for the Sinaloa Cartel and has no compunction about destroying people's lives, I will *not* hurt an innocent person who is just doing his job."

"You remembered that, huh?"

"Yeah, I think so. Now will you answer my question?"

He took a deep sigh and shook his head out the same window I had been staring at before.

"You are a weird fucking son of a bitch." He turned back to me. "You know I worked for the Feds. When you have that in your blood, you never shake it."

"You told the Feds about me?"

"Not exactly, but I sent them your coffee cup to see if you were in any of their databases."

"Son of a bitch." I said it without much feeling. "You took my money and then you did that?"

"You paid me to find out who you were, remember?"

I nodded. "Am I about to get arrested?"

"No."

"Did you get any results?"

"You're not on any database."

"A guy who is not on any federal database, who is not a known felon, kills four dangerous cartel members with brutal, expert skill. How likely is that?"

"Not even a little." We sat in silence for a moment. Then he asked, "What are you going to do?"

"Return the truck. I'm not a thief."

"And after that?"

"I'll find a shrink who knows about amnesia."

"You've remembered something in the last twenty-four hours, haven't you?"

"Maybe." I stood. "But I don't want to test your loyalties, Dave. You're a Fed, and you will always be a Fed. I don't know what I am, and neither do you. Maybe it's best you never find out. Hang loose."

I turned to leave but he said, "Wait," I stopped, looked at him, waited. He held up his cell. "In my contacts I have you as Amnesiac. What should I call you?"

I gave a small smile, "Rogue. Call me Rogue,"

Out in the reception area, Betty regarded me with pinched lips. I paused at her desk and frowned at her like I cared. "We could have been friends, Betty," I said. "But destiny was against us. Maybe at some other time, in another life..."

I pushed out of the door and trotted down the steps, smiling to myself. So I killed drug dealers and I had a sense of humor. I wondered what else I was going to find out about me. So far, I was beginning to like me.

SIX

THIS TIME I HAD LEFT MY TRUCK IN DAVE Marshall's parking lot, at the bottom of the outside staircase. I climbed behind the wheel and called Dr. Elizabeth Grant's receptionist. She told me who I was calling, then asked how she could help.

"I need an appointment with Dr. Elizabeth Grant today. It's urgent."

"Oh, I am not sure..."

"It has to be today. It's a matter of life or death, and I mean that literally. I am not being figurative or metaphorical."

"Please hold the line."

"Tell her it's the guy with amnesia."

The line went quiet, and a couple of minutes later, Dr. Grant came on the line.

"This is Dr. Grant. Are you the gentleman I spoke to in the bookstore?"

"How many other guys do you know with amnesia? Yes,

it's me, Rogue."

"Look, Mr....*Rogue*, I treat people with serious problems who need real help. If this is some kind of prank—"

"It's not a prank, Doctor. Why would you think it is? I need help, and I need it very urgently. I need it now."

"I'm finding it hard to see how—"

"I think I may have killed somebody. I think that may have caused the amnesia." She went very quiet. I went on, "I need your help to try and remember what happened."

"All right. Can you be here in an hour?"

"I can be there in an hour."

She hung up, and I fired up the truck.

Forty-five minutes later, I arrived at Flower Street. Her building managed to be ugly and uninteresting all at the same time. The architect had obviously thought it would be a good idea to make it matte black with five stories of identical, featureless windows. If his objective had been to achieve soulless functionality, he had achieved it.

I left the car in the underground lot and took the elevator to the fifth floor. The reception was everything you'd expect from a successful psychologist in downtown Los Angeles. The walls were paneled in oak, the reception desk was a slab of polished, black marble, and there were real palms in huge, terracotta urns in the corners.

I told the receptionist who I was, and she eyed me up and down, buzzed the doctor, and told me to go through. But as I headed for the door, it opened, and the doctor was there, watching me approach. She allowed me in and closed the door behind me.

The room was large. It too was paneled in oak, but all the walls were lined with books. A quick glance told me ninety percent of them were read often. The other ten percent were valuable first editions.

Her desk was also oak and large with a big black leather chair, and to one side, there was a large, leather reclining armchair with a more modest chair beside it. That, I figured, was the famous couch. She pointed to the desk as she closed the door.

"Shall we sit at the desk to start with?"

As we sat, I noticed a handwritten letter on her blotter. It was a letter she was writing to somebody else. She removed it and said, "You have to understand—"

"I don't have to understand anything."

Her face flushed. "That kind of thing is not going to help."

"I am not here to help you, Doc. I am here for you to help me. I am lost. I am in a tiny pool of light surrounded by blackness. I need you to help me find my way back into the light." I paused while she took a deep breath and sagged back into her chair. "Don't tell me I have to understand your situation and how you might feel threatened by an unusual case. Patients should not be expected to fit a doctor's requirements. Doctors should be expected to adapt their skills to the needs of their patients." I offered her a humorless smile. "Or have I jumped to the wrong conclusions about what you were going to say?"

She took another deep breath. She placed her hands on the edge of the desk and looked at them for a moment. "If you persist in this confrontational, point-scoring attitude, I will not be able to help you."

"Then I'll stop," I said. She frowned like she was having trouble understanding me. I went on. "But you need to understand that I do not know who I am or what I am like. So I don't know if you can trust me, and I don't know if your misgivings about me are correct or not. That's why I am here asking you for help."

She was quiet for a moment. Her face told me she was wondering how to retake the initiative and assert some authority over the situation. I shut up and waited, and after a moment, she nodded. "On the telephone, you said you thought you might have killed somebody."

"Four men, yesterday or the night before, on Ocean Boulevard. You might have read about it or seen it on the news."

She tried to hide it, but she went pale. I could see she was struggling to form a question. In the end, she said, "Okay, tell me about it."

I told her about it: about waking up in the truck with blood on my hands, about going into the house and finding the bodies and then driving back to the apartment in Nevin, where I found the weapons. She listened without looking at me, making notes.

"When did it first occur to you that you might have killed these men?"

I felt a stab of irritation. "Isn't it obvious? I was sitting outside the house with blood on my hands and my memory blanked out!"

She raised her head and watched me in silence for a moment. Then she said, "When did it first occur to you that you might have killed these men?"

"Again?"

"And I will keep asking until you answer the question. Rogue, do you want me to help you, or do you want to teach me how to do my job? Now do yourself a favor and think about the question. When, precisely, did the thought first come into your mind that you might have killed those four men?"

I took a deep breath and let my mind roam back over the last couple of days.

"I guess it was today, when I spoke to Dave." But even as I was saying it, I knew it wasn't true. She was making notes again and said absently, "Really?"

"No."

"When, then?"

"Maybe—" My mind went back to when I was sitting in the Coca Cabaña, watching Jesus Sanchez and Pete and Steve. "Maybe when I was in a bar last night, having a beer." She looked up from her notes. "But no, I guess I already knew then. It was before that. It was when I went in the house and saw the bodies."

"That was when it first entered your mind that you might have killed them?"

I thought about the question, like she'd told me to, and said, "No. That was when I knew I had killed them."

"Are you telling me you remember killing these men?"

"No. I don't remember the event, but I know I killed them."

"And this has come to you since you walked through the door ten minutes ago?"

"I guess nobody asked me the right question. I haven't spoken to many people since I woke up."

There was skepticism in her face, but she seemed to take it onboard. She thought for a moment, then said, "So, Rogue..." She paused, like she was savoring the word. "This is the name you have chosen for yourself. What is it about the word rogue that makes you want to use it as a name?"

I shrugged and shook my head. "Nothing. You're reading too much into it."

"And if I wasn't, what would it be?"

I shrugged again, looking around like I was searching for meaning somewhere in the air, among the wooden panels and the books. "I don't know. Not belonging to the group..." I smiled, realizing a second too late she had tricked me. "Okay, smart. I guess that's the reason. I feel I no longer belong to the pack."

"You said *the* group. What group?"

"It's just a manner of speech—"

"Don't dismiss it. What group? Feel the question, palpate the question, explore it. *What group?*"

I took a moment and did what she said, then shook my head again. "I don't know. I don't want to go there. Not yet."

"Okay. So, Rogue, what are you not telling me?"

I was surprised by the question. "What makes you think I am not—"

"Don't answer a question with a question, Rogue. Let's make that a rule. You want to know who you are? Then face every question head on and answer it, even if the answer is 'I don't know.' Face it head-on and answer it. What are you not telling me?"

"There is nothing I am not telling you."

"Why are you lying to me?"

"I'm not—"

"Take those two questions home with you and think about them. Ask yourself those two questions. They are important." She didn't give me a chance to answer her. She pointed over at the recliner. "Let's move over there. I want to do some preliminary hypnosis with you."

I watched her stand and cross to the recliner. There she stood and looked back at me.

"Are you regretting starting this process?"

I shook my head and stood. "No. You're going to hypnotize me?" I went and lowered myself onto the seat. "I don't think I am hypnotizable."

She sat behind me where I couldn't see her. "You drive a car, don't you?"

"Of course."

"Just close your eyes while we talk." I closed my eyes. She went on. "You read books, don't you?"

"Sure. What's that got to do with—"

Her voice had become a little more mellow. "Just do me a favor, Rogue. Do yourself a favor and relax. Do me a favor and don't ask questions. Shut down the questions. Press the button and shut down the questions. Just give answers when I ask for them. Red light for questions, green light for answers. Just for a little while, let me do *my* job, and you do *your* job, and one step at a time, we can start to achieve something. Something good. However small. So you read books sometimes?"

It was nice to relax. She had a nice voice, and I took a deep breath and let it go. "Yeah."

"And sometimes you watch TV."

"Yeah."

"So, Rogue, if you drive a car, and you read books, and you watch TV, you can go into a light hypnotic trance. Because each one of those activities that you do will put you into a mild trance. A trance, Rogue, is a very natural state of mind that we all go into a trance from time to time..."

I was aware that her grammar had strayed, but I didn't really care because I was relaxing, and it felt like a long time since I had really relaxed. And I had to admit that her voice was nice to listen to, even though she was using an odd kind of rhythm, like every third or fourth word went down a tone.

"When you're doing, a long journey, on a long road, your mind begins, by gentle stages, to focus only, on the long road..."

I could see the road. It was a long, black ribbon through the desert, and she was right: Even her voice was filtering out. She said something about filtering out, but I couldn't remember what it was. All I could see was the road and hear her gentle voice in the background, fading.

Then she was telling me something about a book, and there were so many truths hidden between the lines of words in the book. And if I allowed the book to relax and go soft and subtle, perhaps the book would allow those truths to emerge for me from among the lines.

After that, she was telling me I could go deeper, and that sounded nice. Because the deeper I went, the more comfortable and peaceful I felt. It was a good feeling.

"And Rogue, if, you do feel, you want to, filter my voice out, so that only your unconscious, your unconscious can hear every word I am saying, your unconscious, can understand, every word I am saying is going deep into, your unconscious..."

I knew that what she was saying made no sense grammatically, but she had told me to filter her out, and I did, and

I knew that her words had become like secret medicine feeding into my unconscious, and I followed her words into the darkness and began to heal.

Then there was a TV. I was watching a TV. And there was a guy with his back to me on the TV. He had a wakizashi in his right hand, and he was facing another guy, and the terror in that other guy's face burned a hole in my gut and started my heart pounding.

"No!" I heard myself say it, but my arms and legs were paralyzed. "*No!*"

"That's okay, you are detached from it. It's happening on the TV, Rogue. You are detached. It's on the TV. Do you want to switch off the TV?"

"Yes. Now."

"Tell it to switch off. Tell it with your mind. Has it switched off now?"

"Yes."

"Relax now. All the way down, and listen to my voice. I am going to count down from ten backward, and as I count, you will feel life coming back into your limbs and body. Ten, nine, eight into your fingers, wiggle your fingers and move your hands. Seven, six, five, move your toes and your feet and stretch your legs. Four, three, two, take a very deep breath, stretch and one, open your eyes."

I did everything she said and sat up. She was smiling at me.

"How long do you think you were asleep?"

I frowned. "I have no idea. A couple of minutes?"

"Can you normally tell?"

"Yes. What happened?"

"You can't remember." It was a statement, not a question.

"There was a TV, right at the end. It scared me."

"I asked you your name. You told me you were Rogue, and I suspect you are going to hold on to that for a while. I told you to play out on the TV what happened the night before you woke up in the truck. You got as far as the man with the..."—she checked her notes—"wakizashi sword, and you began to become distressed."

"How long was I asleep?"

"You weren't asleep, Rogue. You were in a pretty deep trance. Just short of an hour."

"I didn't think I would be susceptible."

She nodded for a moment, like she was thinking and agreeing with her own thoughts.

"There are two groups of people who are really excellent subjects for hypnosis. One group is composed of soldiers and policemen. That is, people who are accustomed to following orders and instructions. The other group is composed of people who meditate a lot. Meditation and self-hypnosis are almost identical processes."

"The Japanese weapons. Martial arts and meditation are closely connected."

She nodded some more. "That might be a clue." She stood. "I strongly suggest, Rogue, that you go home and try to meditate. See how it goes. See if it comes naturally to you, and if it does, meditate on that possibility. Do you practice a martial art? Are you involved in that world?"

She moved to her desk, and I stood. "That's it, after an hour? I looked at a TV and panicked?"

She gave a small laugh as she sat. "No, but you need to trust my professional judgment, and in my professional judgment, you are not ready to hear the rest. Make an appointment with Alice to come back for another session. Make it less than a week."

I took a step toward her, feeling a hot coal of anger suddenly burning in my belly.

"I have a right to—"

"Take one more step, say one more word, and these sessions end now. *I* am the therapist. *I* decide how the sessions go. You don't like that, find another therapist or meditate. What's it going to be?"

I took a deep breath. "I'll make an appointment with Alice, Doctor."

"I'll see you then."

I turned and left her office.

SEVEN

I SAT FOR A WHILE AT THE WHEEL OF THE TRUCK. My mind was blank, but every now and then, I would get a flash of the guy with the wakizashi. I could see him only from behind, but I knew it was me. And the guy in front of him was the guy I had found on the sofa. His face was branded into my brain. There was terror in every twist of his face, but I didn't feel compassion or pity for him. The burning in my gut and the pounding of my heart, when I explored them coldly, were excitement, hatred, rage, and if there was any fear at all, it was fear at what I had become— fear of what I was capable of doing.

I fired up the big truck and drove easily and steadily to my apartment. There I collected one of the sports bags full of cash, slung it in the back of the truck, and found my way to Alameda Street to join I-10. I followed I-10 forty miles east as far as Rochester, then joined I-15 and followed it north and east for two hundred and twenty miles toward Vegas.

On the way, I kept going over what the doc had done. On reflection, it had been subtle and smart, like she was gently allowing me to find myself. And that had made me start to question something. If I had killed those men, it was because for some reason I had learned to hate them. The killings were, as I had thought from the beginning, rage killings. But would I steal a truck from a complete stranger? Was that the kind of guy I was? I didn't think so. Or, more precisely, I didn't *feel* so. If I was really honest with myself, I did not feel to myself like a bad guy. And I did not believe I would walk into Caesar's Palace parking lot and steal a random vehicle. Especially as it was even chances that guy would come for his car having lost his shirt in the casino.

That wasn't me.

Which meant, if I had taken this guy's car, it was for a reason. He had some connection with the four dead bodies in the house.

At Prim, just over the state line, I pulled in for gas and put my theory to the test. While I was filling the tank, I called the number.

"Yeah, who is this?"

"You heard from Ochoa?"

He was silent for a count of four, but he didn't hang up. Instead he asked again, "I said, who is this?"

"Don't get your panties in a twist, Rick. This is a friend. How about Nestor, Oliver, and Eulogia, you heard from them?"

He didn't say anything, but he still didn't hang up.

"No? No news? I brought your truck back. It was just a loan, Rick. I have some money for you, for the inconvenience."

"You gonna tell me who the fuck you are? Or do I have to beat it out of you with a tire iron?"

"That's up to you, Rick. From what I'm told, you're at Decatur Boulevard, right by the secondhand car lot and the mall. I have five grand for you, Rick. Instead of beating me with a tire iron, why don't we have a beer? You let me apologize and give you your money."

He didn't sound like a man who had just been offered five grand. He said, "Beer where?"

"We'll meet at the Parkway Tavern, on the corner of Flamingo and Decatur. We can chat, I can give you your money, and we can be friends. That sound good to you, Rick?"

"When?"

"Give me forty-five minutes. I'll be sitting in a booth and I'll have your RAM's keys on the table, and a bag full of cash."

Finally he said what he'd been dying to say since I'd called him. "Why do you keep asking about Felipe and the boys?"

I put a frown in my voice. "Do I?"

"You asked before..."

"I think I only asked once, Rick. I don't think I keep asking. Is there a problem? Do you have a problem with Felipe and the boys?"

"No."

"Good. I'll see you in a little while, Rick. Like I said, I have some money for your inconvenience, and then, if you can help me out, maybe I have a little more cash for you."

"Help you out with what?"

"I'll see you in a while, Rick. Like my gran always used to say to me, be good, but if not, be careful!"

I smiled to myself. Curiosity and greed would get him to the meeting, and I figured I had planted enough of a seed of doubt in his mind that he'd be prepared to betray 'Felipe-and-the-boys' for the right price, especially if that price was the alternative to castration with a blunt knife. I was pretty sure all that was going through his mind right then, and he was going to show at the tavern with just about the right attitude.

Vegas is my least favorite city on the planet. It's like the people who created it made a conscious decision to combine all the ugliest elements you could find in a town to attract all the ugliest people to go there and do ugly things. If that was their purpose, they succeeded and created a town that was both big, brash, and crowded, and small, shallow, and empty. It was a town made of empty, neon dreams and broken promises.

I pulled into the parkway parking lot and left the RAM outside the main entrance to the bar. I found a booth inside and sat by the window with my sports bag and keys on the table. I watched Rick arrive in a seventeen-year-old red Mustang Shelby GT 500. He was six-one, in his fifties, with permed gray hair swept back. I was pretty sure I had never seen the guy till then, but I had an instinct for who he was, and when he came through the door and stood looking around, I was sure it was him. He spotted the bag and the keys and walked over.

"You the guy who called me?"

"Are you Rick?"

"Yeah."

I gave him a lopsided smile. "Then I'm the guy who called you." I nodded at the window. "Nice wheels."

"Yeah. I gave it a makeover. Back in the day, off the assembly line, it was putting out five hundred horses at six thousand RPM. Now it puts out five hundred and sixty. It's got manual transmission. Not everybody likes that, but I figure if you're a real driver, y'know, you like that control..." He trailed off and sat opposite. "What do you want? I ain't heard from Felipe for a while. You said you had some cash for me?"

The waitress came over, and I ordered a couple of beers. When she'd gone away, I said, "I'll tell you what I want, Rick. I met with Felipe and the boys in Los Angeles—" I laughed and leaned forward, guy to guy. "I want to say yesterday, but actually it was the day before yesterday, but things dragged on into the dawn right there by the beach. You know what I'm saying? Those boys can party."

He tried a smile and almost made it. "Right? It's in their blood."

"So Felipe told me about what you guys had discussed." I spread my hands. "I take care of things on the West Coast..." Another laugh. "He calls me the man with no name."

We both waited, watching each other. I was hoping he would fill the silence by telling me what he and Felipe had talked about. But he was waiting for me to tell him what I was talking about. Finally he said, "I still don't know what you want from me. What's this about?"

"No, man. This is not about what we want from you. I told you, I have some cash for you. Five K for your trouble and expense because I took your wheels, man. I'm sorry about that. I had no choice. This is about what we can do for you. Felipe said you'd fill me in. Like I said, I take care of things on the West Coast."

He was frowning and a little confused. It was like I had him, but he was slipping through my fingers.

"You know, they were in New York and they were on their way to Los Angeles, stopped over in Vegas and he told me they wished they'd been able to spend more time with you. But business is business. You were at Caesar's, right?"

"Yeah." He looked up at the girl as she delivered our beers. Then narrowed his eyes at me. "What did you say your name was?"

"Clint. Like the actor."

"And what is it, exactly, you are offering me help with?"

It had been a long shot, and I had blown it. I frowned hard and glanced at the bag, then back at his face.

"I..." I trailed off. "Rick, there seems to have been a mistake somewhere along the line. Seems I have to apologize to you not just for borrowing your car, but also for wasting your time. I understood..." I trailed off and made to stand. "It was obviously a misunderstanding."

I could see his eyes on the sports bag. He swallowed hard and said, "Well, hang on, I mean, maybe..."

I winced and sat back down. "You have to understand, Rick, a man in my position, working for Felipe and *his* boss, I have to be real discreet. But Felipe led me to understand that you..." I gestured toward the window, toward the direction he had come from, and left the end of the sentence wide open for him.

"The club?" he asked. I made a face that suggested, 'Well, duh!' and he went on. "They knew about that before they arrived here." He gave a small, nervous laugh. "Those guys do their homework,"

"Oh." I nodded. "Those guys do their homework!"

"They had looked at just about all the clubs in Vegas. Obviously some are protected."

I nodded. "Right."

"But there are a handful of independents, like mine."

"So Felipe offered to bring you under his wing."

"Right, and take care of the supply side."

"Oh, sure, straight from Mexico. Where'd you get the supply before?"

"Mainly local adds, or the net." That made me reach for my beer to hide the surprise. He didn't notice and went on. "Mainly independents. They're pretty clean and reliable in Vegas. But like Felipe said, they take a big cut these days. On the other hand, if you bring them in from Mexico, they're practically free."

As it dawned on me what he was talking about, I could feel the heat in my belly seeping up into my chest and then my head. I fought to control it, hiding it behind a small laugh. "Oh, right. I talked to Felipe like two minutes on the phone. If you're drinking with him, he'll talk for hours. But business is two minutes. After that, you gotta sort it yourself. So he is supplying dope and girls?"

He glanced around, like somebody might be listening. "Yeah, that's what he said. I was running a pretty small, independent operation, but he said that was"—he shrugged and swallowed—"he said it was kind of dangerous these days. A guy could get hurt. So he took a couple of my girls, said he was going to introduce them to some guys in LA. I can't remember the names—"

"Don Jesus? Pete..."

"Yeah, Don Jesus, I think he said. They didn't want to go, but I persuaded them it was best."

"Latinas?" I was thinking of the girls I had seen with the guys that night.

"Yeah, Carmen and Becky." He was trying not to look queasy. "So Felipe said he was going to be in touch. But I haven't heard from him." He gestured at me with both hands. "Except, of course..."

I grinned. "You mind showing me the club?"

"If you think... I mean, they saw it already."

I raised the bag. "Then I get a chance to play Santa Claus."

"Sure."

I paid, and we went out to the parking lot. There I gave him the keys to the RAM and held out my hand. "I'll follow in the Mustang."

He hesitated for just a second, then handed over the keys. I slung the duffel bag in the trunk and followed him a mile down Decatur Boulevard, where he pulled across the road into a parking lot outside what was advertised as a gentleman's massage parlor. Across the road was a second-hand car dealer that specialized in American muscle cars and foreign sports models. He jerked his head at it. "That's mine too. I wheel and deal. I like to diversify. I try to keep honest." He laughed. "It's not always possible, but I try."

I followed him inside, through glass doors that he had to pause and unlock. "We open after eight," he told me. There was a reception desk and a coat room. A passage led off to the left, and to the right, a couple of palms framed the entrance to a small bar. He led the way and switched on the lights.

"You want a drink?" He moved behind the bar and gestured at a table. "I think I need a whiskey."

"Sure. Irish. No ice."

I sat, and while he got the drinks I checked Google on my cell, looking for a report on the Ocean Boulevard murders of Ochoa, Gavilan, Peralta, and Borja. By the time he joined me at the table, I had found them. We toasted and drank.

As I set down my glass, I smacked my lips and sighed. "Rick, I am going to come clean with you."

He didn't look like that made him happy. "Yeah? You a Fed?"

"No, but I killed Felipe Ochoa, Néstor Gavilan, Oliver Peralta, and Eulogio Borja the night before last. It was ugly. You can find most of the details on the *Los Angeles Daily Graphic*."

"Jesus Christ..."

I was surprised at the sincerity in my own voice when I told him, "They were very bad men, Rick."

Dawning horror made his eyes wide, and he shook his head at me. "I didn't go looking for them. They came to me. They gave me no choice. They told me what they'd do to me. My girls were always clean, they had insurance, regular checkups. They were independent. We split the proceeds sixty-forty in their favor, and we never dealt in drugs. I swear. You wanna bring your own coke or marijuana, I'm gonna turn a blind eye. But I don't sell the stuff, and you bring anything stronger in here and I have the boys kick you out.

But they came in here and they scared the shit out of me. I had no choice. I swear."

"I know. I have nothing against you, Rick. All I want is information. They took you to Caesar's Palace?" He nodded. "And you spent most of the night there?"

"Till about four a.m. When I went for my truck and it was gone."

"You didn't see me that night?"

He shrugged and spread his hands. "I seen so many people that night. And I was pretty preoccupied with Felipe and those guys. If I saw you, I never noticed."

"They talk a lot?"

"Felipe was pretty gregarious. He didn't seem to give a damn who heard him. He was talkin' about how the border was open for them now. They were expanding their operations in the States and they needed reliable distributors and they needed high class clubs where people with money could enjoy coke and good whores. We call them sex workers, but he called them whores."

"And he told you he'd come from New York. That's where he was based before."

"That's what he said. But now they had to attend to business in Vegas and Los Angeles."

"He didn't say what the business in Los Angeles was?"

He thought about it for a moment. "Not exactly, but he kept going on about how the border didn't exist anymore. He said Sonora and Baja in Mexico and California were now just going to be an extension of Sinaloa. I gotta say I didn't understand what the hell he was talking about, but I told him what I thought he wanted to hear, that that was fantastic news."

I visualized it on a map in my mind, and it made sense to me. "Anything else he said that struck you as weird or interesting?"

"Only that he talked a lot about this Jesus Sanchez. He said the head of the biggest cartel in Mexico—"

"Sinaloa."

"Right. Sinaloa. The head of that cartel was getting old. He's like nearly eighty, and there are people beginning to move in to take over when he dies. There were two guys who were his partner's kids—"

"The Chapitos."

"I think that's what he said, and then there was this guy, Jesus Sanchez, who was moving to take control of prostitution and distribution in the States. Because he said whoever controls drugs distribution and prostitution in the States controls Sinaloa."

"Right." I sat and thought while he watched me. After a moment, I focused on his face. He looked scared. I sighed. "You know what, Rick? Drugs, prostitution, it's not a good business for a man. A man should be able to look at himself in the mirror and feel respect for the guy he sees looking back. You"—I gestured at him—"you can't do that. My advice to you is get out. Do something else. Sell cars." I shrugged. "That's just my advice. It's your life. But you know, something ugly happened to you because you were in an ugly business. Get deeper into that business and uglier things will happen."

I reached in the bag and pulled out ten thousand dollars, which I handed over to him.

"Five grand for the inconvenience of taking your truck

and another five for the bargain, knock-down price you're giving me on the Mustang."

"I am?"

"In gratitude for returning your RAM and not blowing your head off for allowing that son of a bitch to take two girls you were supposed to be protecting."

He nodded several times. "Oh, okay." He watched me stand and asked, "What about the paperwork?"

"I don't know who I am, Rick. No paperwork." I smiled the kind of smile you never want anyone to give you. "But if you report that car stolen, I will come and find you. You don't want that to happen. Read the article in the *Graphic*."

EIGHT

THE MUSTANG'S FIVE HUNDRED AND SIXTY HORSES got me back to Nevin a little before nine p.m. I didn't stop at my house but drove to the Coca Cabaña, parked there, and pushed inside. It wasn't as full as it had been the night before. They were playing Latino music, which would normally make me leave, but it wasn't too loud. They had football on the screens, and only a few of the tables were occupied.

There were two guys behind the bar. One was young, washing glasses, the other was an older guy talking quietly and seriously to Pete. I ignored them and made my way to a booth. My waitress from the night before came over and smiled at me like she liked me. I returned the smile and said I'd have a beer and a hamburger.

The older guy behind the bar glanced at me and kept on talking, quietly and seriously. He had that *Don't look now, but...* expression on his face. I pulled out my cell and made like I was reading messages. In my peripheral vision, I saw her pulling the beer at the bar while Pete and the older guy spoke to her. Her answer was brief, and she looked pissed.

When she brought me the beer, I set down my phone.

"Thanks. What's your name?"

"Ernestina."

I gave it a beat while we both smiled. "You don't want to know my name?"

"Sure." Her smile turned to a grin.

"My name is Roger, but at school they gave me the nickname Rogue because I was so disobedient. So now everyone calls me Rogue."

"Rogue? It sounds cool."

I noticed for the first time she had a slight Latino accent.

"What time do you finish work?"

She rolled her eyes. "Oh, four, five, six in the morning? When the bar closes."

"So if I want to take you out I have to take you for breakfast?"

She laughed. It was a nice laugh. "See? That's why I have no boyfriend!"

"You're obviously hanging with guys who have no imagination. How about a breakfast of eggs Benedict with salmon, an English muffin and Hollandaise sauce, accompanied by a very cold Dom Perignon at Shutters on the Beach in Santa Monica, while we watch the sunrise?"

Her eyes were bright. "Wow, are you serious?"

"Why not?"

"Okay, you're on, mister. I hope you can stay awake that long!"

I wrote my number on a napkin. "I'll have my burger, go

shower and change, and come back for you at five. If you finish earlier, call me."

I had my burger and drained my beer, paid up, and stepped outside as the bar was filling up and the music was getting louder. The night was balmy, and I paused outside the door to look up at the orange ceiling the city lights had placed under the stars. I knew that somewhere, at some time, I had looked up at a different sky and seen the Milky Way as a blazing trail across an infinite sky. But I couldn't remember where.

I turned toward the Mustang and heard a voice behind me.

"Nice ride."

I glanced over and wasn't surprised to see Pete. "I like it."

"Didn't you have a RAM last night?"

I thought about asking him what damn business it was of his, but this wasn't the time to kill him. For now, I needed him. So I smiled instead.

"Yeah, I stole it from a guy in Vegas. I took it back today and swapped it for the Mustang." I leaned on the top of the windshield, holding his eye. "I told him if he didn't make the swap I'd cut him open."

His eyes moved over me, like he was calibrating me. "Is that so? All the way to Vegas? They don't have GT500s here in Los Angeles?"

I shrugged. "I had other business in Vegas, and I wanted to return his Dodge. I'm not a thief."

He pulled a pack of cigarettes from his pocket and shook one free. As he poked it in his mouth and lit up, he said, "A killer, but not a thief. You'll take a guy's life but not his property."

"A killer?" I frowned.

He inhaled deeply through his mouth and let the smoke out through his teeth. "You said if he didn't let you have it, you'd cut him open, remember?"

"Oh." Another smile. "I was just joking. Someone has to do something real bad for me to kill them."

"Yeah?" He flicked ash and looked down at his shoes. "Like what? What's real bad?"

"I don't remember," I said quietly. "But I know it was real bad."

I opened the car door. He said, "It's been nice talking to you. What's your name?"

"They call me Rogue."

"Peter."

"Good to meet you, Peter. We must talk again soon, over a beer."

"Count on it."

I climbed behind the wheel and drove away, down the road to my house.

Upstairs, I stood under the shower letting the cold water batter my head and my body, turning things over in my mind. Peter knew. He had seen my truck, and he had come back to ask about me. The older guy behind the bar must be the owner. That's why he was talking to him. And they had both spoken to Ernestina. I would have to play my hand with care. With great care.

I rinsed off, dried my hair, and lay on the bed. I got four hours' sleep, and at four-thirty, she called to say they were letting her off early. I wasn't surprised. I dressed quickly, stuffed a few grand in my wallet, and drove around to collect her. The place was full and noisy, but Pete and the older guy were gone.

I stood in the doorway and saw Ernestina behind the bar, taking her apron off. She waved to me and squeezed her way through the crowd. When she reached me, she clung to my arm laughing, saying, "I didn't think you were serious. I really didn't think you'd come!"

"Well, here I am. It's a little early for breakfast. What do you say we go get a drink somewhere before we go to the beach?"

She gripped my arm and looked up into my face. "Sounds good. Let's go."

She said she wanted to go to a place in Skid Row called High Tide. It wasn't far, and at that time, there was practically no traffic. I cut under the I-10 overpass on South Central Avenue and cruised up as far as East 4th. On the way, I didn't talk. I watched the empty streets and the dull, silent pools of lamplight as they slid by like sentinels outside the dark houses.

She talked. She talked about her brother and her mother, who was a saint but never stopped nagging.

"It's hard sometimes," she said. "It's your family, you know? Family is a big deal for Mexicans. So you're tied to them. But sometimes all you really want is to be free of them. I feel bad saying that."

"You're Mexican?"

"Everyone in that neighborhood is Mexican. This is it." She pointed up ahead, and we pulled up outside a little bit of Los Angeles that would be forever 1960s San Francisco. It was painted a really ugly blue-gray, and looking at the glass doors and windows, you'd be forgiven for thinking it was a thrift store, but it had a nice art deco mural on a terrace wall that told you it was a bar and maybe a restaurant too. It depicted a flamingo surrounded by lots of tropical plants and a big, pale pink squirrel that said *High Tide* in the center.

Inside it was like Hendrix and Che had met up in the long, dark night of the soul, where it's always three o'clock in the morning, and decided to roll a joint and take some acid before setting off in the yellow submarine to overthrow the Illuminati. It was dimly lit with another big mural of flamingos in a lake. There were two guys sitting at the bar with a beer each, chuckling and sharing a cigarette. Ernestina held my arm and led me out to a patio where there were lots of palm trees and colored lights concealed among ferns.

We ordered a gin and tonic and an Irish whiskey. The waitress went away, and we were alone under the palms. The purple light among the ferns lay across the planes of her face, and it struck me I hadn't noticed till then that she was beautiful.

"Was that your boss behind the bar? The older guy?"

"Agustin, yeah."

"He Mexican too?" I smiled. She smiled back. "Is that why you brought me out, to ask about Agustin? Is this where you come out and tell me you're gay and you like older men?"

"No and no and also, no."

"So?"

"I like you. You look good, and you have a personality I could grow to like a lot. But you are right: There is something I want."

Her smile became rueful. "Ain't that just my luck."

I gave a small shrug. "One thing doesn't cancel out another. I could have approached you another way, and right now I could have kept my mouth shut. But I want you to know I'm straight—in every sense."

She arched an eyebrow. "Gee, you sure know how to flatter a girl, Roger."

"That's not my name."

"You're going to tell me you're undercover FBI or CIA or—"

"Hey." I cut her short quietly. "I'm sorry you've been let down and disappointed. But I am not to blame. We don't owe each other anything yet. I like you, you liked me, we wanted to know each other. So give me a chance. Let me tell you what it is I want, aside from getting to know you better."

Her face wasn't welcoming, but she jerked her chin at me and said, "Hit me."

A girl with blue hair and a stud in her nose brought our drinks. When she'd gone, I said, "I have total amnesia."

Her expression was incredulous. "*What?*"

"I woke up the day before yesterday with no idea who I was. I made it back to my house by pure muscle memory. It was like the car knew where to go. When I got there, I kind of recognized it, and I had a key to the door. But there was nothing in the house to say who I was—no photographs, no contracts, nothing. Part of the reason I went into the Coca Cabaña in the first place was to see if anybody recognized me. But it seems I was more like a newcomer."

She still looked skeptical, but she said, "I'd never seen you before."

"But I think Pete has."

She went very quiet, staring down at the ice in her drink. After a moment, she looked up at me, straight in the eye. "I don't want to get in the middle of anything."

"I don't want you to get in the middle of anything either. And that's part of the reason we're here. I need you to answer a question, and I need you to be real honest. When I came in tonight, earlier, Pete and Agustin were talking at the bar. You went to get my beer and they told you to find out about me, didn't they?"

"Son of a..."

"Did they?"

"Yes! Yes, they did. And you know what I told them? The same thing I'm going to tell you. To go to hell!"

"What did he say when you told him to go to hell?"

Her face said that wasn't the answer she was expecting, and she gave a small shrug. "He told me to be smart and do as I was told."

"So...?"

"So tomorrow I hand in my notice and start looking for a job where I get respected by the management *and* the clients."

I sighed and sank back in my chair. "I respect you, Ernestina. That's why I'm here with you, talking to you. What do you know about Pete?"

"I am not a grass. I am nobody's informant, and your story sucks!"

"You're right. The story sucks. Do I look stupid to you?"

"Yes!"

"Don't be a wiseass. It's a serious question. Do I look stupid to you?"

She sighed. "No. To be honest, I am real disappointed."

"So if I was going to make up a story to get close to you, do I look stupid enough to go for total amnesia as a cover?" I waited, but she didn't answer. She just watched me. "I can tell you I hired a private detective yesterday to trace the plates on my truck, and I started seeing a psychologist on Flower Street. She is using hypnotherapy on me to try and restore my memory. You are more than welcome to go to both or either and check. I have lost my memory, and I have practically no idea who I am."

She was shaking her head. "I don't need this."

"Yeah, I agree. The problem is, you have it, and if I am right, Peter is a dangerous man and you don't want to get on the wrong side of him."

She frowned. It was hard to tell if she was mad or scared. I figured for her maybe it was the same thing. "What are you saying?"

"I'm saying, I noticed the way Pete and Agustin spoke to you and how they looked at me. I'm saying I know Pete is interested in me, and I don't know, or I don't remember why. And above all, I'm saying to you that you should do whatever you have to do to stay safe. Make no mistake. He is a dangerous man."

She held my eye a moment before answering, like she was trying to work me out.

"How do you know that?"

"The more I tell you, the more at risk you are."

"How do you know he's a dangerous man? I don't need a nanny."

"He's just taken over distribution in Los Angeles for the Sinaloa Cartel."

She flopped back in her chair, and her jaw actually sagged. "How the hell would you know that?"

"Am I wrong?"

She shook her head. "I have no idea whether you are right or wrong, but if you have total amnesia, that is one hell of a thing to remember!"

"Who says I remembered it?"

"So once again, how do you know?"

I sat staring at my whiskey for a moment. I hadn't touched it yet. "Information is power," I heard myself say. "But the wrong information can be a death sentence."

"Who said that?"

I looked up, surprised. "I did."

"No." She shook her head. "Somebody else said it. It was like a famous quote or something. On TV."

I shrugged and echoed her head-shake. "I have no idea, Ernestina. What I am saying to you is that I can tell you things I have learned in the last two days, but the more I tell you, the more I put you at risk."

"I'm going to tell you one more time, Roger—"

"That's not my name."

"And Rogue is?"

"I think so. Maybe."

"I don't need a nanny."

"You said yourself you don't need this problem, either." She watched me, waiting. "I have some kind of a nagging memory. It has to do with drugs and drug dealers."

"What kind of memory?"

"I hate them. It's a very strong feeling. So strong it seems to have survived the amnesia. It's like a driving obsession. I

—" I hesitated. "You said you were going to hand in your notice tomorrow?"

"If there was any doubt before, there isn't now."

I took a deep breath. "I followed Pete and Steve last night. Pete dropped Steve at his house and went on. I went in and spoke to Steve. He told me they'd been having a meeting at the Coca Cabaña with Jesus Sanchez, who is a big shot in Sinaloa, and Pete had agreed a distribution deal with them. They are not just into narcotics. They are into sex trafficking too. You want to stay away from this guy, Ernestina. Even if you never talk to me or see me again. You have to stay away from him."

"You followed them last night, and you went into Steve's house after Pete dropped him off. To get information from Steve."

"Yes."

"So you killed Steve."

"Yes."

NINE

I WAS EXPECTING HER TO STAND UP AND WALK OUT. It's what any smart woman would have done. I started to say, "Before you go—"

"I'm not going anywhere."

We sat and stared at each other for a long moment. She picked up her drink and took a pull. As she set it down, she said, "You asked me out for a reason. And that reason was not to warn me that Pete was working for Sinaloa. Or to tell me to go ahead and sell you down the river."

I took a deep breath and picked up my own drink. I looked at it a moment and set it down again.

"You're asking me questions I'm not sure I have the answer to. I asked you out because I wanted to ask you about Pete and Agustin, but especially about Pete. At least, that's why I thought I asked you out."

"Don't sell me a line, Rogue. You don't need to."

"I'm not selling you anything..." I felt a sudden rush of irritation and narrowed my eyes. "Whatever else you might have against me right now, you at least have to admit I am being honest with you. I could have told you any number of lies tonight that would have made life a lot easier for both of us. But I have screwed things up by being honest. So I am not selling you any kind of line." I paused. "When we were in the car, you told me all about your family. Now that we are sitting here..." I took another deep breath, sighed, and spread my hands. "I still want, probably *need*, that information about Pete, but I also feel that, even more important than the information about Pete is that you and your family should be safe." Another rush of irritation made me snap, "And I'm sorry if that is contemptible, unbelievable, or brings out the cynic in you. It just happens to be true!"

She was quiet for a long moment. When she spoke, her voice was quiet.

"I don't think you're contemptible or unbelievable, and I am not a cynic." She gave a small shrug, and her head did a little sideways twitch. "Well, it is a little unbelievable, but I guess I believe you anyway. It's too crazy to be made up."

"Thanks."

"Rogue, you're a Fed. It's obvious."

"No. The private detective I hired ran my DNA and my prints through the Federal databases, and there was no match."

She was quiet with her eyes flitting over my face, like she was looking for something. Finally she said, "You went rogue and started killing suspects?"

I gave a small snort of a laugh. "Right? But I'd still be on their databases. Even more so."

She squinted at me. "Are you for real?"

"Yes, unfortunately I am for real."

"What made you kill Steve?"

I glanced at her face. "You knew him?"

"Only from that night. What made you kill him, Rogue?" Then she added, "You've got to admit, that name..."

I ignored her last comment and cut her short. "I first noticed it when I went in to the bar that first night. You served me, and they were in the corner, Jesus Sanchez, another guy in a linen jacket, Pete and Steve. And I knew then, suddenly. I knew like I know I am sitting here right now. I knew what they were. And I felt..."

I looked down and saw that I had clenched my fist in front of my belly without realizing it, expressing the clenched burning I felt there.

"I felt hatred. It was deep, it was hot, in my gut. And I wanted to kill them right there where they were sitting. I don't know why. I don't know what caused that hatred." I picked up my glass again and muttered half to myself, "Not that you need much reason. What's not to hate?"

I took a pull, and as I set the glass down, I started to speak again. My brain was telling me I shouldn't tell her, but I couldn't seem to stop.

"When they all left, I wasn't aware of having any particular intention. It was like I was acting on instinct. I followed them, and when Pete dropped Steve at his house, I waited for a bit till he was inside. Then I went and knocked on the door. I persuaded him to let me in, asked him some questions about Jesus Sanchez and about Pete..." I trailed off.

"And then?"

"I shot him in the head." I held her eye, and she held mine. "I felt nothing," I told her. "No compunction, no guilt, no remorse. He had to die." I rubbed my face with my hands and sighed loudly. "I'm sorry. I don't know what's wrong with me." A small, bitter laugh escaped my mouth. "How could I know what's wrong with me? I don't know who the hell I am. I shouldn't have burdened you with this. Only, please, be careful with Pete, and especially with Jesus."

She didn't say anything. She was looking down at her drink, as though she was mesmerized by the bubbles moving slowly to the surface.

I said, "You want me to drop you somewhere? Or they could call you a cab."

Now she looked up. "You want to get rid of me already? I thought you were inviting me to breakfast."

I frowned. "After what I've just told you?"

"I don't know how much of what you've told me is true or how much is madness or bullshit. But my intuition is pretty good, and my intuition tells me you're on the level. If Steve was trafficking drugs, if he was planning to bring in heroin and fentanyl for those hijos de puta in Sinaloa, if he was willing to help in the traffic of women and girls for sex, then I am going to speak plain with you, Rogue, he deserved to die and you were too compassionate shooting him in the head. I would have cut off his balls and let him bleed to death."

"Wow."

"My parents came here when I was eight years old, but my memory goes right back to when I was real small. We lived in Peñasco, right on the north shore of the Gulf of California. It was a nice, pretty town. In that part of Mexico, there was not much problem with drugs. We were happy. But you know that part is Sonora, and it lies between Sinaloa and the US border. So Sinaloa started to move in to north-western Sonora because the routes through Texas, New Mexico, and Arizona were becoming more and more difficult. Border control was getting tighter, and the Gulf Cartel was controlling that side. So they start to look for more easy routes, like from Baja into California. It was easy, an obvious choice. Baja had no real drugs problem, and California was an open door for Mexico. So Sinaloa started to focus on northwest Sonora. And Peñasco was perfect. It was desert, it was fifty miles from the border with a big nature reserve, and it has its own port. So by road they are taking it into Yuma, or Indio and Palm Springs via Salton Sea. Or from the port by sea, they were registering yachts in France, Spain, Italy, and sailing from Peñasco into Los Angeles, San Francisco, or a hundred small ports and beaches along the coast, like they were European boats."

She took a long pull on her drink, and as she set it down, she looked into my face.

"Suddenly, my cute, pretty town was full of killers and drug traffickers from Sinaloa, and they were recruiting the young guys and taking control of the police and the local government. Everyone from the mayor down to the lowest cop was given the choice: accept the money we gonna pay you, or we kill your family and then you. My father was the local magistrate."

"What happened?"

"He called friends in the DEA, they pulled strings, and me and my mother came for a day trip to San Diego to do some shopping. We never went back. The officials we talked to told us my father had been shot dead as he was coming out of his office. He was going to get in his car, to come and join us here, but a truck drove by, and he was shot outside the court. There were no witnesses, no evidence was found. You know the story."

"Sinaloa had arrived."

"Right. So now my mother cleans houses, my brother has joined a local gang whose great ambition is to become part of the Chupacabras, and I work in a bar which belongs to a guy who used to be a sicario, an assassin for Sinaloa." She laughed. It was startling and loud. Then she leaned forward and held my wrist. "You know? They want to keep the borders open so that Mexicans can escape from the drug cartels and start a new life. But what they do is make Mexican ghettos where the cartels retire their killers to oversee the distribution of drugs in USA." She sagged back in her chair. "So I got no problem with you taking out Steve, or Pete, or Jesus."

I smiled and gave a small shrug with my eyebrows. "This is unexpected."

"You want me to get you information about Pete?"

"Not if it puts you at risk, no. I'd rather you and your family moved where they can't find you."

"How are we going to do that?"

I gestured north and east toward my apartment. "I have like two million bucks in various duffel bags in my apartment. I don't know how I got it." I paused and smiled. "But I can imagine. I took about five hundred grand from Steve."

She shook her head. "I don't want that money."

"Be smart. These people could become very dangerous, not just for you but for your family. If they suspect you are feeding me information..."

"You talk like a cop."

"Don't change the subject. It's a big risk, and I don't want you getting hurt."

"Then kill them, Rogue. Kill them all. I'll get you whatever information I can."

"Then we do a deal. You give me what information you can. I get rid of this dirty cash and make it legitimate, and you get yourself and your family to safety."

She gave me a real nice smile, then spent a while turning her glass in circles. "I hope," she said after a while, "when you're done, if you get your memory back"—she paused and raised her eyes to meet mine—"I hope you're not married with two kids and a home, and crazy in love with your wife."

I smiled at the implied compliment. "That's the nicest thing anyone has said to me in, well, forty-eight hours."

She didn't laugh. "What do you think? What do you feel? Are you married? Are you a family man?"

"It's a blank. It's more than a blank. It's a black hole. A place I am not allowed to go. An empty place."

"I'm sorry. I shouldn't have gone there. It was selfish of me."

I shook my head, surprised at my own reaction. "No, it kind of helps to be able to talk about it. And"—I smiled on the side of my face where it was rueful—"if I were married, I think she might be quite like you."

She screwed up a paper napkin and threw it at me, but she was smiling.

We talked some more. Some of it was about what she knew about Pete. A lot of it was speculation about who I might be, some of it was about what she would like to do with her mother and her brother, getting them to a saner, safer place where law enforcement and government did not live in fear of organized crime and terrorism, but most of it was just idle chat, and we laughed a lot. I found there were songs, books, and films I remembered, some she liked, some she'd never heard of. And there were songs and books and movies she told me about which mostly I didn't remember or never knew.

And as the horizon started turning gray, we drove down to the beach and had a breakfast worthy of the gods. We watched the sun rise over the San Jacinto mountains and turn the ocean and the sky first pink, then violet, and finally blue. And after that, in the morning's early light, with the soft top down, I drove her home to her house on East 25th Street. Before she got out, she reached across and kissed me on the cheek and whispered in my ear, "Call me?"

"I will."

I watched her turn the key and go inside the house, and I watched the door close. Then I drove back to my place, climbed the stairs, and collapsed on the bed. I looked at the clock on the bedside table. It said it was eleven thirty-five in the morning in big, red digits. Then I slipped into a deep, all-absorbing darkness.

TEN

EARLIER THAT SAME MORNING, PETE HAD RUNG the bell and knocked softly on the door at the corner of East 25th Street. For a while, nothing had happened. So he did it again. It was eight in the morning. He knew they would all be at home. Agustin had told him their routine. Ernestina worked late and slept late. Her mother cleaned and didn't leave the house till nine, sometimes later, and the boy Nelson didn't get up till one. He was out all night snorting coke and smoking marijuana with his teenage gang.

He rang again, and the door opened an inch. It was the mother.

"Yes?"

He smiled. "Mrs. Carmen Lopez? I am sorry to call so early. I am a friend of Agustin's, Ernestina's boss. I have something important to discuss with you and your children."

"Important?"

He sighed and broadened his smile. "I do apologize. I

have a flight to New York later this morning, and I was hoping to have this settled before I left. I wanted to offer Ernestina a job, and possibly you and your son, too. Agustin said you'd be grateful of it. It pays well, managing a quality café down on the beach, at Venice. You know the Ocean Front Walk? I just bought a property there..."

He trailed off. She had seemed to give a little jump when he mentioned the address. "Oh, Venice? Ocean front is nice. You better come in."

She unlatched the door, stepped back, and opened it wide. Pete gave her a big, friendly smile and stepped over the threshold. She ushered him into the sitting room, talking all the while.

"They are both still in bed. Young people today! It was different when I was a kid! You must have been up real early to be here at this time. Of course Ernestina works long hours at night. I have some coffee brewing. Will you have some? I'll call the kids."

She hurried down the short passage, past the kitchen. He could smell the rich coffee on the air. A door opened. He heard murmured voices, one male, sleepy, the other Carmen's. The door closed, and another opened. Silence. Then Carmen was coming down the passage again looking distraught.

"Nelson is just getting up. He is out late most nights." She spread her hands, shrugging, shaking her head. "Ernestina is not home yet! She works sometimes till four in the morning. Maybe she stayed with one of the other waitresses. She should be back soon. I can call her."

He knew where she was. She was with the son of a bitch who'd killed Steve and Jesus' men. He paused and thought, smiling at her the while. Waiting would be a waste of time. If she was getting close to the asshole, that was a good thing. So the choice was, wait here for her and give her a surprise when she got home, or leave and come back for her later.

He reached in his pocket and pulled out a card, which he handed to Carmen.

"Tell her Pete was here. I would really like her to do this job for me. It pays very well. Tell her Agustin and I will be very grateful, and her whole family will benefit. Tell her to call me when she gets in."

"I will, Mr. Peter. I am so sorry she was not here, and my son sleeping. I will tell her to call you. Venice? On the beach?"

He shrugged. "Young people. Yeah, Venice, on the beach. You'll love it."

She sighed and let him out just as her son was emerging from his room, bare-chested and sleepy in just his jeans. Pete paused in the doorway and looked at the boy. They held each other's eye for a long moment.

"Good morning, Nelson. Don't go anywhere. I might have some well-paid work for you."

He winked and left. They watched him drive away in his dark BMW, Carmen sighing and shaking her head. "Where is your sister? An opportunity like this comes, and where is she? She didn't come home last night, and now look!"

He didn't answer. Nelson turned and went into the kitchen, muttering, "You made me get up for this? Where's my breakfast?"

———

JUST TWELVE MILES to the west, Dave Marshall sat in Special Agent Elroy Jones' office. Jones was behind his desk, and sitting beside Dave was Assistant District Attorney Serenity Hamilton. Her face was as severe as her gray wool suit, and her hair was pulled back so tightly you could almost hear it scream.

"Do you mind explaining to me, Mr. Marshall, why you have taken it upon yourself to share confidential information of your client's with Special Agent Jones and myself?"

Marshall suppressed a frown of incomprehension and shook his head. "Not at all. I have shared it because the law requires me to do so. This man, whose identity we still don't know, came to me claiming to have total amnesia. He claimed to have awoken outside the house on East Ocean Boulevard where Ochoa, Gavilan, Peralta, and Borja were found, on that same morning, with no idea of who he was or how he came to be there."

He paused and glanced at Jones, cleared his throat, and went on.

"The reason he came to me, he said, was that he wanted me to trace the plates on his truck, to see if that would give him some clue to who he was. A little digging showed me the truck was registered to the owner of a club in Vegas. It had been reported stolen a couple of days earlier, from the parking lot at Caesar's Palace, at the very time Ochoa, Gavilan, Peralta, and Borja were staying at that same hotel." He held up both hands. "Already we're crossing state lines, but that in itself does not signify. However, what *might* signify is that those four gentlemen are known by the Federal Bureau of Investigation to be heavily involved in drug and sex trafficking, as well as murder and extortion, on behalf of the

Sinaloa Cartel. And the very night after this guy comes to me, Steve Schneider, a small-time pusher who was actively trying to make it into the big time, gets killed in his house. All five kills were clearly professional. So"—he spread his hands and made no effort to conceal the sarcasm in his voice—"and please forgive me if I have overstepped the mark, but it seems to me that there is an at least even chance that there might be at least one more professional hit on the way in the near future, that it might be related to trafficking for the Sinaloa Cartel, and it might be professionally executed. I think that places a legal obligation on me to come forward, and the narcotics and the cross-border nature of the Ochoa hit bring it within the jurisdiction of the Bureau."

She regarded him with hooded eyes. She didn't like him, and he wondered why. He suspected it was because he was a man. She turned her hooded eyes on Jones.

"What is your opinion, Special Agent Jones? Is Mr. Marshall just trying to get his job back, or is there something in what he is saying?"

Jones arched an eyebrow at the edge of his desk and rumbled.

"Dave can have his job back any day he likes, Ms. Hamilton. Nobody here wanted him to leave. And I agree with him. It looks very much like somebody has put a contract out on Jesus Sanchez and his network in Los Angeles—"

"Was Steve Schneider involved with the cartel, or is that just an assumption on Mr. Marshall's part?"

"I'm right here. Why don't you ask me?"

She didn't look at him. She said, "I am asking Special Agent Jones."

Jones made another, lower rumble. "Ms. Hamilton, I

cannot speak for what assumptions Dave has or has not made. I know he is a damned fine professional, and we miss him at the Bureau. For my part, seeing the string of events so closely connected in space and time, and this man with no apparent identity at the scene of Ochoa and his boys' murders, I'd say a person would have to be pretty damn stupid not to suspect a causal link."

Her large brown eyes became even more hooded. "Are you implying, Special Agent—"

"No, ma'am, it would never cross my mind to imply anything. I am just saying that I believe Dave has made a very good point, and suspecting that a major, violent crime might be about to be committed, he is required by law to inform us. I also believe that this case falls within the jurisdiction of the Bureau."

"How do you intend to proceed?"

"We've spoken to the Long Beach PD and requested their files. The first thing I aim to do is talk to this guy and have him checked out by a shrink. I also want to have a close look at the forensics and see if this guy fits the bill. Whoever killed the Ochoa boys was one tough son of a gun. I want to know who this guy is and whether he is my prime suspect or not."

"Keep me informed. If there is one thing I don't want in my city, it's the Sinaloa Cartel." She got to her feet. "Good morning, Special Agent Jones."

Dave Marshall watched her cross the room to the door.

"Good morning, ADA Hamilton," he said as she opened it. She didn't answer. She stepped through and closed it behind her.

Marshall turned to Jones and spread his hands. "What is

her problem? What, in future I should keep my mouth shut and ignore my statutory duties? She's mad at me for alerting you to a probable violent crime?"

Jones shrugged. "She thinks she has something to prove."

"Well, she sure proved it to me. What do you want me to do if this guy contacts me again?"

Jones stood, took his jacket from the back of his chair, and shrugged it on. "I'm going to go see him now. If you hear from him, tell him to go to your office and keep him there. Let me know and I'll come and talk to him. If I don't find him at home, I'll call you. I want to talk to this guy. I want to know who the hell he is, I want to know what his intentions are, and if he works for somebody, I want to know who."

Marshall smiled. "I think he feels the same way."

They rode down together in the elevator. In the shadows of the parking garage, Marshall bad his friend farewell and headed for his office.

Jones drove first to Ocean Boulevard, where Ochoa and his boys had been slaughtered. There he took his time going over the house, taking in the details and visualizing the events—first in the living room, then in the dining area, then upstairs in the bedroom, and finally in the bathroom, where there had been a violent struggle. Here the killer had shown not just a lack of compassion, but an active will to make the victim suffer. Him and the guy in the bedroom. He had suffocated both of them, denying them air, the very ability to breathe. He had been fearless, stealthy, highly professional, and cruel. Jones decided there had been deep, personal hatred in his actions.

Which meant that they had had some prior personal connection with their killer. New York?

The previous afternoon, he had been to Steve Schneider's bungalow. The crime scene officers had made it clear Schneider had allowed the killer in, and there had been no sign of violence prior to Schneider's being shot. In as far as any execution could be compassionate, this one had been: a single shot to the brow at almost point blank range would have caused instantaneous death with minimal suffering. That single, important detail set the two crimes apart from each other.

So what connected the two?

He went to the window that overlooked the front lawn and stood with his back to the glass, surveying the long room, trying to visualize the events. Somehow the guy had opened the door. The positions of the bodies ruled out anyone letting him in. So the Crime Scene Unit believed he had picked the lock. If he had, he was skilled because he had left no mark. The TV had been on, so nobody had heard him. He had come into the room, and as Ochoa had stood from the sofa, he had disemboweled him and stabbed him in the heart in a single, fluid movement.

He must have moved with speed and zero hesitation, crossing the room as Gavilan got up and came at him. Gavilan must have been still wondering what the hell was going on as he split his head down to the collar bone. And upstairs nobody heard a thing.

Bold. Bold and fast. Bold and paradoxical because displaying the rage and hatred he had displayed, he was cold, calculating, and professional.

Jones moved to the stairs as the killer had done. He had

gone up silently to where Peralta was in bed. Again, he must have been fast and silent and driven a second sword through his diaphragm, leaving him to suffocate. But he saved up all his rage and violence for the last victim, in the shower, knowing nobody would hear him.

So what connected the two was the boldness, the cold professionalism, the proximity in time and space, and the nature of the victim. But where the second-rate German American pusher got a compassionate execution, the four high-powered Mexican Sinaloa men got the full treatment.

His cell rang.

"Jones."

"Elroy, it's Marcia from the lab. I've been looking over the stuff from Steve Schneider's place."

"Yeah? Anything?"

"Well, there are a couple of things. They'll be in the report, but I thought you'd like to know right away. You remember the panel that had been pulled away from the old fireplace?"

"Sure."

"We found prints there, on the wall and on the panel. Most were too smudged to read, but a couple were viable, and we put them through the database."

"You got a hit?"

"Peter Barta, originally from Russia, came to the States as a refugee claiming Putin's regime wanted him dead. Got involved in drugs, prostitution, and extortion but has so far been too smart to get caught."

"Too professional." He said it half to himself.

"You could say that. There is something else."

"Yeah?"

"His cell shows a string of calls in the last few weeks to and from a number. We managed to trace that number to Peter Barta."

"Thanks, Marcia, that's good work."

"Sure, you got it."

He went out to his car and sat on the hood, looking down 4th Place toward the ocean. He knew about Pete Barta. He had been on the FBI radar for a while. Ex Russian special forces, did his time in the FSB, and when it came to cold professionalism, he took second place to nobody. But was he stupid enough to take on Sinaloa? Unless he'd struck a deal with somebody. The Gulf Cartel? He didn't have the kind of army he would need to deal with El Mayo's retribution, but if he had backing...

The specter of a war between the two biggest Mexican cartels fought on Californian soil sent a chill down his spine. Especially as, in his view, there was no political will to face such a prospect, much less stop it from becoming a reality.

It was all speculation, he told himself, and what he needed was hard evidence. He needed to talk to Pete Barta, but before that, he needed to talk to this guy with no memory. He pulled open the door of his Honda and climbed in, spun the wheel, did a U-turn, and headed north toward Nevin.

Half an hour later, he pulled up outside the address Dave had given him. He spent a while letting his eyes rove over the area. Despite the broad streets and the California sunshine, there was a brooding darkness about the place, and those dusty streets were practically empty.

He got out of his car and slammed the door. The bleep of the lock was loud in the mid-morning emptiness. He crossed the road and climbed the wooden stairs to the upper floor. There he rang the bell and hammered on the door. Nothing happened, but below, in the street, he heard a car accelerate and, as he glanced down absently, he saw a red Ford Mustang GT500 speed past with the top down.

He pulled his cell from his pocket and called Dave.

"Yeah?"

"He's not here. Has he contacted you?"

"No. I'll try and call him and get him to come here."

"You said he drove a white RAM, right?"

"With Nevada plates. He may have gotten rid of it by now. He said he was going to return it to its owner."

Jones peered down the road in the direction the Mustang had taken.

"Yeah," he said. "Maybe he did that. Okay, keep me posted."

ELEVEN

THERE WAS HAMMERING IN THE DARKNESS. I struggled out of the blackness, opened my eyes, and sat up. I reached for the BUL under my pillow and crossed the room toward the door with my mind still struggling to grip on to consciousness. The hammering was still going on, but now I could hear a voice too.

"*Rogue! Wake up! Please wake up!*"

I opened the door, and she burst in, gripping at my shoulders. "You have to help us! Please! You said you would! Please!"

I slipped the pistol in my belt behind my back and took hold of her shoulders.

"Slow down. Tell me what's happened."

"You left me at my house just now! When I went in, my mother told me Peter had been there. He wanted to offer me a job, he said. Some bullshit about he had bought a bar on the beach and wanted the three of us to run it."

"What the hell...?"

She swallowed and took a deep breath, then spoke very deliberately. "He left a message for me, Rogue. He said he and Agustin would be very grateful if I do this job. There is lots of money in it for us, and it will be very good for me and my family. You *know* what he is saying! That is classic Sinaloa—"

"Set me up for the kill, or he will kill your family."

"*You have to help!*"

I nodded. "Oh, I'll help. I'll help, Ernestina, but you need to cool down and start thinking. Did anyone follow you here?"

She stared into my face like she was transfixed. "I—I don't...I just ran here when she told me. I didn't look."

I peered out the door and down the steps. There was nothing. I listened. There was no sound of revving engines.

I went back inside and snapped, "Help me!" She followed me into the bedroom, and as I grabbed my weapons, I said, "Under the bed. Get the sports bags."

She grabbed the three bags and dumped them on the bed. I took all the money out of one of them and crammed it into the other two. I handed them to her and said, "Take them down to the car!"

As she struggled out, I grabbed a few handfuls of clothes and dirty laundry, stuffed them in the other bag, and followed her out. From the top of the stairs, I pressed the fob and unlocked the car. The lights flashed and bleeped in the empty street. She opened the trunk, and we stuffed the three bags in. I slammed it shut and got behind the wheel, and she climbed in beside me as I raised the soft top.

I took it easy going down Compton Avenue, scanning

for any car or person that looked out of place. But as usual, the streets were empty. I turned into East 25th and stopped outside her house. I climbed out and stood staring up and down the street. Still there was nothing. I leaned in the window. "Okay, get out and go into the house. Leave your car door and your front door open. Go."

She did as I said, and I heard raised female voices inside the house. I followed her inside, and the woman who was obviously her mother stood in the middle of the floor staring at me. Ernestina's brother, a boy of maybe eighteen, was standing by the kitchen door. He was also staring at me with an ugly mix of resentment and curiosity.

I spoke to the mother. "You speak English?"

"Of course."

I turned to the boy. "I am going to tell you this once. I am not going to argue with you. We have zero time to waste. You both understand?"

They didn't say anything, but their faces said they understood. "The man who came this morning is called Pete Barta. He works for Jesus Sanchez, who is a senior member of the Sinaloa Cartel. He is a drugs trafficker and a killer. If he comes back here, he will kill you all."

The mother went pale and put her hands to her mouth and looked up at Ernestina. The boy frowned and looked down at his feet.

The mother said, "Who is this man? Why is he saying this? The man this morning, he was a good man, well-dressed..."

Ernestina was shaking her head. "No, Mama. I know that man. He and Agustin sell drugs, I know this."

"*And you work there?*"

I said, "We have no time for this."

The boy interrupted. "Is true, Mama. He let me know when he was leaving. He was offering me a job."

"You guys need to get your money, your cards, the absolute essentials, and we have to get out of here now."

Her mother threw her hands in the air. "But this is crazy! Esta loco! This again! We come to the States to get away from this! I don't believe you!" She shook a crazy finger at me. "No te creo! No te creo!"

She was shouting, advancing on me. I looked at her son. "Get her in the car." I turned to Ernestina. "Get everything that's essential for the three of you. Make it fast. Driver's licenses, credit cards, cash. Whatever you need to survive. But no cells! You understand that? No cell phones."

The kid was pushing his mother out the door. I went out ahead of them, scanned the road, and waved them into the back of the Mustang. The mother was weeping, saying in Spanish I was crazy and I was going to kill them.

"Esta loco. Nos va a matar a todos..."

Ernestina came out running with a plastic grocery bag full of purses and junk. I dropped the passenger seat, and she got in. I climbed behind the wheel, made the engine roar and made a U-turn, then swung back onto Compton Avenue and roared past my place. As we passed it I spotted a Honda Accord that hadn't been there when I left, and in my side mirror, I saw a black guy in a suit standing at my door.

Even at this distance, I could tell. He was a Fed. He had it written all over him. I had little doubt that was Dave's work. But they'd be looking for a white Dodge RAM, not a red Mustang. What I had to do now was get Ernestina and her family out of harm's way, and I needed to think.

I needed to think hard and fast.

I spent half an hour making random figures of eight around southern Los Angeles with one eye glued on my mirror until I hit Route 91, which I followed as far as I-15 at Corona, and then headed north toward the mountains and the desert beyond. All the while Ernestina's mother had been whimpering and praying in Spanish. Now as we headed out of town through Sierra Lakes, I asked her, "What's your name?"

She sniffled a bit and said, "Carmen. You gonna kill us?"

In the rear view, I gave her the closest thing to a human smile I could muster.

"If I was, don't you think this would be a pretty stupid way to do it?" I gave her a moment to think about it. Then I told her, "I'm a friend of Ernestina's. We've known each other a while, right?"

I glanced at her, asking her for confirmation for her mother's sake. She said, "Yeah" and gave a small laugh, then more quietly, "A while."

Knowing she'd back me up, I began to improvise. "I used to work in law enforcement, Carmen, and I know this guy. He is dangerous and he is on the FBI's watch list. I am not going to hurt you. I'm going to take you somewhere safe for a few days while we deal with this. You'll be with Ernestina and your boy..." I glanced at him in the mirror. He muttered, "Nelson."

"Nelson. As soon as this is over, in a couple of days, I am going to come and get you. But you have to trust me on this, and the three of you have to promise me you will make no telephone calls to anybody. You will keep quiet, keep a very low profile, watch lots of TV and tell nobody, absolutely nobody, where you are. Agreed?"

They didn't say a thing.

"Guys, you have to understand this. If you give him the smallest opportunity, he will find you, and he will kill you. Do you understand that?"

Nelson nodded and said, "Yes." Ernestina echoed him, and finally Carmen said, "Okay, de acuerdo."

We came out of the mountains at Cajun Junction, and at exit 141 I headed north into the desert. I didn't know where I was going, but I was learning to trust what went on down there in the darkness of my unconscious. I joined Route 395 and just kept speeding into the desert in a long, straight line past Adelanto and empty miles of dust and dirt until we came to Atolia and Searls and finally, after more than an hour and almost a hundred miles of flat emptiness, heat, and dirt, we came to an intersection with a turn-off for Ridge-crest. When I saw that sign, I knew this was where I was headed.

Ridgecrest is a neat, prosperous town set on a desiccated desert plain surrounded by the Sierra Nevada mountains to the west, the Cosos mountains to the north, the Argus Range to the east, and the El Paso Mountains to the south. But the land surrounding the town itself is flat and dusty and populated by little more than dry, gnarled scrub, snakes, and bugs.

In among the well-kept streets, however, there was an abundance of pine trees, plane trees, oaks, and others I could not identify, and each house had its own brilliant green, irrigated lawn. Hi-tech and the Navy drove the economy in this place, and between them, they were turning the desert hi-tech green.

At the intersection of Upjohn Avenue and South China Lake Boulevard was the Quality Inn. There I pulled in to the parking lot, killed the engine, and took Ernestina around to the trunk. I opened it, making sure we blocked any view of its contents, and unzipped one of the bags. From it I extracted fifty thousand dollars in mixed bills and stuffed it in the plastic grocery bag. I saw her draw breath and cut her short.

"This is not for you. So you can't refuse it. This is for your mother and your brother, and you have no right to put their lives in jeopardy just to protect your own pride."

It came out with more aggression than I had intended, and I saw her cheeks color. She stepped back and scowled at me. I handed her the money and spoke more gently. "They should not have to pay for the mistakes that we have made. You take this money, you look after them, and you keep them safe."

She hesitated, then took the bag. I pulled the BUL SAS from my belt and handed her that too. "Nobody is going to come for you because nobody knows where you are. But if something goes wrong and they do come, you kill them. You aim for the body and you pull the trigger. Do *not* let your brother see the cash or that you have a weapon. You understand?"

She nodded and took the pistol.

"Now go book a room for the three of you, out of sight of the road. They must not see me. When you have the room, you come back, and we drive to the door."

Fifteen minutes later, they climbed out of the car and

hustled into the room at the back of the motel, taking their few possessions with them. I followed them in and closed the door behind me. Nelson sat on a chair, Ernestina sat on the bed, and her mother lay next to her, weeping with one arm over her eyes. I pointed at Nelson.

"This is not about you." Then I pointed at Carmen and Ernestina. "And it is not about you, or you. Whoever you are, it's about the other two. You cannot give in to your pride, or your fear, or some stupid need to talk to a friend or relation on the phone.

"If it is just your life on the line, you can. You take the risk, you pay the price. But when it's your brother, your sister, your mother, or your children's lives on the line, you can't. You do not have that choice. Because it's *their* lives that are on the line, not yours."

I waited. They all averted their eyes, but nobody spoke.

"I just need a couple of days. There is a shopping mall half a mile up the road. I'm going to go there and buy a cell phone. I am going to leave it with you, Ernestina. You call me only if there is an emergency. I'll be back in a day, two at most, and you'll be able to go home."

It was Ernestina who spoke first. "What are you going to do?"

"You don't want to know." I half-smiled. "Remember, information is power, but the wrong information can be a death sentence."

"I remembered who said that," she said, but I didn't listen.

"I'll be back in twenty minutes, half an hour tops. Stay here, keep quiet, and don't do anything stupid."

I got in the Mustang and drove half a mile up South

China Lake Boulevard to the Ridgecrest Plaza Shopping Center. There I bought food for three people for a week and a few bits and pieces of DIY hardware I needed, including a car battery. I also bought a couple of burner cell phones. When I got back, I left Carmen unpacking the groceries and took Ernestina outside. She sat with her ass on the hood of the Mustang, and I handed her the two burners.

"This one, the red one, is for you to call me if there is an emergency. Do not under any circumstances use it for anything else. I've got the number on my phone, and I'll call you if I need to. Okay?"

She nodded. I pointed to the other phone.

"The black one is for you to call Pete."

"*What?* Are you kidding me?"

"You tell him we want to meet him. You tell him you'll be with me. You'll hand me over, but you want ten thousand dollars and a guarantee he is going to leave your family alone."

"No! I won't do that! Anyway, like I'd take his word for anything!"

"No." I shook my head. "Don't think about you. Think about him. What is he going to believe? What does he see when he looks at you? He sees a frightened, naïve girl that he can control and dominate."

"Is that what you see?"

"Stop it. Focus on the job. We don't have the time to be personal or emotional."

She closed her eyes and took a deep breath. "Where?"

"Topanga Beach, just before the lagoon, you come off the road and you go down the drive to the sand. There's a parking lot down there, and an old house. I think they're restrooms now. Tell him to park there and we'll meet him on the far side of the lagoon at ten tonight. It'll be just you and me, and he should come alone."

"He won't."

"I know that."

"And you *will* be alone."

I gripped her shoulders and pulled her close, looking hard into her eyes. "Do your part right. I'll do my part right, and everything is going to work out fine. Trust me."

She sighed and smiled. "A guy who doesn't know who he is tells me to trust him as he prepares to go and shoot a Sinaloa gangster." She nodded, watching me with weary eyes. "And I do."

I returned the smile. "Who said I was going to shoot him?"

I got behind the wheel, pulled the soft top down, fired up the big V8, and rolled out of the lot. All the while she stood there, watching me.

I didn't go back the way I'd come. I took State Highway 14 and blasted across the eighty miles of desert through Red Rock Canyon to Mojave, and then didn't take my foot off the gas till I reached Palmdale and started to climb into the mountains, leaving a cloud of dust behind me eighty miles long.

It took me forty minutes to cover the eighty miles, but from Vincent to Topanga, the roads were not so straight and the route was convoluted and twisted, through mountains and through some densely populated areas. It was a little over sixty miles, but it took me an hour and a quarter to cover the distance, and it was closing on four p.m. by the time I got there.

At the bottom of Topanga Canyon Boulevard, I pulled into the gas station and filled the tank. I also bought four gas cans and filled them too. Then I cut across the Pacific Coast Highway and down onto Beach Drive. At the bottom of the drive, I parked in the parking lot and sat staring out at the sea, thinking about how I was going to kill Pete Barta.

TWELVE

TOPANGA CREEK SPILLS OUT OF THE BROOKSIDE Canyon, among the mountains that rise sharply above Topanga Beach, runs under the Pacific Coast Highway, and forms the Topanga Lagoon, which divides Topanga Beach in two as it runs out into the ocean.

On the east side are the old restrooms, the parking lots, the shaded gardens, and the drive that leads up to the highway. On the west side, the lagoon is flanked by big rocks and trees, and the parking lot, such as it is, is just sand and scattered bushes and weeds—one rare place in Southern California where paradise hadn't been paved to put up a parking lot.

I spent a half hour or a little more mooching around the area exploring. I was curious on two levels. First of all, I wanted to recon the area for what was coming later, but I was also curious because I had realized when I was talking to Ernestina that I knew this place. I was familiar with it. But now, as I explored, no bells were set ringing. Nothing leapt out of my memory.

There were not many people there—a couple of families under bright umbrellas, a girl in a pink bikini reading a book —and as the sun began to decline, those began to gather their stuff and leave. That was when I started setting the scene and making the arrangements. It took a while, but by seven p.m., it was all ready, and I took the Mustang to the upper parking lot and crossed the road to get some food from the Seven Eleven.

I took the food and a drink down to the far side of the Topanga Lagoon, along with the duffel bag I had stuffed full of clothes and dirty laundry, and sat at the foot of a palm tree to eat bread and cheese and drink a cold beer. From where I was sitting, I had a clear view of the lower parking lot, and I was not surprised to see a couple of cars pull in at nine-thirty and park at the bottom of the drive, opposite the restrooms. One of the cars looked like a dark BMW, the drug dealer's vehicle of choice. The other was a dark Audi, the discerning criminal executive's choice.

They stood in a small group on the edge of the sand, looking around. They were silent. I pulled the .357 from under my arm and raised my voice.

"I told you to come alone, Pete."

They all froze, and I smiled to myself. After a moment, he said, "You said you were coming with the girl. Where is she?"

"She's here, with me, where I can protect her. I don't blame you for bringing protection of your own, Pete, but if we are going to talk, your boys stay by the cars."

"So you can put a bullet through my skull like you did with Steve?"

He was scanning the darkness, trying to fix where my voice was coming from. I gave a small laugh.

"I'd have to be pretty stupid to do that, Pete, wouldn't I? There are six of you against me and a girl. You think I didn't know you'd bring your boys? I'm not stupid, and I am not a novice. But I do know that when you hear what I have to say, you won't want to kill me. Not yet."

He had stopped scanning, and he and his boys were all looking at the same spot, right at me across the sand and the shallow water of the lagoon where it spills into the ocean.

"You're at the palm tree."

"Take it easy, Pete. What I have to talk to you about starts with two and a half million bucks that I have taken from schmucks like Steve from New York to Vegas and now LA. I am ready to make a trade, but we need to talk, you and me."

"I ain't stupid. I am not going over there without—"

"You bring one guy and you cross the stream of the lagoon. Your five other boys stay on the other side where I can see them. You'll see a stack of driftwood. They come no closer than that. If they do, I'm out of here. If I do anything stupid I'll have five armed men from Sinaloa on my tail. I'm not that much of an asshole, Pete. That situation is exactly what I'm here to try to avoid. Now you want to talk about two and a half million bucks, or you want to tell me how chicken shit scared you are?"

There was some murmuring and muttering. Then the group started to move across the sand. Fifteen yards from the stream that carried the water from the lagoon out to the sea,

I had made a stack of driftwood. There the group stopped, and Pete called out, "Okay, where are you? You at the palm tree?"

"Where am I? I am out-gunned six to one, that's where I am. Your bodyguards stay there where I can keep an eye on them, and you and one of your boys cross that shallow stream and stop. Then I will come out with a bag containing the six hundred grand I took from Steve. After that, we will talk about where the rest is and how you can get your hands on it. Are we on the same page, Pete?"

He had not expected this, and he was struggling to decide how to handle it. That was what I was banking on, and I started to pressure him.

"I have a bead on you, pal, and if you're not already bleeding out in the sand it's because you are more use to me alive than dead. Keep thinking and I am out of here. Your friends Ochoa, Gavilan, Peralta, and Borja will tell you I'm not stupid, Pete. So either get on board or get the hell out of here. Do you want the money or not?"

He glanced at the guy next to him, and they walked forward. The stream was maybe twelve feet across, but it was no more than six inches deep. They waded in, with the rippling water glinting and reflecting the street lamps from the highway above. The slosh of the water blended with the thud and sigh of the small waves on the shore. Above, a bus hummed past and vanished into the night toward Los Angeles.

I stood, keeping myself behind the trunk of the palm tree, and took hold of the duffel bag I had brought with me, packed full of old clothes and laundry. I swung it and threw it down the beach. It landed maybe twelve feet from where Pete was standing.

"That's a show of good will. You can check it while your boy covers you. You got five other boys behind you. Try to be a man, Pete."

They knew exactly where I was by now. Pete turned to the guy next to him and nodded. His boy drew his piece and pointed it in my direction. I hunkered down and reached behind a rock.

Gasoline is volatile. Leave it in a warm place, under the sun or under a stack of wood, and it wants to evaporate, but if it is contained in a plastic container, what it does is start to build up pressure.

I had made a small hole in just one of those containers and I had inserted a length of electrical wire of the sort you'd use for a lamp. I had stripped the ends and wound them around a half inch of copper wire. Then I had sealed the small hole with electrical tape to keep the pressure in.

The wire I had bought was long, long enough to run under the sand from the stack of wood, across the stream and all the way to the palm tree where I was hunkered down. There, one of the ends was connected to the negative pole of the car battery I had bought. Now, as Pete trudged through the sand toward the sports bag full of junk, I connected the other wire to the positive pole.

For a second, nothing happened while the small copper element resisted the flow of electrons and grew hot among the fumes of the gasoline. Then the heat reached a critical point, the copper made a small bang and ignited the fumes, and four gallons of gasoline blasted in a ball of fire out of the woodpile, engulfing the four men standing there, igniting their clothes and their skin in the searing heat. They screamed and writhed like dancing demons in the night.

Pete and his man turned to stare. It was a stupid thing to do. I didn't waste time. I already had his guy in my sights, and I put a slug right through his heart. Then I was running hard across the soft sand toward Pete.

He turned as I collided with him, and we hit the ground sprawling. But this guy was tough, and if I had hoped to wind him, I was sorely disappointed. As I straddled him and hit his face, he was pounding my sides with his fists, twisting and thrashing. I fell to the side, and he was scrambling to his feet. He struck out with his foot and kicked me twice, hard in the thigh before I could roll away.

By the time I was on one knee, he was pulling his piece from behind his back. I didn't think or hesitate. I charged him, scooping up sand in my hand and hurling it in his face. He fired wildly as I dodged to his left, but I felt the heat and the pop of the rounds as they skimmed past my head. I reached for his arm, but he staggered past me, running for the lagoon. I went after him as he plunged in, splashing water into his eyes and wheeling around, looking for me, flailing his gun at the same time.

The water and the mud slowed me down, but I got close enough to grip his gun barrel with my left hand and deliver a powerful right hook to his face. I missed his jaw and caught his cheekbone, but it was enough to make him stagger. I didn't let go of the gun, but I stepped in closer, and the next right hook went to his floating ribs. I needed the son of a bitch conscious. He retched, and as he doubled up, I tore the weapon from his hand, took a handful of his wet hair and shoved the cannon in the back of his neck. Far off, I could hear a siren.

I snarled, "You want to avoid an intimate one-on-one with the Los Angeles Sheriff's Department? Then get moving. Fast!"

We half-ran and half-stumbled across the sand, past the smoldering bodies that were still twitching beside the burning driftwood. We ran up the steps that led to the parking lot, and I shoved him toward the Mustang. My plan had been to stick him in the trunk, but the approaching howl of the sirens meant there was no time. I pulled open the passenger door and snarled at him, "Give me trouble and I'll blow your kneecap off. Do we understand each other? Do I need to prove I'm serious?"

He looked pale and sick and shook his head. I figured I had five minutes before he gave me trouble again. I got behind the wheel, the engine roared, and I did zero to sixty out across the Pacific Coast Highway and back onto Topanga Canyon Boulevard in less than four seconds. I kept the headlights off so the cops arriving behind me would not see me, and in another four seconds I was doing a hundred miles per hour, making the tires complain on the winding bends.

I glanced at Pete. "I think you might die tonight, Pete. You fancy fighting for your life at a hundred miles per hour, climbing into the mountains? I need both hands for the steering wheel. You want to give it a go?"

He scowled at me, but he didn't answer, and he didn't try it.

It took me fifteen minutes to get to Woodland Hills. By that time, we were deep in sleeping suburbia, and I eased the speed, but I also picked up the Glock I'd taken from him in the lagoon and held it on the wheel. I told him, "I need you to think, Pete. I could have shot you dead along with your friends, but I didn't."

He darted a look at me. There was fear in his eyes.

"What do you want?"

"I want you and Jesus Sanchez off my back. You can do what the hell you like with Ernestina. But I want you off my back." I turned onto the Ventura Freeway and began to accelerate. "Now I am smart enough that I know if I kill you, Jesus Sanchez will have to come after me, to protect his reputation. So what I need you to tell me is, what do I need to do to get you and him off my back?"

He didn't answer right away. He was watching the city slipping by outside and wondering where the hell we were going. At the interchange at Sepulveda, I took I-405 headed south, back down through the mountains toward West Los Angeles and Santa Monica. He had gone very still and very quiet.

"What's the matter, Pete? You're not answering my question. This all looking familiar to you? It's where you live, Pete. I am taking you home. But I need something from you. You have seen what I am capable of, Pete, but I am willing to leave you and Jesus Sanchez alone. I know when I am outgunned. But you have to tell me: what do I need to do to get you guys off my back?"

I came off at Exit 55A onto the Santa Monica Boulevard and followed it all the way down to Ocean Avenue. When he spoke, his voice sounded different, like he was scared, disoriented, and being real careful.

"I guess, if you returned the money that would help,

plus interest." He glanced at me. I was nodding. He went on, "You said a couple of million…"

"Two and a half is what I have available right now."

"That, and maybe hand over the girl. Somebody has to pay, right?"

"Right. So she pays for what I did, as an example to others. That makes sense."

"Right? I can talk to him. Mediate…"

"Good. That helps." I flashed a grin at him. "See? We don't always need to be killing people, right?"

His laugh would have been pathetic if it hadn't been so nauseating.

Now I followed Ocean Avenue through winding streets where the owners were too rich to bother with the grid system, until we came to Corona del Mar, a short road that housed ten small mansions. There I pulled into the crescent drive of the smallest one, halfway down the road. I killed the engine and pointed the Glock at the very same spot where I had shot Steve, making a triangle with his eyes.

"You going to invite me in for a drink? We have plans to make." He swallowed and nodded. I said, "I get out first. You do something stupid and I will not kill you. I will shoot you in the knee, in the hip, in the stomach. All those places where it really hurts, Pete." I shook my head. "Don't make me do that. Let's solve this problem, right? So we can both go on our way."

He nodded. "Okay, I get it."

I got out and covered him as he climbed a couple of steps to the porch and slipped the key in the door.

THIRTEEN

The front door opened into what modern architects like to call a space. A space is the same as a room, only you save money by not having to build walls around it. This space had parquet floors strewn with bull skins and a couple of Persian carpets. There was a large fireplace with an iron poker hanging from a stand with other tools. The furniture was a set of two big, overstuffed calico armchairs and an eight-foot sofa, all positioned around the fireplace, with a huge, ethnic coffee table designed to bruise your shins after you'd snorted your coke. At the far end of the space, beside the glass doors that led to the lawn and the pool, there was a large, oval dining table with eight chairs. A French dresser against the wall held expensive china and crystal. It was hard to imagine this guy entertaining people for dinner, but who knew?

I closed the door and watched him go to the dresser, where he poured himself what looked like a brandy from a crystal decanter. I moved a bit closer. I had tucked the Glock into my waistband and had the .357 in my hand.

"You going to offer me a drink, Pete? We are supposed to be working on a friendship here, remember? We're going to be pals. I give you two and a half million bucks and you use it to get Jesus off my back."

"What do you want?" He asked it without looking at me.

"Scotch or Irish, neat."

He spoke as he poured. "Where is the money?"

"I will give it to you as soon as we have a plan worked out."

He came toward me holding two glasses. I raised the weapon, and with my left hand I pointed toward the big, ethnic coke table. He set the drinks down and sat. I sat opposite him and took a pull on my drink.

"Is Jesus settled in Los Angeles?"

He shook his head. "No, he has a house here in Beverly Hills, on Rexford Drive. It belongs to one of his money laundering companies. But he lives in Mexico. He has some kind of palatial ranch south of Guamúchil, Reino Sinaloa."

"So how come he's here?"

"I don't know."

I smiled at him. It was the kind of smile you don't want to see late at night in a dark alley. "Be cooperative, Pete. Why is Jesus Sanchez in Los Angeles? Don't tell me you don't know because you were at the Coca Cabaña talking about it with him."

He took a deep sigh and a pull on his drink. "It looks like there is going to be a change of leadership in one of the cartels—"

"Ismael Zambada, el Mayo, the head of the Sinaloa Cartel, is dying. That is the last warning I am going to give you, Pete. I am trying to do this nice so we both benefit. You keep trying to play me and I am going to take off your kneecaps." He had gone pale. I showed him the revolver, aiming it at his leg. "It's a .357 magnum. It will tear your leg in half. The game has changed. Be smart."

He swallowed and nodded. "El Mayo is dying. He's almost seventy-six years old, and he suffers from diabetes. They reckon he might have only a couple of years left, if that."

"So there's going to be a palace revolution."

"That's what Jesus wants to avoid. Sinaloa has been so successful because El Mayo managed to enforce unity and loyalty. If there is a civil war, the whole thing could collapse."

I nodded. "Okay, I'm being patient. How does that bring Jesus Sanchez to LA?"

"He owns the corridor from Guamúchil and Los Mochis up through Sonora to San Diego and Los Angeles. But from the border into the States, distribution nationwide is haphazard and sometimes chaotic. Sometimes some stupid asshole on the street can get an important guy caught or even killed because he's not professional. He's careless. Add to that the Gulf Cartel causing problems in Texas and the east, and suddenly Sinaloa has distribution problems.

"So what Jesus is trying to do is take some control over the distribution network, get it working smooth from San Diego to New York, Miami to Seattle. He's been planning it for a couple of years because he figures when the time comes that will put him in a position to take over the cartel with a minimum of conflict. I think he's right, and people can get very rich." He shrugged. "The state the US administration is in, they could end up controlling the US the way they control Mexico."

I did a lot of nodding. I couldn't remember what condition the US administration was in, but I had a gut feeling he was right.

"Ochoa and his boys, they were in New York..."

He was warming to his subject. Maybe he was thinking that if he kept talking enough I might not kill him.

He interrupted me. "Yeah, Jesus thinks New York is key, at least as important as Los Angeles. It's the financial heart of the United States. You buy yourself a couple of judges, some senior cops, the DA, and the mayor and you own New York, man, and through New York, you can run the biggest laundering operation in the history of international crime. Sinaloa makes billions every year, tax free, selling coke, fentanyl, heroin, and women. You put that money through the New York financial institutions and man, you could own the fuckin' Federal Reserve, and with it the fuckin' White House." He stared at me, and after a moment shook a finger at me. "It's not hard to do. The administration in New York is very corrupt. There is *a lot* of corruption in New York, at all levels, but to exploit it, you need an organization that works efficiently. Sinaloa is very powerful because they are very violent and willing to use violence. But they are not efficient."

"Not like the Russian Mafia."

He gave a scornful laugh. "Sinaloa has the product. If we had that product? We would rule the world. Is like the fuckin' Arabs, right? They got the oil. So what can you do?"

"Take over."

"Right."

"So Ochoa and his boys were in New York trying to put efficient distribution in place."

"Yeah, and Jesus was there too. Then those guys get killed in Los Angeles, like some fuckin' ninja!"

"No kidding."

"Yeah. You saying now it's you. And then Steve. And you take his money—*their* money. But you asked me about his reason for being here. Distribution. He is making better distribution."

"And he is here now, in Beverly Hills?" He nodded. I thought for a second. "You got a den, or an office?"

"Upstairs."

"Okay, let's go."

He sat staring at me, and for a moment, I thought he was going to cry. "Are you going to kill me?"

"Not if I can avoid it, Pete. Jesus! You don't listen, do you? Come on, if you want to live, man up and get with the program. Upstairs."

I followed him up polished pine stairs to a broad loft area with exposed beams and skylights. There was a large desk that looked like it was made of black glass, a big black leather chair, and a computer. There were no books, but there was a single filing cabinet and a large safe in the corner. I pointed to the safe.

"Open it." He hesitated. "That's the last time, Pete. You can open it or I can torture you till you give me the code. Now I am being nice to you, and I am getting mad because you are unappreciative. Open the safe or give me the code."

He went and hunkered down, and you could tell from his movements that he was beginning to panic. He felt he was losing control, and he was right. He had lost control a long while back.

He pulled open the safe. I could see his hand was shaking. Inside the safe there were a few documents and a stash of money that was at least as much as I had taken from Steve, probably considerably more. He looked up at me.

"You want Jesus Sanchez not to go after you, but if you kill me and take my money, you will make him real mad, and he will go after you, to the end of the world. He will never stop until he kills you."

"For the last time, Pete. I do not want your money, and I am not going to kill you. Now go to your desk and write down Sanchez's full address and his telephone number. I am going to call him now, and we are going to talk. Sit down and relax."

He moved to the desk and scrawled an address in Beverly Hills on a piece of paper. Underneath it he scrawled a cell number, then held out the paper. I jerked my chin at him.

"Call him."

He hesitated, then dialed the number on his cell. I said, "Put it on speaker."

He did so and set the phone down on the desk. It rang four or five times, then a man's voice came on.

"Peter. I hope this is important. It is not smart we call each other."

I answered. "Hello, Mr. Sanchez, you don't know me, but you know of me. I am sitting here with Pete Barta in his house. It has been a very busy day. Four of his men were incinerated down on Topanga Beach, and another was shot through the heart. But I have to say, I can't complain. I seem to be growing rich pretty fast. I think I am crowding three million dollars right now." I smiled at Pete, who looked like the world was crumbling under his feet. "But I digress, Jesus. The reason I am calling you is because I gather you are looking for me, and you sent Peter here to find me. Well..."

I cocked the gun, and the magnum round exploded and punched the hollow point slug right through his forehead. At that short range, the back of his head erupted across the wall behind him.

"He won't be able to look for me anymore, Jesus, because he already found me, and now he's dead. But I wouldn't worry about that, Jesus, because you don't need to find me. I am coming to find you."

I hung up and went to search for a bedroom. I found one next door and, in the closet, I found a duffel bag. I took it back to the den and hunkered down in front of the open safe. I threw in the files and counted the money, which was bound up in neat parcels. There was eight hundred thousand dollars. That went in after the files. I took his cell, showed it his face, re-set it to open to my face instead, slipped it in my back pocket, and made my way downstairs.

I fired up the Mustang and cruised slowly back toward Santa Monica. I could not risk going back to my place in Nevin. I didn't know who knew about it or how much Dave Marshall had told the Feds.

And now it began to dawn on me how different it was for a rogue. If you were a drone, if you belonged, you could go to a hotel, rent a room, even find a new apartment, and you would have all the bank accounts, documents, and plastic cards you needed to secure your position, your status, and your credibility within the community. Because the hive would have you located, registered, and controlled at all times.

But if you were a rogue, you would have none of those things. If you have no identity capable of being registered, then as far as society is concerned, you do not exist, and if you do not exist, you cannot rent a room in a hotel, you cannot rent an apartment or buy a car or a house.

I took a moment to focus my memory, then punched a number into my cell. It rang twice before Dr. Elizabeth Grant answered.

"Hey, Doc, it's Rogue."

"It is very late, Rogue. You have to phone—" She stopped dead, and when she spoke again, there was a frown contracting her voice. "This is my personal number. How did you get it?"

"You were writing to a friend. The letter was on your desk, and it had your private number under your address. It turns out I have an eidetic memory. Isn't that ironic?"

"You absolutely cannot call me at my private number. This is an invasion of my personal, private space!"

"I won't call you again. But I need your help."

"Rogue, this really—"

"I have had to leave my house because they are trying to kill me. I have about three million dollars in cash but no credit cards or debit cards. And I have nowhere to sleep tonight."

Her voice was almost shrill. "I hope you're not expecting to stay at *my* house!"

I laughed with little humor. "Good lord, no! You'd never get the blood and grime out of your satin sheets."

"Well, what *do* you want? I don't know how you think I—"

"Elizabeth." I said it quietly, but it made her shut up. "You should really see someone about those anxiety attacks. Now do me a favor. Book me a room at a nice boutique hotel, explain I am a friend and I have been mugged and had my wallet stolen with all my papers but it is all in hand and being seen to. Meantime, you will cover everything with your credit card. I will pay you with interest at our next session."

"You must be out of your mind!"

"That is a nice thing for a psychiatrist to say to her patient. 'You must be out of your mind.' I think I could probably report you for that and have you struck off."

You could almost hear her closing her eyes and covering her face with her hand on the other end just by the tone in her voice. "Dear God! I am so sorry. I really am. I didn't mean, oh sweet Jesus...!"

"Relax, will you? I am not crazy, and you are only human. It was a long shot, but I thought I might as well try. I have nowhere to stay, and I am hurt and pretty bruised. You can't help, or you don't want to. That's fine. There's no reason why you should—"

"Rogue, wait."

"What?"

She took a deep breath and sighed noisily. "I have a house out in Williams Canyon. It's about an hour from here. I use it as a refuge at weekends. You can stay there for a week or a few days while you sort yourself out."

"That's real big of you, Doc. I mean it."

"Well, we can't have you sleeping on the street, can we?

You'd better spend the night here on my sofa, and I'll take you up there tomorrow morning."

"Thanks. I appreciate it. Where is here?"

"Venice. Dell Avenue." She gave me the number. "It's the black house over the bridge, completely hidden behind trees."

"I'll be there in ten minutes."

"Oh, that soon?"

"Is that a problem?"

"No! Not at all. Have you eaten?"

I couldn't remember whether I had eaten or not, but something made me say, "No, I haven't eaten. Shall I bring some wine?"

"No, thank you, Rogue. This is not a social meeting. What I would like you to do is behave yourself."

I smiled. "I'll be there in ten."

FOURTEEN

She fed me in the kitchen. It was just a steak and some fries, but it was good. I ate in silence while she sat in her pajamas and watched me, like she was fixing me and wanted to know if I worked properly.

"You're different," she said at last. "There is something different about you."

"Yeah?" I shrugged with my eyebrows as I wiped my mouth with a piece of kitchen paper. "I wouldn't know."

"Have you remembered anything?"

"No."

"Are you sure?"

I frowned at her, trying to wrap my head around the idea of not being sure whether you remembered something.

"I mean, how would I know...?"

"You want a drink?"

"I could use one."

She led me into the living room. It was large, broad, and in good taste. The sofa and the armchairs did not belong to a set, and they were distributed around the room, not nested in front of a TV. There was also no coffee table strategically placed to damage your shins and stop you from standing up. Instead, the chairs and sofa had lamp tables beside them where you could put your drink, your book, and maybe your pipe.

The sofa was big, overstuffed, and covered in suede. The armchair in the far corner by the drapes looked like a genuine, ancient chesterfield. The nearer one was chunky and more comfortable than aesthetic, upholstered in some kind of heavy-duty canvas. She had a large Persian rug on the floor. Where most people would have a television to receive their daily dose of conditioning, she had a wrought iron fireplace and on either side of it were dark wooden dressers topped by bookcases.

She pointed to the nearest dresser, where there was a silver tray with decanters and glasses.

"Mine's a cognac."

I poured her a generous measure into a delicately hand-cut balloon and gave myself another generous measure of Scotch into a Waterford tumbler.

She was sitting on the sofa and pointed to the ancient leather chair as I handed her her drink. I paused, holding her eye.

"I am disobedient by nature," I told her.

"Is that something you remembered? It's fine, but it's easier for me to talk to you if you sit just there."

I sat. She sipped and said, "Most people don't think about how we think." I frowned at her. She went on. "We think mainly in pictures, then we also think in sounds, and then smells, tastes, touch, and feelings generally make up what we call kinesthetics. Every sense we have generates thoughts on what we think of as the inside of our minds."

"Why are you telling me this?" I thought I knew, but I asked anyway.

"Because that's how we make memories. Think about how we bumped into each other in the shop. I mean that, actually think about it."

"I am."

"You have a short, slightly hazy movie in your head, right?"

"Yeah."

"But you also have a soundtrack."

I nodded. "You were laughing at the noises I was making. I said, 'Half of them tell you you have to find your-self, the other half tell you to destroy your ego. Ego is I in Latin, so who is doing the destroying...?' Etcetera."

"But you were also feeling something."

I nodded and thought about it. "I felt surprise, pleasure, attraction..."

"So if you said you remembered meeting me in a book-shop, that simple statement conceals a whole plethora of memories you didn't even know you had. Many of them, especially the feelings, you would not even have thought of as memories."

"That's why you asked me if I was sure I didn't remember anything."

"Images and sounds we remember with our intellect, but feelings, Rogue, we tend to remember with our bodies. Because feelings are organic, not intellectual. Have you been remembering with your body?"

I looked at the glass of whisky in my hand and wondered. Had I?

"I think I have a memory of..." I trailed off. "It's hard to put it into words. It's like a need or a hunger."

"For what?"

"I want to say justice, but that doesn't cover it." She waited. I said, "Retribution is closer, but there is more anger and rage in it than the word retribution can express. Not even revenge expresses the feeling."

I took a pull on my whiskey. As I swallowed, she asked me, "If I said to you that somebody in the recent past had hurt you very badly, would that ring true?"

I nodded, more to myself than to her. "It is so obvious, isn't it? It was staring me in the face, but I had never put it into words."

"One of the jobs of your unconscious, Rogue, is to protect you from thoughts and feelings that are too painful for you to deal with consciously. It's exactly like forming scar tissue over a wound, only the wound is in your mind, not on your body."

I stared at her for a long moment. Then I asked her, "Are we in session?"

She looked vaguely surprised. "I don't know. I don't normally cook my clients dinner and give them whiskey. Why?"

"Because if you're my therapist, there are things I can't tell you."

Her surprise turned into a frown. "Haven't you got that the wrong way around?"

I shook my head. "California State law requires you, as my therapist, to inform the authorities, and intended victims, if you believe I am a potential danger to myself or others. That obligation is much more vague, and the facts are much harder to prove, among friends."

She threw her head back, like she was staring at the ceiling, but closed her eyes and sighed loudly. "Jesus Christ, you don't let up, do you?"

"I don't know."

She lowered her head and eyed me for a moment. "I am going to say that because of your amnesia you have no real understanding of who you are, or what your limitations are in your personality. And because of that and your strong feelings of resentment, you believe you are capable of murder. *I* do not believe that you are."

"So this is a session, not a conversation among friends."

"Rogue, we hardly know each other."

"Or ourselves."

"What are you trying to tell me?"

I took another pull, savored the strong, peaty flavor, and swallowed. When I spoke, I surprised myself with the strength of my feelings.

"I need help, Elizabeth. But I need to trust somebody. I don't know if I can trust you as a friend. Like you said, we don't know each other. Hell, I don't even know myself, how can I expect to know you? But I do know that as a therapist I can't trust you because your first loyalty is not to me; it's to the State of California and the law."

She looked away with another sigh. "Boy, you are some kind of heavy dude."

"I can't argue with that."

She put her glass down carefully on the lamp table beside her and spread her hands. "Let's—" She paused and then went on. "Let's talk hypothetically. Let's say that, in this room, during this conversation, I am neither your therapist nor your friend. I am just a person here listening to what you say. And let's say also that nothing you say is to be taken as literal truth. Okay? In this conversation, you can say whatever you like because it is just a crazy release for your fantasies in the hope that that freedom will allow you to draw out and explore your repressed memories. So nothing is to be taken as true or real in this room. How would that work?"

I turned my gaze on the hot embers in the fireplace and smiled. "It sounds like the kind of thing a psychiatrist would dream up." I turned the smile on her. "But it might work. Sophistry aside, can I trust you not to report me to the cops?"

"Yes."

"I have a murderous hatred of drug dealers, especially those associated with the Sinaloa Cartel in Mexico. When I see them, I have an overpowering need to kill them."

"A need? Not a desire, a need?"

"Yes."

"Do you act on that need?"

"Yes. I am driven. First I entrap them, then I interrogate them, sometimes using torture, then I kill them and take their money." She had gone pale, but that was the only sign that my words had had an impact. Something made me smile and say, "You said fantasizing was okay, right?"

Her glance was almost grateful. "Yes, of course. You said you interrogate them. What do you interrogate them about?"

"Where they get their supplies from. Who is above them in the chain of supply and command. It's like a thread, a line that leads from the junkie dying on the street to the guy at the top—the one I want to get."

"There is one special guy?"

"Yes."

For some reason, her next question surprised me and confused me. She said, "What makes him special?"

I frowned. Several thoughts rushed me at the same time, and I had the image of bodyguards closing around the man they were protecting. I wanted to say, "Well, isn't it obvious?" But instead I heard myself saying, "He's responsible —" But I had to stop there.

"Responsible for what?"

I waved my hand around. "For all of this. For everything. For all the junkies in the doorways, for the tent cities under the highway overpasses, for the dead kids and the people whose lives are being destroyed and thrown away. For all the suffering and the death." I stared at her and narrowed my eyes. "He has to be stopped. He has to be killed."

"You said earlier that you felt anger, rage. You said it was like revenge."

"Yeah." I nodded.

"How do you know?"

I screwed up my face at her. "*What?*"

"How do you know?" She said it more forcefully. "I know I am hungry because I get an empty feeling in my belly and I start imagining the taste of certain foods. I know I am tired because my body stops wanting to move, my eyes feel heavy, and my brain wants to stop thinking. How do *you* know that what you are feeling toward these drug dealers, and this one particular man at the top, is revenge and not just, say, prejudice and hatred?"

"How do I know it's revenge and not prejudice or hatred?"

"Yes. I am not challenging you, Rogue. I am asking you to examine the feelings and find the difference."

For a moment, I felt anger and frustration toward her, but I set that aside and tried to turn my attention inward toward the feelings of revenge, anger, and hatred. They were similar, but she was right. They were also different in some ways. I could sense they were different, but at first, as I struggled with them, I couldn't see what those differences were. She said, "Rogue, what is the difference between revenge and hatred?"

I sat forward with my elbows on my knees. "I'll be damned!" I turned to look at her face. "Again? These things are so obvious, but I am not seeing them."

She held up her hand. "How far is my hand from your face? Seven, eight feet? But if I got up and pushed my hand into your face—an eighth of an inch from your eyes—would you see it?"

"I guess not. You showed me two things tonight that I had right in front of my face. Both were too close for me to see. I have been hurt so badly that I have suppressed the memories of my entire life. And I blame Jesus Sanchez, the man who will soon be the head of the Sinaloa Cartel, or I blame the whole cartel itself. I want to punish them because I hold them responsible for the pain I feel."

She waited a while. I sipped my drink and stared at the small flames twitching among the embers. Finally, she spoke quietly.

"Does this give you any clue as to who you are?"

I pulled down the corners of my mouth and shook my head. "Not really."

"Have you got any special skills, Rogue?"

The answer came automatically before I could even think about it. "Yeah." I studied her face a second. "I am good at killing people."

She took a long, deep, shaky breath. "Dear God...!"

I grinned. "We are still talking fantasies, right? Otherwise I can tell you I am pretty good at driving, and I can put myself to sleep within thirty seconds, even when under stress. And I can tell myself when to wake up."

I was half-laughing as I told her these things, but she wasn't returning the laugh. Her eyes were darting over my face with small, sharp movements.

"Let me ask you something," she said finally. "In the last couple of days, has any particular place come repeatedly to your attention?"

"A place?"

"A neighborhood, a state, a country, a city..."

"New York. Vegas and New York, but mainly New York."

"In what context?"

The humor faded from my face and from my insides. I held her eye. "I told you I killed those four men on Ocean Boulevard."

"You told me you believed you had. I wasn't sure I believed you."

"I knew I had."

"Okay."

"They had come from New York. I think I followed them from New York. I also found out that their boss, Jesus

Sanchez, had been in New York, organizing a more efficient distribution system for imports from Sinaloa."

"You haven't got a New York accent." She smiled. "You don't say caw-fee, or Noo Yawk."

I thought about it. "Where is my accent from?"

She shrugged. "It's just what they call GA, general American. I couldn't place you from your accent."

I grunted. "That would be too easy. I think I have to go to New York."

"And do what? And where in New York? There are eight and a half million people there, spread over more than three hundred square miles and five boroughs."

I thought about that too, and all I could come up with was "I don't know."

She surprised me by reaching across and squeezing my hand. "Rogue, you do realize you were hunting these men?"

"I guess I was."

"That narrows things down a bit."

"What do you mean?"

"As a working hypothesis, we can say that the Sinaloa cartel hurt you really badly. Okay?"

"Okay."

"Now either they hurt you because you were hunting them, or you were hunting them because they hurt you. Does that make sense?"

"Yeah. It does."

"Okay, but now stay with me. We are saying that your amnesia is traumatic, caused by what they did to you. And we are saying that your amnesia starts just a few days ago on Ocean Boulevard. So that means you were hunting them before the amnesia started and before whatever they did to you. Does all that make sense?"

I nodded. She paused a moment, then asked, "So you weren't hunting them because of what they did to you, right? Because you were hunting them before that. So I have to ask you, who hunts the Sinaloa?"

I stared at her. "The DEA? The FBI?" I shook my head. "But they'd have a record of me. My prints would be on file. And I am not on any of their databases."

"There might be an explanation for that. Has it occurred to you that if you entered that house while on active duty, you may have killed those men in self-defense?"

The images flashed into my mind. It was hard to imagine it as self-defense. Her voice came to me again.

"If you had gone in there with the intention of killing them, don't you think you would have used a different weapon? A gun, a rifle, a shotgun?"

"I don't know."

She patted my wrist. "Come on. Let's get you some sleep and rest. We'll talk more in the morning."

I stood. She took my hand and led me up the stairs. She opened the door for me and pointed out the en suite bathroom. Then we stood in the doorway a moment, looking at each other. She said, "This would be a really bad idea."

"Most of the best ideas are bad ideas," I told her quietly. "You just have to make the most of them."

FIFTEEN

Special Agent Elroy Jones looked out at the dawn seeping over the Pacific. He had been born and raised in Boston. In Boston, the sun rose like bulging, molten lava over the sea at dawn. In California, it rose from behind the mountains, making the ocean gray and the sky pink. After twenty years, he still couldn't get used to it.

The breeze touched his face and made him shudder and sigh. He felt tired and a little nauseated. Reluctantly, he looked back at the twisted, partially carbonized bodies on the sand. However hard you tried, it was impossible not to look at their grotesquely grinning teeth and their staring eyes. Even the ME looked sickened. She was hunkered down peering at the bodies without touching them.

"I ain't never seen such black white men," she said and glanced at him with an apologetic smile. She was Black, like him, so she could make that kind of joke. "You're not going to ask me for cause of death, are you?"

"Not till you get them into the lab." He pointed at the pile of charred driftwood beside them, where the crime scene officers were hunched in their forensic jumpsuits, picking through the ash and cinders. "But I can see the melted plastic containers from here and the charred wire. I'm guessing these guys were not shot. They burned to death."

He stepped closer to the scorched, smoldering remains of the wood, pulling on a pair of latex gloves. Taking his pen from his inside pocket, he pointed into the ashes. "See that, Henk?"

One of the guys in a forensic suit looked closer where Jones was pointing. "What is it, wire?"

"Electrical wire. The plastic is melted and blackened, but you can see the copper. See? The two ends have been pulled apart. You want to lift that with your tweezers?"

Henk took a hold of it with a set of pincers and began gently to pull. As he did so, the wire began to emerge from the ash, and then the sand, until some four feet were exposed. The two men looked at each other, and Jones smiled.

"You a betting man?"

"Not against you."

"This wire is going to run under the sand, across the overspill from the lagoon, and all the way to that palm tree. That's where our man was hiding, and that's where he shot that other lone dude from, on the other side of the stream."

He slipped his hand under the wire and walked steadily across the sand, pulling it up from where it was buried. Henk handed the charred copper end to his colleague and followed Jones across the stream to the palm tree. There they found the car battery sitting in the sparse grass. Here both men hunkered down again. Henk pointed. "Beer bottle. And see where the grass has been crushed? He was sitting here for a while."

Jones nodded. "Are those bread crumbs? He ate here while he was waiting and had a beer. This guy is as cold as my ex mother-in-law's heart." He paused, glancing around. "So what happens? He arranges to meet them here, at a particular spot. They gather where he has told them, down by the woodpile, and he detonates the gas cans. One of them is far enough away to escape the explosion and charges him. But he shoots him dead as he approaches."

Henk rose and approached the body lying face down beside the duffel bag. As he walked, he called to his colleague, "You want to bring me some bags from the truck? I got a bag here and a car battery with thirty yards of wire."

Jones squatted by the body and shook his head. "There is no singeing. That must have been a big fireball, but not even his hair got singed. This guy was already across the water when our man pressed the detonator. He was negotiating with him and threw him that bag. And as he went for it, he ignited the gasoline, and as the guy turned, he shot him. See?" He pointed at the entry wound. "See where the slug went in? At the side of his chest. That's not an easy shot in the dark. Who the hell is this guy? Why was this man negotiating with him?"

As he asked those questions, he was watching a sheriff's deputy approaching from Topanga drive, trudging across the sand. She jumped the small stream but wet her shoes anyway and started speaking as she came closer, a little breathless and shaking her feet.

"Special Agent Jones, you asked us to run the plates of the cars parked at the bottom of the drive. The Audi belongs to PB Imports and Exports, a corporation registered here in Los Angeles. The Bimmer is registered to Peter Barta of sixteen hundred Corona del Mar in Pacific Palisades."

"Peter Barta?"

She looked up from her notebook. "Yeah."

"PB."

She smiled. "Huh, right."

"But I'll lay you ten to one Peter Barta is not here. Deputy, will you do me a favor and call dispatch and get them to send a car to sixteen hundred Corona del Mar in Pacific Palisades. I have a strong hunch we will find Mr. Barta there just a little bit dead."

As she reached for her radio, Jones reached for his cell and called a number he had listed as SA Newton. It rang a couple of times and was answered by a woman.

"Elroy, what can I do for you?"

"I have four men incinerated on Topanga Beach. They were incinerated by an improvised gas bomb. I have a fifth man shot through the chest while trying to collect a duffel bag which..." He paused as he watched Henk open the bag with extreme care. "...was full of dirty linen by the looks of it. And I have two cars, an Audi and a BMW. The Audi is registered to a corporation called PB Imports and Exports, and the BMW is registered to Peter Barta of sixteen hundred Corona del Mar. Both cars are parked on Topanga Drive, just thirty yards from the incinerated men. I have asked the Los Angeles Sheriff's Department to send a car to sixteen hundred Corona del Mar, and I am on my way there myself, because I have a hunch I am going to find a rather dead Peter Barta. I was wondering if you would like to join me so I could have a bouncy surface at which to throw thoughts and ideas."

"That sounds like a very inappropriate suggestion, Special Agent Jones. I'll see you in fifteen minutes."

He took more than fifteen minutes to get there because he spent that long sitting on the low wall that flanked the steps, staring at the beach and trying to visualize what had happened there. Finally he heaved a big sigh, climbed the steps, and got into his Honda Accord.

It was a short drive from Topanga Beach to Corona del Mar. When he got there, he found two patrol cars, a crime scene van, and the ME already there. As he pulled up, parked, and swung down from the cab, he saw Special Agent Cathy Newton emerging from the drive. She startled him every time he saw her. Her hair was platinum, her eyes were turquoise, and her skin was so pale it really was almost white. She was small and looked frail, though he knew that she was anything but. It was odd, but somehow in her, it all came together and worked.

It worked really well.

"Is this what you guys call fifteen minutes in Boston?"

"I was staring at the Pacific. That takes time, especially at dawn."

She gave her head a small shake. "One day you're going to convince me you're a sensitive man. How did you know he'd be dead in here? Did you kill him?"

"If I am right, this man was killed in the wee small hours. You try and get me out of bed at that time of night."

"Is that an inappropriate proposition, Special Agent Jones?"

"In your dreams." They fell into step walking toward the house. "In answer to your question, I didn't, but his cars being parked there along with five dead guys, it looked like he was supposed to be one of them. He wasn't, so the odds were he would be at home, dead."

She shrugged with her eyebrows. "I guess that makes sense to you. You were right, anyway. He's upstairs in his office."

Jones stopped dead and narrowed his eyes. "In his *office?*"

She stopped and smiled with hooded, ironic eyes. "Sitting at his desk. He has a small hole dead center of his forehead, and a really big one where the rest of his head should be."

"At his *desk?*"

"At his desk."

"Let me see." As they entered the house, he turned to the crime scene officer dusting the lock. "I want to know if that lock was picked. Check, double-check. *Was that lock picked?*"

"You got it."

As Newton made for the stairs, Jones stood and stared around the room. "Brandy and whiskey." She paused on the first step and watched him. He glanced at her. "They are sitting here, one here and the other there, and they are talking and drinking. One of them is drinking brandy, and the other is drinking whiskey."

He scanned the room and pointed to the tray with the decanters. "The brandy is Pete Barta's."

She frowned and smiled at the same time. "How do you know that?"

"Look at the brandy decanter. It's three-quarters empty. The whiskey is almost full. Whoever lives here drinks brandy."

"Smartass."

"The other guy drinks whiskey."

"Does this help?"

He stared at her a moment. "I don't know. We'll see."

She jerked her head toward the upper floor. "Come on, Sherlock. He's up here."

Jones followed her up to the big, open-plan loft with exposed beams and skylights. The place was practically empty but for a single filing cabinet and a large safe in the corner. The safe stood open.

And then there was the large desk made of black glass. Beyond it was a big black leather chair, and slumped across the desk was what was left of a man. He had a large hole in the back of his head, and he had bled profusely over the black glass. Behind them, a gurney was being brought up the stairs. The ME, a skinny man with grizzled gray hair, was bizarrely bent over peering into the dead man's head.

Jones gave his face a rapid rub with his palms, then glanced at the chair on his side of the desk.

"Six in one day," he said. "And the least gruesome was the one who was shot in the heart."

"You okay?"

"Yeah. So this whiskey-drinking dude shows up. He has either already killed the dudes on the beach or he is going to —" He glanced at the ME. "Any chance of a time of death?"

"Sure," he said without looking up. "I'll ask Agatha Christie via the Ouija board. Maybe she can tell you."

Jones sighed heavily. "So I'm going to say the meeting on the beach was elaborately arranged. So he went with that first, and when he was done, he came here. I'm going to say if they were drinking downstairs and talking and then came up here. Peter Barta knew his killer and let him in. They talked some more, our man persuaded Peter to open the safe, and once it was open, he had no more use for Pete." He looked at Newton. "Working theory?"

She nodded. "It's a working theory. What about this guy Dave told you about?"

"The guy with the white RAM."

For a moment, that was all he said, but he shoved his hands in his pockets and went up on his toes a few times, looking first at the mess on the black glass desk, and then at the open safe. Then he turned and ambled toward the stairs. Cathy watched him and followed as he took the first step.

"There's some kind of a pattern," he said. "There was Steve Schneider, shot in the forehead in his living room, with the safe open and his money gone."

"Does two a pattern make?" she asked from behind, knowing that in this case, it did.

"What happened just before Steve Schneider got whacked?"

She smiled. "Whacked? Before Steve Schneider got whacked, Felipe Ochoa, Nestor Gavilan, Oliver Peralta, and Eulogia Borja got whacked and diced on Ocean Boulevard."

"And where have I just come from, Special Agent Cathy Newton?"

"Yeah, okay, five men with probable ties to drug trafficking gruesomely killed by unknown parties."

"Party. One resourceful cold-blooded son of a bitch."

They had reached the bottom of the stairs and stepped out into the fresh morning. She studied his face for a moment, thinking he looked tired, but her pale face betrayed nothing. She said, "Didn't you go and talk to this amnesiac in Nevin?"

"He wasn't in, and there was no white RAM parked outside. There was a red Mustang convertible that left while I was knocking. I don't know why, but I felt there was something about it."

"Can you be more precise?"

He shrugged. "It was a nice day, and he had the soft top down. He looked like he was trying not to look like he was in a hurry." He glanced at her. "According to Dave, the amnesiac, as you call him, said he was going to return the RAM. You got anything going on?"

"What's on your mind?"

"Care for a ride to Vegas?"

She smiled. "Who says no to Vegas?"

He grunted as he made toward his car. "Me, for one."

"Yeah, but you're a miserable curmudgeon, Elroy." She stuck her fingers in her mouth and emitted a shrill whistle. He stopped and turned. She pointed to a twenty-year-old Dodge Charger that gleamed in the morning sun like it had just been minted.

"V8, three hundred and seventy-five horses. I figure we'll get there faster than if we go in your Honda. What's that, eighty hearses?" She grinned as he came back to climb in the passenger side. She got in behind the wheel and slammed the door. "Get it, Elroy? Hearses instead of horses? Eighty hearses?"

He looked out the window so she wouldn't see the smile as the big engine roared and she pulled out of the drive.

"That's funny, Cathy," he said, remembering a book by Dashiell Hammett he'd read once. "Deep down funny, where it's not like funny anymore."

"Curmudgeon."

And they roared away toward Vegas.

SIXTEEN

In its passage through Beverly Hills, from the circus at Doheny Drive all the way down to the Country Club, Santa Monica Boulevard is framed on its northeastern side by pretty gardens and lawns. Parkway runs parallel to those gardens, and pretty close to the corner of Parkway and North Rexford Drive stood a relatively unassuming mansion. It was largely concealed from view by a gigantic jacaranda and a number of pin oaks out front by the half-moon drive and a six foot wall at the back, surmounted by another six feet of dense hedge.

The mansion, which had only six bedrooms, stood empty most of the year, as Jesus Sanchez, its owner, was increasingly uncomfortable leaving Mexico. In Mexico, and especially in his home state of Sinaloa, he was confident that the authorities would not dare to touch him. But here in the United States, it was hard to predict what might happen. El Mayo had good friends here, especially within the defense and intelligence communities. They enabled him to stay in power. But the White House and Congress were increasingly in conflict with the Pentagon, and it was hard to know from one day to the next who was your friend and who was your enemy. So most of the time, he stayed put in his fortified ranch in Guamúchil.

Now he sat by his large, organically shaped pool set among the lush, semi-tropical gardens in back of his house and stared at the turquoise water. He had heard the voice of Indio, one of the two men he most trusted in the world: his two bodyguards.

"Jefe, Mateo llegó."

Mateo had arrived. Jesus sighed. Mateo, his right-hand man, was not his other trusted lieutenant. Mateo, he knew, would stab him in the back the moment it became expedient to do so.

"Dile que pase," he told Indio, instructing him to fetch Mateo, still gazing at the turquoise ripples bisected by luminous threads. A moment later, Mateo stepped through the sliding plate glass doors in his three hundred dollar jeans and his five hundred dollar linen jacket. Jesus watched him sit.

Mateo said, "You heard."

"Yes, Mateo. I heard. Peter is dead, like Steve, like Felipe, like Nestor, like Oliver and like Eulogio, and like five of Peter's men, and whoever killed them has more than one million of *my* dollars."

Mateo drew breath to answer, but Jesus cut him short. "I told you to solve this problem. Do you remember? We were at the Intercontinental where I am paying a fokin' fortune for your suite—" He closed his eyes and waved his palm at Mateo, who had drawn breath again. "No, no, Mateo, don't talk. I am happy to pay for that fokin' suite when you are doing a good job for me. In the past, you have done a good job for me. But now, in the present, you are making a *fokin' mess!* I have lost six men and more than a million bucks in less than *one fokin' week!* So you want to explain to me how you are earning this *fokin'* room at the Intercontinental?"

"I will find him, boss. And we will punish him!"

Jesus smiled. It was a warm, friendly smile that concealed a growing desire to kill his lieutenant. "That's good to hear, Mateo. It's what I want to hear. But are you sure we have enough men left? You sure nobody else was killed this morning while you were having your massage after breakfast?"

"No, jefe."

"Or," Jesus laughed, pointing at Mateo, wagging his finger, "or is this killer working for you?"

"Jefe! No! Don't joke like this! That ain't funny!"

Jesus laughed some more, flapping his hand at Mateo. "Come on! I'm joking! But I tell you this, Mateo—" And the laughter fell from his face leaving an ugly, dead expression. "You better find this guy and kill him, because if he doesn't kill you, I will. Find him. Kill him."

"I'm going to find him, jefe. You want to talk to him before I kill him?"

Jesus didn't answer right away, but after a moment, he nodded. "Yeah. How you going to find him?"

"I've been sick all morning thinking about it. This guy is not normal. Four of our best guys, and he kills them with swords, an axe, and Eulogia with the shower curtain, and broke his arms—"

"I know what he did, Mateo."

"So this guy has skills, and thinking about what he did to

Pete's men, with the gasoline, he is a guy who plans. He is methodical, and he makes plans. He has been following us since Vegas, and maybe since New York, getting closer all the time. And he wants you. I am figuring, boss, that this is a guy with a grudge, and he wants you."

Jesus narrowed his eyes and curled his lip. "A grudge?"

"There are a lot of crazies out there, jefe. Maybe his girlfriend came to work in one of our clubs, maybe his brother got killed in a reprisal. Something we did in business he took personally. That's my feeling, and the way he killed the guys on Ocean Boulevard, he was mad. He wanted to hurt them."

"And you think he's after me."

"It looks that way. He is closing in. I get the feeling he is looking for you."

"What's your plan?"

"We get you out of here and back to Mexico on the quiet. I say we get a plumber's van and we park it out front like we have a guy fixing a tap, whatever. You, Indio, and Sicario dress in overalls, you get a toolkit, and you drive to the BLOC parking garage on Flower Street. There you take the overalls off. I will have a car waiting for you there, and you drive across the border back to Guamúchil. Meantime we will have six guys in the house waiting for this son of a bitch to show."

"Sicario stays here. He stays in the house."

"Sure, but take another guy with you. Be safe. Indio and another guy."

Jesus grunted and nodded. "But just waiting for him to show up..."

"No, we are also asking questions in the LAPD, but you

know what it's like these days. It ain't as easy as it used to be."

"Okay. How soon can you get the van?"

"I can have it here this afternoon."

"Okay, do it. Go do it now. On your way out, tell Sicario I want to talk to him."

Mateo rose and went into the shadows through the sliding glass doors. Jesus returned to his contemplation of the turquoise water and the luminous threads that twisted across its surface.

After a couple of minutes, Sicario came out and stood staring down at him. Indio was big and powerfully built with a big chest and strong arms and legs. He had the hawk-like nose and long black hair of an Indian. Hence his name. But Sicario was different. Jesus believed he was the more dangerous of the two. He was thin and wiry, with pale, freckled skin and red hair. Like Indio, he favored a knife, but where Indio used a knife the size of a small machete, Sicario's blade was a vintage Spanish OTF with a long, slender, double-edged blade that was razor sharp. Sicario liked to boast that most of his victims didn't know they had been stabbed when they died.

"Mateo has told me I should go back to Guamúchil, Sicario. What do you think?"

"I think it's good, jefe. Lots of people dying here now."

"What will you do if I die, Sicario?"

"I will find who killed you, and I will do bad things to him. Then I will kill Mateo."

Jesus smiled. Sicario had always had the ability to read his mind. He laughed.

"What if you are already dead?"

"Then you and me, we will go together to the Infierno, jefe, we will find Satan, and we will give him the choice, serve us or die."

They both laughed. Then Jesus became serious. "I will go back with Indio. Find this man who is hunting me. Kill him. Then kill Mateo. I don't trust him. When that is done, I will come back, and we will finish setting up the distribution."

"Okay, jefe, eso esta hecho. *It is done.*"

"Something else, Sicario. I want you to go to the Coca Cabaña. Talk to Agustin. The night we were there with Peter and Steve, there was a waitress who was getting friendly with a stranger, a gringo who was sitting on his own. He had a hamburger and a beer. Outside he had a white truck, a Dodge RAM. I didn't like him. Go and talk to Agustin, ask him about the gringo and about the waitress."

"Okay, jefe."

"But, Sicario, be careful. That was what Peter was doing when he was killed."

Sicario nodded. "Anything else, jefe?"

"No. Go and do it. Keep me informed."

Sicario gave a small nod and left. From the fruit bowl in the kitchen, he took the keys to the BMW, and five minutes later, he emerged through the electronic gates and crossed the Santa Monica Boulevard to head northwest on I-10.

———

MEANWHILE, one hundred and fourteen miles away as the black crow flies, Nelson, Ernestina's brother, was sprawled in an uncomfortable chair at the motel, watching TV but taking in nothing of what was on the screen. In the bed beside him, his mother lay with her eyes closed and occasionally made a whimpering sound. In the bathroom, his sister was taking a shower. He glanced at his watch. It was ten minutes before one p.m. He sat up.

"Mom, I'm going to buy a hamburger. You want anything?"

Her eyes opened in alarm. "Where you goin'?"

He sagged, rolled his eyes, and groaned. "It's just across the road, Mama. The Golden Ox. It's like fifty yards. Please keep quiet. I don't want Ernestina freaking out on me. You want something?"

"No. What I want is for you to stay here and be safe. They gonna kill you, like they kill your papa."

He muttered something sacrilegious under his breath and stepped out of the room. He took a moment to look around. There was no one in the courtyard, so he made his way to the lights on Upjohn and crossed, then crossed South China Lake Boulevard at a run, though the lights were red and there was zero traffic.

The Golden Ox was a small, cute, standalone restaurant they had tried to make look like a Mayan temple, only the steel and glass doors kind of let it down. Inside, it didn't look like a Mayan temple either. It could have been McDonald's, Burger King, or any other fast food burger joint.

He ordered three burgers and fries, and while he waited, he glanced over his shoulder to make sure Ernestina had not come out after him and slipped his cell from his pocket. The guy he assumed was Ernestina's boyfriend had said absolutely no cell phones, but he didn't understand. Nelson had to stay in touch with the

Chupacabras. If they didn't know where he was, there could be trouble.

There was a message from his pal Paquito. He opened it.

Hey, compi, where R U man? U din show las nite.

"Here are your burgers."

He took them and went outside, where he walked around in back of the restaurant into the parking lot. There, he called Paquito.

"Hey man, where are you? Che was mad you didn't show last night."

"Yeah, I couldn't, man. This guy, a gringo, I think he's my sister's boyfriend, he shows up with her and starts giving orders. He says Jesus Sanchez is gonna try and kill us and we have to get the hell out of there. And he said no cell phones, in case they trace us using the GPS or some shit."

There was a long silence. "You kidding me, Nelson?"

"No, man. It's true. He had this red Mustang, and he brought us out into the desert. Some shithole called Ridge something. Ridgecrest. We all stuck in a motel, man, all three of us in one shit room. I'm goin' crazy, man."

"How come you're calling now?"

"My sister was in the shower—"

"*That* I'd pay to see!"

"You watch your fokin' mouth, man! You keep my sister out of your filthy mouth or I'll cut your fokin' tongue out!"

"Okay, okay, okay, keep your panties on! It was a joke."

"You want we should start joking about your momma?"

"Okay, man, I'm sorry. Let it go. So what happened?"

Nelson's voice was sullen. "I came out to get some burgers for lunch."

"So how come this dude thinks Jesus Sanchez wants to

kill your family? I mean, he's like El Mayo's number two. Why does he give a shit about you? No offense, but you know what I'm sayin'."

"I don't know. I got like this guy was law enforcement or special ops or something, and Sanchez wanted him dead."

"And your sister is his girlfriend. She'd give Sanchez leverage."

"Something like that."

"Where you stayin'?"

"The Quality Inn. Why?"

"You want me to come and get you?"

"Nah. I better stay with Mom and Ernestina, just in case."

"K, but you wanna get out of there, you call me, dude. I'll come and get you."

"Thanks. But listen, Paquito, I'm serious. You ever talk like that about my sister, I swear I will cut your tongue out. You disrespect her, you disrespect me. You heard Che: Mothers and sisters are off limits."

"I hear you, man. My bad. We good?"

"We're good, man. I'll see you in a day or two."

Nelson hung up, and a hundred and fifteen miles to the southeast, Paquito hung up too and sat staring at his phone. After a moment, he picked up his beer and took a pull looking over the rim of his glass, out of his booth, at Agustin as he polished the glasses behind the bar.

"Where's Ernestina, Pops? You alone?"

Agustin shrugged. "I ain't seen her, and she ain't called. That's the way it is these days. No respect."

"Right. It was different when you were young, right?"

"It sure was. Small time upstarts in street gangs had

respect for their elders, especially when they knew those elders could have them whipped or get them a special necktie if they wanted to."

"Okay, Pops. I didn't mean no offense. So you had ties with some serious people back home in Mexico, huh?"

"I did my time."

"They look after you?"

"You ask too many questions. Questions get kids like you killed."

The conversation, such as it was, was cut short by the sound of a car pulling up outside. Agustin peered out of the window behind the bar. He saw the dark BMW, and he saw the wiry, redheaded man climb out. He went waxy pale and turned to Paquito in his booth.

"You keep your mouth shut, you understand? You sit, you eat, you drink, and you go. And you don't talk!"

SEVENTEEN

It was four in the morning, and I was awake. Elizabeth, the doc, was asleep beside me. The window was open, and moonlight was reflecting off succulent leaves in a back yard that was more like a tropical garden. I sat up and stood at the window. Somewhere an owl was calling. I knew one type of cry was a male, the other a female, but I couldn't remember which.

I pulled on my clothes, went downstairs, and climbed behind the wheel of the Mustang. It rumbled into life, and I pulled out of Dell Avenue to head north up South Venice. It wasn't a long drive, less than ten miles. At that time of the morning, the traffic was negligible, and after little more than ten minutes, I was pulling off Santa Monica Boulevard and onto Rexford Drive. I crossed Parkway, drove a hundred and fifty yards, did a U, and came back to park thirty or forty yards from Sanchez's house on the opposite side of the road.

It was hard to see much because of the abundance of trees and foliage, but I could see light in one of the upstairs windows. At four-thirty in the morning, I figured maybe his conscience was keeping him awake. I climbed out of the car and walked the short distance to his gate. It was iron bars and electronically controlled. It would be easy to get over, but he was sure to have security cameras. Though something told me his alarm system probably did not alert the cops. They probably dealt with anyone stupid enough to break in in-house.

He had a big, beautiful jacaranda out front that obscured a narrow path down the side of the house. I walked to the far gate on the half moon drive and saw a broad path that led to a double garage. Between the garage and the house, there was another path that led into shadows. I could just hear, but not see, the lapping of the water from the pool.

I walked back to the jacaranda and vaulted the fence. By the time the motion detectors had switched on the lights, I was up in the branches of the jacaranda. But aside from the lights coming on, nothing happened. I kept my eyes on the bedroom window with the light in it, but it didn't open. I eased myself slowly down from the tree, keeping behind the large trunk, then made my way quietly down the path to the back yard. It was large, with a large swimming pool and an abundance of tropical plants and palms. I crossed to the edge of the pool. It had lamps in the bottom, but they were not switched on. I turned and looked up at the windows. I wondered if Jesus Sanchez was in there right now.

I had an impulse to kick in the sliding glass doors and go searching for him from room to room. For a moment, I had a flash of the house on Ocean Boulevard, of kicking open a door, of the terror on a face as I plunged the katana into his diaphragm or ripping a plastic curtain away from a shower, of the struggling body within.

I had to plan it. I had to make sure it worked and paid off. But now I knew where it would happen.

I crossed the garden as far as the garage. The lights came on again, flooding the clear water and the lawn. I walked down between the garage and the house, listening for windows or doors, or shouts, half-hoping I would hear them. I didn't.

I came back to the jacaranda and vaulted the fence again. When I landed, I looked up at the illuminated window again. There was a black silhouette there, motionless, looking down at me. I couldn't make out any features. I stared back for a few seconds, then turned and walked away.

After that, I drove around for a while with no clear destination, just letting my mind roam. I wound up eventually on the beach, looking at the moon rippling on the small waves. Finally, as the horizon started to turn gray, I drove to DK's Donuts on Santa Monica and took half a dozen fresh croissants back to Dell Avenue with me. As I parked and climbed out of my car, I checked my watch. It was a quarter to seven.

When I got into the kitchen, she was sitting at the table with a mug of coffee, watching me.

"Where were you? I was worried."

I smiled and held up the bag of croissants. "I went to DK's and got some hot croissants." I put them on the table and sat. "Are we married now?"

"Don't be patronizing, Rogue. At some point, we'll need to talk about what happened last night, but my being worried had nothing to do with that. One way or the other, I still feel a responsibility toward you."

"I didn't want to wake you. You want to get me a cup or shall I get it?"

She pointed to a cupboard over the sink. "In there. There's hot milk on the stove. The coffee's strong. Sugar's—"

"I take it black, no sugar."

"Of course you do."

I took a small cup and a couple of plates. "You want butter?"

She shook her head, and I sat again. I put a plate in front of her and the bag of hot croissants in the middle of the table.

"You're welcome."

She studied my face a moment and sighed, reached for one, and said, "Thanks. I'm canceling my sessions today. I'm going to take you to my refuge. There's a limit on how long you can stay there. I want to see you three times a week. We have to sort out your Social Security number, find you an apartment and a legitimate income, and start getting you integrated again."

I arched an eyebrow at her as I chewed. "I bet you say that to all the guys."

She kind of sagged. "I'm sorry, Rogue. You are a very attractive man. Don't let it go to your head, but you're hard to resist." She shook her head. "But last night was a mistake, you must see that. And we need to get back on track. I'm sorry if you were hoping for something else."

I smiled. "Don't worry about it. I was going to say the same thing to you." I gestured at the croissants. "I bought these to try and soften the blow. I was going to say, 'Elizabeth, you're an attractive woman and hard to resist, but we need to get on track and sort out my life. I'm sorry if you were hoping for something else.' Seriously, that's what I was going to say."

She studied my face a moment, sighed not for the first time that morning, and shook her head.

"I'm going to shower and get dressed. You'd better get your things together and we'll head out to Williams Canyon."

I nodded and reached for my coffee. "I'm ready when you are."

She went upstairs without answering. I refilled my cup, and I was suddenly aware of observing myself, like I was standing six feet behind me, watching; only what I was seeing was the cup in front of me, the coffee pot, and the black steaming coffee spilling into the cup. And I heard a voice in my head, which I knew was my own voice saying, "I gave up a long time ago trying to understand what makes women get mad."

I put down the coffee pot and sat staring at the cup. I went cold all over as it dawned on me: there was a woman in my life. She would get mad at me and I would react like that, by telling myself only a fool tried to understand women.

I was married. That certainty oozed out of the darkness of my memory and settled in my mind like an immovable fact. I was married, and I didn't know who to. I could feel her, but I couldn't see her or hear her. Her face and her voice were on the edge of recollection, just out of sight, just out of earshot. I felt a sudden unbearable desolation. An urgent, desperate need to get in the car and go home and grip her and hold her close to me. But I had no idea where she was or even who she was.

Time must have passed because Elizabeth was standing in the doorway dressed in jeans and a blouse, and she was staring at my face.

"You remembered something?"

I clenched my brow. "How would you know that?"

"You're crying."

"Bullshit!" I wiped my hands over my face and found they were wet. I stood. "We'll go in my car, and when you need to come home, I'll bring you back."

She gave a single, upward nod. "Rogue, you can't spend the night again. You understand that."

"I understand that, Elizabeth."

By the time we got out and I climbed behind the wheel, the sun was up, and it was a fresh, bright morning. I fired up the engine, and she said, "Take I-10 to Boyle Heights, the I-5 south."

We drove in silence as far as the interchange at Santa Fe Springs, then I said, "I'm married."

She glanced at me, but not in surprise. "Is that what you remembered?" I nodded. She said, "Do you remember who to?"

"No."

"Anything about her?"

"No."

We drove in silence for another fifteen minutes along the vast, concrete chute of Interstate 5. Eventually, she pointed ahead and said, "Take exit one hundred and follow Jamboree north."

After a while, we began to climb among low hills, and

there were fewer buildings and more space. It was surprisingly green and fresh, and I began to relax. Eventually, just short of Irvine Park, she told me to turn right onto the Santiago Canyon Road, and finally we were out of the city, among birds and hills and grass and trees.

"It hit me in your kitchen," I said. "While you were showering. It felt like a marriage." I glanced at her. "I realized that I knew what that felt like, and it came back in a flood. And I knew. I *know*. I'm married." I shook my head. "But I have no idea who she is or where she is."

She didn't answer, but pretty soon we were in the land of cute villages, white picket fences, and rather incongruously, cowboys. Because here the cowboys didn't drive cattle and drink whiskey. Here the cowboys owned wineries called Cowboy Canyon Winery.

"Git on your horse and drink your wine," I said absently. She didn't laugh. She pointed ahead again and said, "Follow Pleasant Moon almost to the end, then turn right, and my cabin is at the top of the track, surrounded by trees."

Pleasant Moon was the name of the road we were on. I followed her instructions, and pretty soon I pulled up outside a large, two-story cabin made of huge tree trunks. Large plate glass windows on both floors gave panoramic views of the canyon and the mountaintops all around us.

While she opened the door, I opened the trunk, hauled out my few possessions, and followed her inside through the open door.

It was one of those places that are divided into spaces instead of rooms. There was a huge open fireplace with a stack of logs beside it, a big sofa, and four eclectic armchairs in the area that would have been the living room, and bear skins were scattered around the wooden floors.

At the near side of the space, there was a second, smaller fire and a long dining table with six chairs. A broad staircase made a dogleg from the living area up to a galleried landing where I counted four bedrooms.

She stood in the middle of the floor, watching me.

I said, "Who chops the wood?"

She shook her head. "Ask me again when you remember who you are, who your wife is, and what your Social Security number is."

"That's harsh."

"Life is harsh. The world is harsh."

"You sound how I feel. You want rent for the time I'm here?"

"No."

"Why not?"

"Rogue—"

"Last night, we were friends. You actually seemed to give a damn. You invented your elaborate get-out clause so I could feel safe and open up to you. I actually believed you cared and wanted to help." I gestured at her. "I must be one hell of a lover. Four hours in bed with me and I've turned you into an ice queen. I feel like a parasite abusing your good nature. If this is inconvenient, I can take you back home, and if there is one thing I know for *damned* sure, it's that I'll survive!"

A deep anger had suddenly twisted my gut. She waited. A heavy silence descended on the cabin.

"Are you done?"

"I don't know," I snarled. "Don't patronize me."

"Are you ready to listen to me without insulting me? Can you close the door, sit down, and have a drink with me?"

I sighed, closed the door with my foot, dumped my bag on the table, and sat beside the cold fire. She poured a couple of drinks, handed me one, and stood by the fireplace.

"It is practically impossible for a therapist to help a client if they get involved in an emotional, romantic relationship. I have no doubt that you are a very strong, capable man, Rogue, but it would be stupid and naïve to pretend that you are not in desperate need of help. I can help you—and believe me, there are very few therapists who would take on a case like this. I didn't want to. But now, knowing you and having gotten this far, I can help you, and I *want* to help you. If we become intimate, if we become a couple, I won't be able to."

She waited. I nodded. She went on.

"And you have just remembered you are married! How does this work? What if tomorrow morning, when we are tangled in sheets upstairs, you suddenly snap your finger and cry, 'Jane Harrison! Forty-Two Haight Avenue, the Bronx!' Where does that leave her? Where does it leave me? And where does it leave you?"

"You're right." I said it to the floor.

"You need," she said, "a central point of reference."

I frowned. "A what?"

"A central point of reference. One solid thing you can hold on to, and from there begin to make sense of everything else."

"Information is power," I heard myself say.

"What?"

"Information is power," I said again louder. "But the wrong information is a death sentence."

"What are you talking about, Rogue?"

"I don't know. When you said that—" I closed my eyes, struggling. "Little sayings that sum up a situation, an attitude." I snapped my fingers several times. "Reality is plastic, truth is concrete." I pointed at her, suddenly excited. "If they kill you for telling the truth, you will live forever!" I sagged back into my chair. "It's gone. It was there. I had it. Like when a name is on the tip of your tongue. But it's gone."

"What was it?"

"Her. She had these sayings. I think she got some of them from her grandmother, but she made most of them up herself." She watched me, silent and immobile, waiting in case it came back. I said again, "A fixed point of reference. You need a fixed point of reference, and everything else will make sense."

EIGHTEEN

WE SAT AND TALKED FOR A COUPLE OF HOURS. Then we took a walk through the countryside, among the pines and the rocks and bushes to the top of what she called Jackson's Peak. From there, we could see for miles over Lake Forest and the Old Mission and the dim haze over the ocean fifteen miles to the west. There was a big round boulder on the peak, and we climbed it and sat on the top in silence.

"Like two eagles," she said. "Waiting."

"Waiting for what?" I asked.

After a long moment, she gave her head a small shake. "I guess we'll know when it comes."

It was a comfortable, companionable moment, sitting there. For a few minutes, I was able almost to forget the madness of the last few days. I glanced at my watch and saw it was lunchtime, and almost simultaneously, I felt the twist of a pang of hunger in my belly.

My skin went cold. The hair bristled on my head and on the back of my neck. I smelled moussaka and heard a door open and close as I held the round handle, a voice—my voice —and a woman's voice, light, pretty, as familiar as my own in my ears. The breeze from an open window on my skin.

"It wasn't the Bronx."

She turned to look at me. "What?"

"You said forty-two Haight Avenue, the Bronx. But it wasn't the Bronx." She waited, watching me. I said, "It was the Upper West Side. There are two trees outside." I looked at her and laughed. "Two ginkgo trees, one on either side. If I look to my left, I can see trees, uh linden, and London plane trees. Lots of trees and grass."

She was smiling. "Are you looking out of a window?"

"Yeah." I closed my eyes. "It's a...uh...it's a sash." I made the action with my hands, pushing up the sash window. I heard the clunk of the wood, heard the sliding weights in the wells.

It faded as fast as it had come.

"I was hungry. She made a good moussaka."

"Rogue, that's fantastic. It's coming back to you. Two ginkgo trees side by side on the Upper West Side should not be that hard to find. By the sounds of it, it's quite close to a park or a lawn."

I felt my heart pound hard in my chest. I tried to speak, but the words seemed trapped in my throat and in my chest. She was still talking.

"I don't know New York that well, but I know the Upper West Side has Central Park to the east, and on the west you have all those lawns and parkland between River-side Drive and the Hudson." She smiled again and reached for my hand. "I am so happy for you. You are so much closer than you were yesterday, even an hour ago!"

I slid down from the bolder. "Let's go get some lunch. You have stuff at the cabin?"

"Sure." She slid down and stood beside me. "You okay?"

I tried to speak but shook my head instead. I started walking, and she fell into step beside me.

"Rogue, a house, even an apartment, on the Upper West Side, within sight of a park, you are talking about very serious money."

"I guess so."

"We had talked about the possibility of your being in law enforcement, but I don't think even the highest paid cops in New York could afford a place on the Upper West Side."

"What are you driving at?"

She took hold of my arm. "I'm not really driving at anything, but I wonder if you—or we—need to broaden our ideas of who you *might* be. Perhaps we have been blinded a bit by the circumstances in which you woke up and the fixations you seem to have developed. They are obviously important, but maybe they don't *define* you as much as we think they do. Maybe—*maybe*—you are not the person you think you are."

"I don't know who I think I am," I said quietly.

She was nodding before I had finished. "Oh, yes, you do. You think you're a professional killer. You think you are some kind of monster whose only redeeming feature is that you go after men who are even more monstrous than you are. But maybe that is *not* who you are."

I watched her face as we walked. I had never stopped to think about it, but I knew that what she was saying was true. I had seen myself do monstrous, inhuman things, and I had felt no compassion or remorse. And I knew that made me a monster.

"I mean"—she stood back, half-laughing, and gestured at me—"look at you. Okay, you dress like you get your clothes from a thrift store, but even dressed like that, you have a bearing, a kind of elegance in the way you walk and move."

"Come on!"

"I'm serious. I am not flattering you, I'm saying maybe we should adjust our focus. Now, another thing: the first time I met you, you were talking like a crazy guy. But you know what stopped me from walking away?"

"My aristocratic good looks?"

"The obvious intelligence behind the crazy things you were saying. You were intelligent and articulate. And you know what I have noticed: With every passing day, with every passing *hour*, your speech and your thinking become more articulate. Frankly, Rogue, you come across as a highly intelligent, educated man." She raised her hands. "I am sure there are some highly educated, intelligent cops. But after ten or twenty years on the front line, their edges have been pretty roughened. You don't come across as a cop."

I narrowed my eyes at her. "I haven't got rough edges? Seriously?"

"No. What you've got is a really bad case of post-traumatic stress. But to me, you living on the Upper West Side makes a lot of sense. I see that."

"But..."

"But it raises some difficult questions. For a start, how does a guy from the Upper West Side in Manhattan wind up two thousand five hundred miles away, sitting in a truck on

Ocean Boulevard with blood on his hands and a house full of dead drug dealers?"

"For example."

"Well, we just have to keep working at it until your unconscious gives up its secrets."

"Find a central point of reference so everything else makes sense."

"That's it."

We had pizza and salad in the kitchen, and at just after three p.m., I drove her home. I promised I'd call her when I got back to the cabin, watched her go in through her gate, and pulled out of Dell Avenue and onto Venice Boulevard. There I called Ernestina. She answered on the first ring.

"Hi! Where are you? Are you coming to get us?"

"Not yet. I still have some things I need to do. Probably tomorrow. I need about twenty-four hours."

"I am going crazy here. Nelson is just being a pain in the ass. He won't settle, he won't help, he is just negative, negative, negative, *all* the time!"

"I know, it's tough. Just hold out one more night, and this will all be over."

"Okay, but what if tomorrow you haven't fixed it? What can we do?"

"I will have fixed it tomorrow. If I haven't, I will give you two and a half million dollars so you can start a new life in Florida, Hawaii, or wherever you want to go."

"You're crazy."

"You got that right. Okay, Ernestina, I want you to hang in there for me. I am on my way to fix this now. Trust me. I'll be in touch."

"Okay, call me as soon as you know something. Okay?"

"You got it."

I hung up and headed north and west toward Beverly Hills. I took my time and arrived at Rexford Drive as the sun was sinking toward the ocean, turning the sea a burnished bronze and the sky crimson and orange. Instead of turning left toward Sanchez's house, I turned right into Civic Center Drive at City Hall and parked the car in the parking garage. I sat a while gazing into the dirty, echoing shadows. An engine growled. A set of tires screamed like a banshee, people going home from work to their families where meals were being cooked, husbands and wives kissing each other in greeting, kids...

I blinked myself out of the reverie, took a deep breath, and climbed out of the Mustang. I went to the trunk, opened it, and pulled out the Smith and Wesson 29, which I slipped into the holster under my arm. It was uncomfortably large, but I knew it wouldn't stay there very long.

The .357 I slipped in my waistband behind my back, and, lifting my right foot onto the rim of the trunk, I strapped the Fairbairn and Sykes fighting knife to my calf under my jeans, tucked into my boot.

Then I took the bags of money and carried them downstairs. They were cumbersome, but I knew I had to take them with me. I crossed at the lights and walked the hundred yards to Sanchez's house and heaved the bags over the fence, into the driveway. After that I went and vaulted the gate by the jacaranda and walked to the front door.

I didn't think too much about how I was going to get away, or what I would do after I had killed Jesus Sanchez. All I knew was that I was going to kill him and everybody else he had in the house. After that, I had to take the money to

Ernestina, but not in the Mustang. The Mustang had served its purpose and would stay in the parking garage. But Ernestina and her mother, and maybe her brother, had to make a new start for themselves, in a world where murder was something you saw on TV.

So I rang the bell and waited. It was opened after a long thirty seconds by a guy in an Italian suit. He had long black hair and the kind of big brown eyes women think are sensitive and guys know are ruthless and predatory. He didn't say anything. He just looked at me.

I struck his windpipe with the proximal phalangeal knuckles of my right hand. Those are the knuckles in the middle of your fingers. If you start to make a fist but stop halfway, those knuckles can be used to destroy a guy's windpipe.

The blow was fast and savage and left him unable to breathe or make any noise other than a soft wheeze. I pushed him back, stepped in, and closed the door. As he started to turn blue, I slipped the knife from my boot and drove the blade down behind his left collarbone.

It's a cut that is not always easy to deliver, but if you can, it's useful because it causes massive hemorrhaging on the inside from the aorta and the pulmonary artery, but you get very little bleeding on the outside. Death comes within seconds.

I lowered the guy to the floor, gave him a couple of seconds to stop twitching, and removed the knife.

I was in a hall about the size of a small living room. There was a dogleg staircase rising to the upper floor with an open door on the left that led to what looked like a study. A closed door on my right I figured led to a living area, and a passage beside the stairs probably led to the kitchen and the pool.

I cleaned the knife on the guy's Armani jacket and slipped it back in the sheath while I listened. I could hear the soft tones of a TV in the living room. It went quiet, and a voice called, "Ismael, quien es?"

The dead guy was Ismael, and his pal wanted to know who had rung at the door. I didn't hesitate. I pulled the Smith and Wesson 29 from under my arm, took two strides, and pushed open the door like I lived there. Take somebody by surprise, and it will take them up to four seconds to process the unexpected information and react. I knew that on my right there would be only a couple of windows, and the bulk of the room would be on my left. So I went through the door with my weapon pointing that way.

There were two guys sitting on a sofa. They had a TV in front of them, and they were both looking at me with wide eyes and sagging mouths. The nearest guy sat forward, and the .44 magnum exploded. The hollow point smashed his ribcage and erupted out his back, where it plunged through his pal's throat and tore into the back of the sofa.

If there was anybody else in the house, they had been alerted.

I went to the sofa to confirm the kill. They were both dead, and the sofa was a mess.

From where I stood, I could see out into the back yard. There was a guy in bathing trunks sitting on a deck chair and another climbing out of the pool. I guess the late sun was reflecting on the glass because apparently they couldn't see me. And the door was obviously triple-glazed, because everything I could see was in total silence. I smiled. They hadn't heard the shot.

"*Don't move!*"

I turned. There was a guy in the doorway. He was in shorts and had rumpled hair. He had both hands stuck out in front of him and he was holding a semi-automatic pointed at me. He was half-crouching and inched closer. There was an absolute coldness inside me and an absolute certainty about what he was going to do next. He inched another couple of steps into the room and looked at the sofa.

As he did, his face registered horror. Who knows why? He must have seen ugly death many times. Maybe these guys were his brothers or cousins or childhood friends. Whatever the case, as he lowered his eyes to look, I shot him in the chest. A .44 magnum round will shatter a concrete cinder block. It hit his chest, ripped through his ribcage, and erupted out his back while he was still looking surprised about his cousins.

I glanced through the glass at the guys by the pool. One of them was drying himself and laughing at whatever the guy in the deck chair was saying. The sun was sinking, and I knew they'd be coming inside soon. I couldn't hear any movement inside the house, but I didn't know if Jesus Sanchez was upstairs pissing his pants in one of the bedrooms.

One thing at a time, I told myself, went back to the hall, and sprinted up the stairs. There were six bedrooms. I worked my way through them methodically, one after another, but they were all empty, as were the en suite bathrooms and the built-in wardrobes.

Jesus Sanchez wasn't here.

Out on the landing, at the top of the stairs, I head a door open, raised voices and laughter. I moved down the stairs and met them as they were coming along the passage from the kitchen. I raised the weapon and lined them up. They stopped dead.

"This is a .44 magnum, punks. It used to be the most powerful handgun in the world, but it can still blow your head clean off. With one of you dead, maybe the other one can get to me." I smiled. "So you have to ask yourselves the question, 'Do I feel lucky?' Well, do you, punks?"

NINETEEN

They didn't feel lucky. They dropped the towels and raised their hands. I stepped back and gestured them toward the living room. They moved in and stopped just through the door. I heard one of them rasp, "Dios santo!"

I told them, "Keep moving."

They moved a few more steps in, and I went in after them and kicked the door closed with my heel.

I jerked my head at the one with wet hair. "What's your name?"

"Ramon. Are you the guy—"

"I ask the questions, Ramon." I looked at the other guy. "What about you?"

"Mateo Guzman. You don't know what you're doing."

"Maybe you're right, Mateo. Who's in charge here?"

Ramon glanced at Mateo, and that was good enough, but Mateo spoke up. "Me. I am."

"Good. Lie on the floor, face down."

He went waxy pale, and I saw two beads of sweat break out on his forehead. He gave his head a small shake. "No, listen—"

"Do it now or I'll blow your kneecap off."

I lowered the cannon, and he dropped to his knees and sprawled on the floor. He also started sobbing. Something inside me stirred, like it wanted to feel compassion. But I made myself remember the thousands of lives he had helped destroy, the women and young girls he had either raped or allowed to be raped, and I felt the hot rage in my head begin to replace those green shoots of compassion.

"Put your hands behind your head with your fingers locked and cross your left ankle over your right one." I looked at Ramon. "What's your function in this setup, Ramon?"

He shrugged with his hands still in the air. Shock must have been kicking in because he had started to shiver. The room was getting dark in the growing dusk. He looked thin, wet, and cold.

"I am protecting Don Jesus. I do jobs for him."

"Ever kill anyone?"

He gave a small shrug. "Sometimes."

"Move drugs?"

"Sometimes."

"Girls?"

"Yeah, sometimes."

I shot him and discovered that Dirty Harry really hadn't exaggerated. On the floor, Mateo's sobbing had turned to whimpering. I walked behind him.

"Mateo, I am going to shoot you in the back of the knee."

He started wailing, "*No, no, no!*"

"I have just shown you that I am capable of doing it. I have killed four of the five people who were in this house. So you know you have to take me seriously. You understand that."

"Yes! Please. I will do anything you say. Please, mister. You are looking for Jesus? You are the guy looking for Jesus? I tell you where is he. I tell you. Please don't kill me."

That made me pause but only for a moment. "Where is he?"

"He gone back to Mexico. He knew you were comin' for him. So he went back."

By the window, there was a dining table. I pulled over one of the chairs and sat.

"He was here setting up distribution, right?"

"Yes. He wanted better distribution in the USA."

"But he's gone back to Mexico without setting up that distribution, just because of me?"

It was hard to believe, but he nodded.

"You're lying. I don't believe you, Mateo."

His voice was edged with hysteria. "How many people you killed? In just a few days? Look at you! You crazy! Fourteen, fifteen guys! And nobody can find you!"

"You been looking?"

"Of course!" He stopped dead and swallowed.

"So he's gone back while you look for me. And when you kill me, you call him and he returns to Los Angeles." He didn't say anything. He just swallowed and started whimpering again. "Who's looking for me?"

"We were waiting for you here in the house."

I laughed. The sound was loud and ugly even in my ears. "*This* was your *trap?*"

"We thought you would come at night. I saw you last night. I thought you'll wait till dark."

"Stupid." I thought for a moment. "Where in Mexico?"

"*You crazy?*"

"Yeah. Where in Mexico?"

"Aguapepas Ranch, on the Mochis Culiacan Road. Is about three kilometers south of Alamos de los Montoya village. Is in Sinaloa. They gonna kill you."

"Sure. Who was out looking for me, Mateo? You were waiting here, but somebody was out looking for me. Who?"

"El Sicario. The boss always goes with two guy. They grew up together. El Indio went with him back to Mexico. El Sicario stayed to look for you."

"Where did he go to look, Mateo?"

I was going cold inside as I thought about it.

"I don't know," he said. "I think he went to the Coca Cabaña. Jesus say he remembered a guy there that night. The waitress was flirting with you. He went to talk to Agustin, the owner, and the waitress."

I shot him in the back of the neck. It almost decapitated him, but it was quick.

I searched the house till I found a fob for a car. It was a BMW. I don't like German cars, but at least the BMW would be fast and reliable. I went out front into the quickening dark and collected the bags of cash, then I took them into the garage and dumped them in the trunk of the BMW.

I turned right out of Rexford Drive aiming to take I-405 up to Santa Clarita. As I cruised slowly among the boulevard lights, I called Ernestina. It rang for a while, then went to voicemail. I tried again as I passed the Getty and again as I passed Woodley. I tried one more time as I joined I-5 at Sylmar and began to climb into the hills. After that, I didn't try anymore because I knew I was not going to get an answer. And I knew why.

I drove fast through the San Gabriel mountains, but even so it took me almost an hour to reach Palmdale, where I could begin to accelerate. I reached Mojave closing on a hundred and twenty, praying the cops would not try to stop me. They didn't, and I came into Ridgecrest forty minutes later standing on the brake instead of the gas. I came in from the north, down South China Lake Boulevard, jumped the lights at Upjohn, and drove into the parking lot at the motel with horns blaring behind me.

I pulled up in front of the room. I had two rounds left in the 29, so I put it in the glove compartment and climbed out of the car. There was no light in the window. I approached the door from the side and blew out the lock. I slipped inside, left the lights off, and closed the door. I had no doubt people would be peering out their windows, but what they would see would be precisely nothing of interest.

Carmen was lying on the bed. For a moment, I felt a stab of hope. That was because in the darkness it took me a moment to see Nelson slumped in the chair, and the big, dark stain under Carmen's head.

I stayed with them for a while, in the silence and the darkness. I wanted to apologize for having failed them. I had tried to make them safe, but I had failed. And now they were dead. Eventually I went outside into the dark evening, with the dull, dead light making the parking lot into a two-dimensional stage set where nothing seemed real. I climbed behind the wheel of the BMW and sat motionless for maybe five minutes.

Ernestina was not there. Jesus Sanchez had thought that she was flirting with me. It was like a weird kind of synchronicity. My cell rang. The screen said it was an unknown number, but it was plus 52, and I knew that was Mexico.

"Yeah."

"Good evening. You are the man who is trying to kill me?"

"Are you Jesus Sanchez?"

He laughed. "You think I will answer a question like this?"

"That's a yes, then. So my answer to you is no, I am not the man who is trying to kill you. I am the man who is going to kill you, and if your friend el Sicario is there with you, tell him I am going to kill him, too."

"Oh, but you are going to kill everybody. You are a verdugo."

"I am Rogue, Sanchez, out of control."

"I have your little friend, Ernestina here with me. She is a very attractive girl. I can see that any man would want to make her happy. I will make a trade with you, Mr. Rogue. The money you took from Steve and Peter, and two millions in compensation. Is three million dollars, and I give you Ernestina, unhurt and still a virgin."

He laughed lots. He obviously thought it was real funny, like the guys I could hear in the background.

"Where?"

"You come to Tijuana. Is neutral territory. We meet in the Bar Mecha on the Paseo Costero. You bring the money.

We bring the girl. We swap. You go home and I go home and we never see each other again."

"What guarantee do I have that I will get out of Bar Mecha alive?"

"The same as me, gringo. Tijuana does not belong to us. There is a lot of cops there controlling the drugs. If I shoot you, I got a big problem with the cops. If you shoot me, the same. You got a big problem."

It sounded like bullshit and a clumsy trap, but I told him, "Okay. When?"

"Tomorrow, twelve noon. We can have lunch and be like friends for a while."

"Yeah, I can't wait."

I hung up.

I had no illusions about what I was going to find in Tijuana if I went. Ernestina, assuming she was still alive, would not be there, and neither would Jesus Sanchez. His pals Indio and Sicario might be, but he would be safely barricaded in his fortress ranch in Guamúchil, seven hundred miles to the south.

I called Dave Marshall. He answered after a couple of rings. He sounded tired.

"This is Dave Marshall."

"Hi, this is Rogue. You sound like you're still in your office."

"I was about to close shop and go home."

"I need to see you urgently."

He sighed. He made it loud enough for me to hear. "Can it wait till tomorrow?"

"There's a girl. They are going to kill her, if they haven't done so already."

"Jesus!" He said it wearily, like he had his eyes closed. "What the hell have you gotten yourself into?"

"That's not important. What's important is that this is an innocent girl, her mother and her brother have been killed, and she has been kidnapped. Every moment counts, Marshall. I need to talk to you."

"Where are you?"

"Ridgecrest. If I don't get arrested on the way, I can make it to you in two hours."

"Who's this girl?"

I fired up the car and pulled out of the lot as I spoke.

"Her name is Ernestina. Jesus Sanchez was after her because he thought he could get to me through her. I brought her and her family here to Ridgecrest to keep them safe. But somehow they found them."

"How?"

"I don't know. The boy was involved with a local gang. Maybe word got out. But I just found them in the motel room."

"Rogue, did you kill these people?"

I scowled at my cell on the dash. "Are you out of your mind? I just told you I took them there to protect them. Besides, I was otherwise occupied in Beverly Hills."

He didn't say anything. After a moment, I spoke again.

"Listen to me, Marshall. If you do something stupid like calling the cops or your friends at the Bureau, you could be sentencing a young woman barely in her twenties to death. And not just death. You know what these people are capable of. Just wait for me and hear me out before you go doing anything stupid. I'll report this to the local PD."

"All right, I'll wait for you. I am at my office."

I hung up and called the Ridgecrest Police Department to report a double homicide at the Quality Inn.

It was past nine when I arrived. I parked in his lot. My BMW was the only car beside his, a Ford Ranger with a covered bed. I opened one of the bags full of cash and removed about half, which I distributed among the other bags. Then I took the bag from the trunk, climbed the stairs, and rapped on the door. He opened it after thirty seconds, gave me the once-over, and said, "Come in."

I followed him into his office and dumped the bag on his desk. He was about to sit but paused and said, "What's this?"

"A quarter of a million bucks. It's untraceable. It's yours. I need you to get me into Mexico. You get the other half when I'm across the border."

"Are you out of your mind?"

"Probably, but we have no time for that now. Will you do it or not?"

"Jesus Christ, man!" He sank into his chair. I opened the bag and shoved it toward him so he could see the cash. He stared at it and frowned like he didn't know what it was. "You're nuts. I can't—"

"For Christ's sake, Dave! She's beautiful and maybe twenty-three years old! You *know* what they'll do to her! And when they're done, they'll cut her throat! Do you want to live with that the rest of your goddamn life?"

He closed his eyes and rubbed his face. "No."

"Then take the damned money, put me in the back of your truck, and drive me across the border. Leave me the truck, and you fly back from Tijuana. Once we're across, I'll tell you where the rest of the money is."

"I don't want the goddamn money! But what the hell are you going to do over there? Where the hell have they got her?"

"Sinaloa. I spoke to him on the phone—"

"Who?"

"Jesus Sanchez. He called me. He told me he has her."

"It's you killing all these dealers, isn't it?"

"Yes."

He shook his head, narrowing his eyes in disbelief. "Are you out of your mind? You know the Feds are looking for you?"

"I imagine, probably thanks to you."

"You can't just go around killing people because you disapprove of what they do!"

"No? Should we leave that to law enforcement, since they are doing such a bang-up job? I haven't got time to argue with you about the ethics of the situation. I'm offering you half a million bucks to smuggle me across the border. Nobody will even check you. People get smuggled *out* of Mexico, not in."

"Do you know where she is?"

"Probably at his ranch in Guamúchil. I figure it's about seven or eight hundred miles. I should be able to make it in ten to twelve hours from when I leave you at the airport."

He gave an exasperated laugh and put his fingers to his forehead.

"But—what the hell do you think you're going to do when you get there?"

"Kill them all and bring her back."

He sat and gaped at me. "Kill them all. Just like that."

"I seem to be pretty good at it." He spread his hands

silently. I said, "When I get back, you can hand me over to the Feds, if you can find me. On the other hand, you could take a look at the kind of trash I've been taking out and just keep your mouth shut. Meantime, every minute we waste takes Ernestina a little closer to rape and death. I am the best hope she has, and the only hope she has."

He groaned loudly. "Okay, let's go."

TWENTY

SEVERAL HOURS EARLIER AND TWO HUNDRED AND thirty miles to the northeast, Special Agents Elroy Jones and Cathy Newton had pulled into the parking lot outside the gentlemen's massage parlor on South Decatur Boulevard, opposite the used car lot, in Vegas.

Newton leaned on the bell and hammered on the glass door, and after a couple of minutes, a tall man in his fifties with permed gray hair swept back appeared. He shook his finger through the glass and mouthed, *We are closed.* Newton mouthed back, *No you're not* and pressed her badge against the glass. Jones raised his to be seen. The guy with the permed hair rolled his eyes and unlocked the door.

"Can this wait? I am real busy. Can't you guys phone and make an appointment, like other people?"

"No." It was Elroy. "But we can have the Vegas PD show up with ten cars all flashing lights and wailing sirens. That should do a lot for your business, Mr. Henson. Now we only want five or ten minutes of your time, so maybe inviting us inside is your best option."

He sighed and rolled his eyes again and stepped back to let them in. They followed him past a reception and through a door into a bar, where he had accounts strewn on a table. He gathered them up, slipped them into an attaché case, and gestured to the agents to sit.

"What can I do for you?"

Newton answered, "You own a Dodge RAM 1500 that was stolen a few days ago."

Henson gave a small laugh of relief. "Is that what this is about? Well, I'm sorry you guys wasted your time. The guy who stole the truck returned it."

Newton narrowed her eyes under contracted brows. "*He returned it?*"

Henson gave a small, uncomfortable laugh. "Right? Weird. But that's what he did." He spread his hands. "I mean, it was never anything for the Feds to get involved in, but he showed up and apologized..."

"Apologized."

"Right?" he said again. "Crazy guy."

Jones raised an eyebrow at him. "We are looking for this crazy guy who brought your RAM back and apologized to you, Mr. Henson. We are looking for him because we believe he is extremely dangerous and guilty of multiple homicides."

Henson's smile became empty and flaccid. Newton said, "Where did you meet? Did he come here? Did he call you? How'd he get your phone?"

Henson's lips tried to form answers to the questions and ended up saying, "I don't know."

"So he phoned you."

"Yes. He called. He said he had my truck and wanted to return it."

Jones said, "What reason did he give for taking it?"

"Well, he didn't exactly..."

Newton snapped, "How long was he here?"

"Well, uh..." He raised a hand, half pointing. Jones cut in, reading the gesture. "You didn't meet here? Where did you meet?"

"The, the, the uh—"

"You don't remember where you met?"

"How long was he here?"

"No, yes, at the Parkway Tavern, down the road."

Jones asked, "What did he drink?"

"Uh, beer, I think."

"And you?"

"Beer, beer. We both had beer."

Newton said, "So he was here long enough for you both to have a beer at the tavern, but in all that time he didn't explain *why* he was returning it or why he took it in the first place?"

"Well, uh..."

Jones cut in again. "What *did* you talk about?"

"Uh..."

Newton leaned forward. "Come on, Hanson. He was here what, fifteen, twenty minutes, and in all that time you just stared at each other? What did you talk about?"

In desperation, Hanson exploded, "He pretended he was with a gang!"

"What gang?"

"There were four guys. I was at the casino at Caesar's, and these guys approached me. Uh, Felipe Ochoa, Néstor

Gavilan, Oliver Peralta, and Eulogio Borja. They said they'd been making a study of clubs like mine, massage parlors, gentlemen's clubs, that kind of thing, in Vegas. And they said a lot of them were owned by the Mob, and independent clubs like mine needed to be protected. They said they would provide me with merchandise—"

"What kind of merchandise?"

He went pale and pasty. "Drugs and women. I told them no way!" He waved his hands in the air. "I told them that wasn't my scene and I didn't want nothing to do with it. And I went to get my truck, but it was gone."

Newton was watching him closely. "So this is what you talked about."

He froze, licking his lips. "Well, I mean, he..." He glanced from one to another. "He—at first he said he was a friend of Felipe Ochoa. But then, when we came here—we met in the tavern but then he said like we should come here. And he told me a different story."

Jones asked, "What did he tell you here?"

"He told me to read the *Los Angeles Daily Graphic*, where it said Ochoa, Gavilan, Peralta, and Borja had been murdered in LA. He said he had done that. He had killed them. He wanted to know what they told me about expanding their operations and improving their distribution in the States."

"He wanted to know about that?" It was Newton.

"Yeah, he asked about that. He asked a lot about them. He was also curious about the fact they'd come from New York." He thought for a moment, remembering. "He was real interested that they told me Sonora in Mexico and California were going to be an extension of Sinaloa. I didn't understand what the hell they was talking about, but he thought it was real interesting. That and the fact they talked a lot about this guy called Jesus Sanchez. He said he was the head of the Sinaloa, biggest cartel in Mexico. He knew all about that.

"They told me the head of that cartel was getting old, and this guy, Jesus Sanchez, was going to take over, and he was going to start by taking control of the States. Because so he says, whoever controls drugs distribution and prostitution in the States controls Sinaloa, and he was real interested in that too." He shrugged. "After that, he gave me ten thousand bucks. He said that was for the inconvenience he'd caused me, but also because he was taking my Mustang."

Jones sighed. "Your Mustang."

"Yeah, I had a real nice red Mustang Shelby GT 500 putting out five hundred and sixty horses. He took it."

Newton pulled her cell. "Tell me the plates." To Jones, she said, "I'll put out a BOLO."

Jones nodded at her, and she rose and went out to the parking lot. Jones turned to Henson. "Did he give you a name?"

Henson frowned. "Yeah, he said Ochoa called him the Man with no Name, like the guy in the movies. But then he said his name was Clint." He shrugged again. "Like Clint Eastwood, who played the man with no name, right?"

"Yeah. The man has a sense of humor, apparently."

Five minutes later, he joined Newton. She had her ass on the hood of the Charger and was just hanging up the phone.

"We have a situation," he said.

"You think?"

"This is some kind of vigilante on steroids. He is

hunting down the whole goddamn Sinaloa Cartel single-handed." He reached for his cell. "I better have the PD send a car around to the Sanchez place in Beverly Hills. He's in Los Angeles right now."

She held up her phone. "Done it. Told them to be on the lookout for a pretty red Mustang too. Shouldn't be hard to spot."

He grunted. "Assuming he's still got it. This guy is smart." He gave her something almost like a smile. "Told Henson his name was Clint. The man with no name."

She snorted. "Clint my ass."

"Come on, we better get back to town. I want to go talk to Sanchez."

They had gotten as far as Borax when Jones' cell rang.

"Yeah?"

"This is Detective Fokes of the Beverly Hills Police Department. Am I speaking with Special Agent Elroy James?"

He put it on speaker and said, "Yes, this is he."

"Special Agent Catherine Newton contacted us a little over a half hour ago about a BOLO on a red Mustang with Nevada plates and asked us to look in on the Jesus Sanchez property on Rexford Drive."

"Yes. What have you found?"

"I don't really know how to put this, Special Agent. What we found was carnage. There were five dead men in that house. They had all been shot with large caliber bullets, and they were a mess."

"Was Sanchez among them?"

"We're not sure yet. The crime scene team is on its way and so is the ME, but I am figuring this is part of your wider investigation, and you had probably better get here and have a look at the scene yourself. Have we got a gang war going on here, Agent Jones? How many dead is that in the last few days?"

"Fourteen that we know of, Detective. We're just leaving Vegas. We'll be there in about four hours."

Newton snorted. "Make that three."

"Sure. There is just one other thing, Special Agents..."

He had to raise his voice over the sudden roar of the big engine as Newton put her foot down.

Jones asked, "What's that, Detective?"

"We also found the Mustang."

Jones sighed. "It can never be easy, can it? Where was it, Detective Fokes?"

"Just across the Santa Monica Boulevard in the City Hall parking lot."

"Okay, thanks. We'll be there in—" He glanced at the intense concentration on Newton's elfin face and gave a weary nod. "In an hour and a half."

He hung up. "The son of a bitch is cool. He took the Mustang there, left it in the parking lot, crossed the road, massacred five members of the Sinaloa Cartel, and walked away."

"Drove away."

He eyed her a moment, distracted for a moment by the incongruous beauty of her face, then nodded. "Yeah, drove away. He takes cars like a woman trying perfumes in a superstore."

She grinned at him. "You were married, right?"

"I was married, right."

"What happened, she dumped you because you were so

damn downbeat?" She was still grinning, and he couldn't help a brief laugh.

"Mind your own business, Newton." But after a moment, as they hurtled past Prim and into California, he said, "What about you? You hitched?"

"Nah!" She shook her head. "Guys my age are all assholes, but if you go with older men, you get a reputation. People say you've got daddy issues."

She frowned at him for a few seconds too long, which made him glance at the road and point. She nodded.

"I got it. The road is straight, and there's nothing ahead. And yes, if you were going to ask, I have kinda got daddy issues." She raised her left shoulder a quarter of an inch and opened her right hand on the wheel. "Just not like that."

"Right. I shouldn't have—"

"You know that song? 'Daddy Lessons'?"

"No."

"Yeah. Well, that was my dad. Only he was a white supremacist on a Harley. Taught me to shoot when I was four. I'm a good shot. Daddy said shoot."

Jones looked at his watch. Still over an hour to go.

As they wound up into the hills, past Wheaton Springs, she smiled at the road ahead and said, "Funny, isn't it?"

"What is?"

"You told me this guy has amnesia. That's why he went to your pal, Dave."

"Yes. Why is that funny?"

"Not funny haha. Funny interesting. Because *he* doesn't know who he is, it makes it that much harder for *us* to know who he is." She shifted her ass in her seat and gestured at him with her right hand. "For example, if he knew who he was, if he had a driver's license, passport, some kind of document, he would do something stupid like rent a car. Right? And we could trace him. But he can't do that, so he is forced to be more resourceful. He kills these dealers and he takes their money and their cars. Okay, in Rick's case, he didn't kill him, he just took his car. But you see what I mean. When we get the Mustang, all we can do is trace Rick. We can't even model his behavior because he doesn't know himself who he is. He is just adapting to survive."

"No, he is doing more than that. What *do* we know, Catherine? We know he is a stone cold killer. You don't bang your head, lose your memory, and become a lethal killing machine. Besides, we have to assume if he went to Dave the same day he woke up on Ocean Boulevard when he killed Ochoa and the others, he knew who he was. It was during or after that massacre that he lost his memory."

"Yeah, okay. So we can say we know he has some kind of training."

"Marine, Special Ops..."

"Something like that. And we also know that he is so deeply committed to hunting down Jesus Sanchez and his gang that his compulsion survived his traumatic amnesia."

"Good point. And we know he started his hunt in New York." She gave a tiny shrug. "Who knows if he stole a car there and swapped it for the RAM in Vegas?"

Jones pulled his cell from his pocket and dialed.

"Special Agent Jones, this is Detective Fokes. How can I help you?"

"In the garage and Sanchez's place, would you say there's a car missing?"

There was silence for a while. When the detective's voice

came again, there was a hollow echo. He said, "Yes, it's possible. There's space here for two cars, but it's empty. I'll make a call and see what cars he had registered, and we'll know what's missing. By the way—"

"Yeah?"

"None of these guys was Jesus Sanchez. He either got out before this guy arrived or your guy took him."

"Okay. When you get the license plates for Sanchez's car, put out a BOLO on them, will you?"

"Of course."

Newton narrowed her eyes at the speeding road hurtling toward her and thumped the wheel thoughtfully with her balled fists.

"Question: assuming Clint-with-no-name had found Sanchez at home and killed all the guys, what would make him then take Sanchez with him?"

Jones shrugged. "To torture him? Make him suffer?"

"He couldn't do that at Sanchez's house? He seemed to manage okay at the place on Ocean Boulevard."

Jones grunted. "So when Sanchez sees his men going down like flies, and Steve Schneider and Pete Barta go down, he ups and runs, leaving his boys to finish off the vigilante."

Newton nodded. "So Sanchez is on his way to the border or already in Mexico headed for his fortress in Sinaloa, in one car..."

"And the vigilante is behind him in the other one."

It was as they entered Cajon Junction that Jones' phone pinged. When he checked it, it was a message from Fokes. He read it and said, "The missing cars are a dark Audi Avant and a BMW. Bolos out on both."

After a moment, Newton said, "The Audi's already

across the border. And if the man-with-no-name took the Bimmer, he's already dumped it for something else." She gave her head a small shake. "It's like chasing a ghost."

"It *is* chasing a ghost. Whoever he was, this guy is the walking dead."

TWENTY-ONE

WE DIDN'T GO VIA SAN DIEGO. WE WENT VIA Arizona instead so I could make a couple of purchases on the way. I had no idea whether Sanchez was going to send a reception party to meet me at the Bar Mecha in Tijuana. I didn't know how stupid he thought I was. But I figured there was an even chance, and when I didn't show, he would be alerted to my possibly knocking at his front door in the near future. So it followed that if he was alerted, I had to be prepared to do something unexpected.

I had Dave drive me to the New Hope Gun Store, just forty-five miles over the border along I-10. As we'd left Ehrenberg behind and kept driving into the graying dawn, he'd glanced at me and asked, "Do you know this place? Do you know where we're going?"

"Looks that way?"

"But you don't remember consciously?"

"Some part of me remembers."

Forty minutes later, as we approached exit 45, I pointed and said, "Slow down. We get off here."

As he took the exit, he said, "You're remembering, man. How much are you remembering?"

"I told you, some part of me remembers. There's a gas station and a Pizza Hut. You go past that. There's a gun store."

"So you've been here before."

"I don't know, Dave! I don't remember. There." I pointed ahead as he turned onto Vicksburg Road. "On the right. It's not open yet."

"Yeah, that might be because it's seven in the morning."

We got coffee and donuts at the gas station and sat in the truck for an hour and a half until a bald guy with a tattooed head and arms like tree roots pulled up in a sixty-year-old Land Rover. As he set to unlocking the door, I swung down and approached him.

"Don't open till nine, pal."

"How about if I pay double?"

"How much you lookin' to spend?"

"Whatever it costs."

"In that case, I am open right now. Tell your pal to come inside and close the door." He flipped some switches, and lights winked on in a small store with a glass-fronted counter and a very wide selection of guns. "What do you need?"

Dave came in and closed the door as I approached the counter. He was studying my face, and I was searching his.

"I had an accident," I told him suddenly. "I lost my memory. I have total amnesia. Do you know me? Have I been here before?"

He glanced briefly at Dave, then his eyes became hooded,

and he shrugged elaborately. "Same thing happened to me. Had an accident and got total amnesia. What do you want?"

I sighed. "I want forty pounds of black powder. I'm paying cash."

He glanced at Dave again. On an impulse, I said, "He's okay. He looks like a cop, but he's cool, and I'm paying him."

It was like he hadn't heard me, but he stopped looking at Dave. Instead he said, "You filling rounds or you want to blow something up?"

"I want to blow something up."

"In Arizona?"

"In Mexico."

He smiled. "You want something lighter with a bit more kick?"

"What have you got?"

"I got some C4 somewhere out back."

I returned the smile. "C4? How much can you give me?"

"You going cross country?"

I nodded. "Some."

"I can put twenty pounds in a rucksack for you. I don't think you'll need more than that." He turned to Dave and pointed to a chair. "You want to wait there for a bit?" To me, he said, "Come with me."

I followed him through a military green steel door into a small warehouse. The walls were untreated concrete, and there were six rows of steel shelving. I followed him down the row on the far right, and at the end, he hunkered down and pulled out a steel trunk. He unlocked it with a key from his pocket and pointed to a shelf behind me. "You got your rucksacks up there. Grab one down for me. You need guns, ammo, anything else? You got a knife?"

I thought about it. "I could use a semi-automatic."

He nodded as he slipped the cakes of plastic explosive into the rucksack. "You'll want a Sig Sauer or a BULL, right?" He stood and went to a wooden box on the far side of the shelf. He came back with a P226 and handed it to me. "This one's on the house. We'll pick up some ammo on the way out. You need a rifle?"

I shook my head. "No. I need to keep a low profile, at least till I get there, but I do need a high-powered scope or some binoculars."

"I hear you." I followed him past a couple of aisles where he stopped and handed me a pair of military binoculars. "From what you're not telling me, I figure you'll need some night vision goggles too." They went in too.

Then he pulled a small crossbow off a shelf, along with a magazine with twelve short bolts, each with a razor-sharp broadhead. He slipped them in the rucksack. "That's a hundred times more silent than a suppressed semi. Eighty pound draw weight. It'll kill a rhinoceros, and he won't even know he's been shot."

After that, he supplied me with a box of .44 magnums, another of .357s, and a couple of boxes of 9mm.

When I was set up, he stood looking at me.

"Is it true you got amnesia?"

"Yeah. Why? Do you know me?"

He shook his head. "Never seen you before in my life, man." He opened the door, and as I went to go through, he spoke quietly. "Come and see me when you get back from Mexico."

I studied his face for a moment, but there was nothing to be seen there. So I nodded once and said, "I will."

At the counter, I asked him, "How much?"

"Fifteen K."

"You said you were going to charge me double."

"That was before you told me you were going to Mexico." He raised his shoulders an eighth of an inch. "You can pay me thirty if you want."

I gave him fifteen grand and slung the sack over one shoulder. As he took the cash, he said, "That's going to be some party. I wish I could join you."

"Yeah." I nodded. "It's going to be fun. Take it easy."

By the time we climbed back in the truck, the sun was climbing over the horizon, and the air was warming over the red dust. Dave looked very unhappy. He slammed his door and fired up the ignition.

"You want me to drive across the border with you and that arsenal concealed in my truckbed."

"Yes."

"Do you know what will happen to me if I get caught?"

"I'll say I slipped in while you were having breakfast."

"Jesus Christ!"

"Listen to me, Dave! You have a clean, respectable-looking truck, a clean, respectable-looking face, a two hundred dollar shirt, and a hundred and fifty dollar haircut. At the time we'll be crossing, they will be busy, and they won't waste their time on a guy like you. Besides, cars get stopped leaving Mexico, not going in. If Ernestina gets raped, tortured, or murdered, I will hold you responsible."

He scowled at me. "Take it easy, will you!"

"Get moving."

We drove east for just short of an hour and at Buckeye took Route 85 south. At Why, just thirty miles from the border, we stopped and had late breakfast at Granny's Kitchen, and at nine-thirty, I clambered in the back with my rucksack, Dave covered me with some blankets and a couple of suitcases, and we headed for the border.

It was a half hour from Why to Lukeville. It was cramped and uncomfortable, but I figured the best way to get through it was to sleep. So I closed my eyes and one by one switched off my feet, my calves, and my thighs, and by the time I'd gotten to my back muscles, we were slowing to a halt.

Then we were inching forward and stopping every thirty seconds, which told me they were not being real thorough at the checkpoint. As we stopped and started, my mind went back to Los Angeles. I reviewed everything I had done. The truth was I had done practically nothing to avoid the cops tracking me down. I had left fingerprints everywhere, all over the cars I had used and the houses where I had killed Sanchez's men. It was like in some part of my mind I had decided I didn't care.

I thought about my heart rate and my adrenaline levels and realized I was calm. I wondered absently if the LAPD or the Feds had a lead on me. I knew Dave had told them something, but I didn't know how much or how much they had learned from Steve's and Pete's deaths. I didn't know if they had found the bodies and Sanchez's house, and if they had, how much that would tell them. Was there a BOLO out for the BMW?

That made me frown. If there was, they would find it at Dave's office. Would that set them looking for Dave's truck?

I didn't think so. Dave had telephoned his wife and told her he wouldn't be home till later today. If the Feds checked, she'd tell them that.

The most likely scenario was that if Border Control was looking for anything, they were looking for the BMW I had taken from Sanchez's house, not Dave's Ranger.

It was as that thought passed through my mind that I heard the truckbed cover open and felt the morning air creep in. I froze, and Dave's voice came to me.

"Yeah, you know, Baja is just fantastic. And Puerto Peñasco, we just love it. We try to come at least once a year."

The next voice sounded like it had heard it all and really didn't want to be Dave's friend.

"Are you traveling alone, sir?"

"Yeah," he laughed. "I'm the advance party. Wife's coming tomorrow."

He was like a damned amateur. He was explaining too much.

"Are you carrying any drinks, prescription drugs, or explosives?"

"No! Good Lord, no."

"And what is the purpose of your visit to Mexico?"

"Oh, just to kick back and relax for a few days."

"Work or pleasure, Mr. Marshall?"

"Pleasure."

"These are all your bags?"

"Yup, my wife is bringing the rest."

There was a long silence. Then a question that sounded wrong. "You are a private investigator?"

"I am. Yes."

"But you are not here working?"

"No, just resting. I used to be with the FBI, you know? And that was twenty-four-seven. Now I work for myself, and I take a rest here in Baja every chance I get."

There was another long silence. Then, "Okay, Mr. Marshall. Enjoy your stay."

"Thank you! I am sure I will."

The door slammed, then the driver's door slammed, and we were moving. Slow and steady for a couple of minutes through town. Then a bend to the right and another to the left, right and left again, and then we were accelerating, and after a few more minutes Dave's voice came to me in a loud cowboy hoot.

"Man! Wow! Dude, we are in the desert! There is not a soul around. I am going to take a piss, and while I do, you can get in the passenger seat."

He pulled over, and I heard the tires on sand and gravel. Then the cover opened, and I scrambled out, shading my eyes from the sun. I scowled at his back while he relieved himself among the bushes.

"Dave, I thought you said you were in the Feds! What the hell were you thinking back there? You sounded like a fucking amateur explaining your whole life to that cop!"

He burst out laughing, bending his knees as he did up his pants.

"I was in the Feds. I was." He was still laughing. "But I was in forensic accounting. I never did field work. I was shitting myself back there! But wow! Man! What a thrill! That's better than sex, man."

"Man, I better get you to the airport before you get yourself arrested and executed."

He laughed some more but with a little less feeling and

climbed in the passenger side while I got behind the wheel. We drove on, on the Sonyata Puerto Peñasco Road, headed for the port town. After another ten minutes or so, he became serious and said, "You've done this kind of thing before."

I studied him a moment. "You think?"

"You are so cold, man. You kill, you face death, you face arrest and possible execution, and you don't react." He wagged a finger at me. "I'll tell you something else. You and that guy at the gun shop. You knew each other from before. You felt that too. I saw it on your face."

I grunted. "You're better off not noticing that kind of thing."

"See? That's what I mean." He narrowed his eyes. "Are you remembering something? I have had the feeling all night and this morning that you are remembering something."

I shook my head. "No." Then, "I don't know. Maybe."

"You want to talk about it?"

"What are you, now? My best friend or my therapist?"

"Hey! Come on, man!" He looked genuinely upset. "You don't need to do that. I'm doing this for you, and I am not taking your goddamn money. The least you can do is be a bit respectful."

I didn't answer, and we drove on in silence moving through the growing heat and glare of the sand. We crossed the dry riverbed of the Rio Sonoyata, and as we passed through the tiny, sun-blasted village of Nayarit, I said, "Something about New York. I'm not sure. Snatches."

I smiled at him. What he'd said was true. He had put himself at risk for a kid he'd never met. "Thanks. And by the way, if you talk to your pals at the Bureau and they pass it on to their pals in Mexico, I could end up a little bit dead. I'll call you if and when I get north of the border. Then you can tell them whatever you like. Deal?"

"Deal."

His flight back to the States was a special charter from the Aeropuerto Internacional Mar de Cortés, which was a wasteland of concrete and tarmac with a couple of shacks halfway along the runway. The eight–seater would fly him back to Phoenix. From there he would make his way to Los Angeles. I covered the tickets and his time, but he had refused to take a dime more.

As he opened the door to climb down from his own truck, he paused and looked back at me.

"I don't know who you are or whether I will ever see you again. But I've seen what you'll do to save an innocent girl, and I've seen what you'll do to men who traffic in girls and drugs. I hope I see you again, and I want you to know you can count on me as a friend. I'm not going to sell you down the river, Rogue." He swung down, slammed the door, and patted it. "Bring them both back safe, dude."

I gave him a single nod and drove away.

TWENTY-TWO

I DIDN'T STOP AT PEÑASCO. I KNEW I WAS ALREADY
out of time, and I needed to get to Guamúchil by yesterday.
It was over five hundred miles as the crow flies, but more like
six hundred by road along Highway 15. It was going to take
me twelve hours if I didn't sleep, and I had already been on
my feet for about thirty.

In this case, caution was going to have to be the better
part of valor because one stupid mistake could have the cops
crawling all over the truck like ants, and if they found the C4
and the weapons, that would be the end of me and
Ernestina. So I stopped at Puerto Libertad, a scattering of
dusty houses and shops a hundred and thirty miles south of
Peñasco. It was hot and sleepy and everything you'd expect
of a remote Mexican village, and it was right on the sea.

I pulled in and cruised around the streets for a while.
There was an apocalyptic feel to the place because the streets
were empty, the doors to the shops and cafés were closed,
and an avenue I cruised down was unfinished and had no

name. It was like they had started the town, but its soul had died before they'd finished it.

But I knew it was not the arrival of the Antichrist or the return of the Messiah that had done this to this small, pretty village. It was the seeping of Sinaloa into Sonora. This was the corridor along which the cocaine, the heroin, the fentanyl, and the girls—children as young as thirteen, enslaved into the sex trade—were funneled for the United States markets.

On Emiliano Zapata Street, I found the small hotel Cirios. It was clean and quiet, and I crashed and slept deeply for a couple of hours, and at three p.m., after grabbing a burrito at La Negra restaurant, I set off on the grueling drive south.

I figured if I drove steadily, without drawing attention to myself, I should make it to Guamúchil by one a.m. I figured it wasn't a bad time to arrive. I knew Sanchez was expecting me, and I knew just about everyone in the area, whether they were members of the cartel or not, would be working for Jesus directly or indirectly, and they would be looking out for new arrivals in town who might fit the bill. He would be immediately informed of any likely gringos booking into any hotel in town or in the vicinity. But with no papers and no passport, I would not be booking into any hotels, and at that time of night, there would be few people around to see what I did do.

The only stop I made on the way was at Ciudad Obregon, at close to seven that evening. I came into town on the 105 and the 128 and made my way to the Tutuli Plaza shopping mall on the Calle Quintana Roo, in the center of town.

There I passed by a camping shop to collect some essentials and then ambled down a side street to a specialist shop. I had phoned ahead, and they had what I wanted. It wasn't cheap, but it was what I needed.

By the time I was done and back in the truck headed for Highway 15, night had fallen, and it was dark. I noticed the road I was on was called No Reelection, and I wondered, not for the first time, what possible future there could be for humanity.

I turned onto the highway and accelerated through the growing darkness toward the 'Free and Sovereign State of Sinaloa' telling myself that, for reasons I could not quite put my finger on, street names like Mulberry Close and Apple Orchard Lane boded better for humanity than the Avenue of the Constitution, Victory and Freedom or Fifth of May.

This, I told myself as the city lights fell away behind me, from the character who'd killed fifteen men in the last three days.

I moved steadily through the night with dully illuminated buildings, gas station and sleeping villages slipping past on my right, and the slow, steady pulse of oncoming headlights on my left, flooding the cab with light, then humming into the dark behind me.

I could have made better progress, but Mexican roads are not great, and I really didn't want to get pulled over for speeding. So I stuck to the speed limits and moved steadily south.

Eventually I passed under a big steel arch with a sign that welcomed me to Sinaloa at well after midnight. The second village I passed after the sign was home to a military barracks and was called El Desengaño, the disappointment, and I was further confirmed in my belief that somebody really needed to talk to the Mexicans about names.

As it turned out, I arrived in the outskirts of Guamúchil at a little after two a.m. I followed the highway through the center of the sleeping city and came out the far end among flat, silent fields, an ocean of shadows under starlight. Here I drove slowly, no more than thirty miles per hour, scanning the sides of the roads. But after a little over five miles, I slowed right down because right there, on my right, was a cluster of steep hills and at the foot of them, less than a quarter of a mile away, was a ranch. There were still lights glowing there, and an illuminated sign over the gate read *Reino Sinaloa*.

The Kingdom of Sinaloa.

For a moment, I considered driving right in and finishing the job. If it had been just my life on the line, I might have done it. Having lost my past and my identity, I had nothing left to lose. But Ernestina's life was on the line, too, and that was worth saving. I had to be smart and stick to my plan.

I spun the wheel left and turned off the road onto a dirt track, pitted and rutted, that climbed steadily into the Mochomo hills that rose there suddenly out of the plain. It was about twenty-one square miles of wilderness, steep mountains and dense forest, traversed by a single dirt track that led to a lake on one of the higher peaks. That was the track I was following now.

I had to go real slow because I had killed the lights, and the trees were growing in density, crowding around the truck and cutting out what little starlight there was. After the drive from Puerto Libertad, it was an exhausting three miles climbing, scrambling, lurching over rocks and into potholes, that took all of an hour to cover, which meant I would probably have gone faster walking, and that I arrived shortly before dawn.

Where I had arrived was a densely forested peak at the southwestern edge of the small sierra, overlooking the valley where Sanchez's ranch lay. I had studied satellite images of the site on Dave's computer in his office, and it had looked promising. Now that I was there, I was not disappointed. The place was hard to get to, but I had managed to find a spot where I had left the Ford concealed among the trees, just fifty yards from my campsite, overlooking the valley.

For the next couple of days, I intended to be invisible. I would not cook, and I would not drive. I would simply lie here among the undergrowth and watch.

And sleep. Right then, I needed to sleep.

I grabbed my rucksack, my new sleeping bag, and a couple of other purchases and carried them to the trees and shrubs that were going to be my home for the next couple of days. I concealed it all in the undergrowth, climbed into my sleeping bag, and went instantly into deep sleep.

I was awoken by the chatter of birds. The first thing I did before climbing from the sleeping bag was to reach for the binoculars and focus in on the ranch below. It had not been clear from the satellite imagery which I had seen on Dave's PC, but now, with the powerful binoculars, it was very clear.

The ranch itself was about a quarter of a mile from the road, and the area around it had been cleared of trees and undergrowth. It rose to a mound roughly in the center. There Sanchez had laid a base of huge rocks and concrete upon which he had built his house, some twelve feet above ground level.

The house itself was on two levels, with barred windows and a tower rising above a red gabled roof. At the back of the house, a large steel gate gave access to the track that led to the road, and at the front, there was a broad terrace and a swimming pool.

I glanced at my watch. It was coming up to seven a.m. At that time of the morning, there was nobody out there but four guards with assault rifles who looked like they'd been there all night and one guy sitting by the pool reading a small stack of newspapers and drinking coffee. It was hard to be sure at that distance, but I assumed he was Jesus. On the tower there was a fifth guy, also carrying an assault rifle.

I counted the vehicles in the parking lot. There were two large pickups, two four-by-fours which might have been a Jeep and a Land Rover, an SUV, and two sedans that looked like Audis.

I rose and splashed bottled water on my face. After that, I spent half an hour doing stretching exercises which seemed to come naturally to me, had a protein bar for breakfast, and returned to my binoculars at eight o'clock.

Now I could see a couple of guys in white jackets setting up a long table by the pool. I counted ten chairs and ten places. A couple of cars had pulled up, and four guys in Bermudas and floral shirts had emerged and entered the house and were sitting talking to the guy I assumed was Jesus. These were not just bodyguards. These were lieutenants.

At a little before eight-thirty, they all moved to the long table, and the guys in white jackets started serving breakfast.

Shortly after that, three girls came out of the house wearing bikinis. Two of them ran to the pool the way girls run, with their arms stretched out and their palms facing forward. They inched carefully into the water and started splashing each other, shouting and laughing silently. The third one sat at the table drinking coffee and apparently joining in the conversation.

I wondered if this was the morning routine. It had that feel to it. They all seemed to know what to do without anyone having to tell them.

A little later, maybe a quarter to nine, a middle-aged woman came out, and everyone sitting at the table stood except the girl, who seemed to ignore her. Sanchez waved his hands about a bit, and people seemed to laugh. She took a seat at the far end of the table from Sanchez, and they all sat.

His wife? Were the girls his daughters?

Before I could give it much thought, four more guys came onto the terrace. They were carrying assault rifles and replaced the other guys, who went inside. Simultaneously a fifth guy replaced the man on the tower.

Ten guys? That would make two twelve-hour shifts each day. I figured it was more likely to be three four-hour shifts. Five guys on watch, five guys available, and five guys sleeping.

I spent the day there, watching, observing, counting, and measuring. Every couple of hours I'd get up and repeat the stretching exercises. And after a while, I started punching and doing high kicks and side kicks. It dawned on me as I did this that I was an expert in some kind of martial arts. A voice in my head told me the kicks suggested tae kwon do, but the southpaw guard and the style of the punches suggested something else. I filed it under 'later consideration' and returned to my observation of the prey.

By evening, as the sun was setting, I had come to several conclusions. The middle-aged woman was his wife. The three girls, who ranged from about fifteen to twenty-something, were his daughters and clustered around her at the table when they settled to eat, and what I was watching that day was the routine they followed when they were at the ranch. It was hard to nail down exactly why I came to that conclusion, but mainly it was because I was on the clock and had to reach a conclusion quickly and because their behavior was so natural. They just looked like they were doing what they did all the time, habitually.

As to the guards, it turned out there were in fact fifteen guys on rotating shifts, and they were very rarely anywhere near Sanchez. One final thing I noted was that there was no sign of Ernestina anywhere. That meant that either she was locked up or she was dead. Either way, as the dusk quickened into evening and night and they sat among flaming torches and candlelight around the table, I chewed on another protein bar and made my plan.

TWENTY-THREE

BRUCE LEE HAD A REPUTATION AS A COCKY PUNK. To some extent, it was a reputation he had earned through being a cocky punk, especially in his youth. But those who knew him well knew it was just a veneer, and that under the show, there was a wise philosopher, gently mocking all the people who were missing the point.

The point was, as he had so often tried to explain, to honestly express yourself. By which he did not mean talking openly about your sexual orientation or parroting all the justifications your therapist had given you about why you were a failure in life. What he meant was to allow your true self to explode into your world like a tornado, driven by your will. And according to this wise philosopher, the best way to do that was by sending your heavy artillery in first.

So as the sun was rising in the east the next morning, I unpacked the drone I had bought in Ciudad Obregon. It was the Aurelia X6 Max. If I'd had more time, I could probably have found something better suited to my needs, but this was good enough and readily available at short notice. Off the shelf, it could do thirty-five miles per hour and had a payload of thirteen pounds, but over the phone and in the shop, he had told me how I could customize it and get another ten miles per hour and another two pounds on the payload. It cost me an extra thousand bucks, but it was worth it.

Once the drone was set up and its payload fixed, I went back to watching the happy family down below. I figured my best approach was to come in high, at the drone's flight ceiling of ten thousand feet. At that height, it would be invisible. I would then drop to fifteen or twenty feet a quarter of a mile to the west of the ranch, where the two-story building would hide its approach and the hum of its engine. I would come in skimming the roof and strike.

That was the plan.

By four p.m., I had managed to confirm that they went through pretty much the same routine as the day before, except that the four guys in floral shirts showed up in different Bermudas and different shirts an hour later than the day before. But they stayed the day and sat down to lunch at the same long table. The girls went to the pool before breakfast, then sat giggling around their mother at lunch, and while the guys talked business with Dad, the girls sunbathed and the guards took their shifts.

So I packed everything back into the Ranger and crawled slowly down the pitted, rutted track through the forest to a patch of dense woodland by a dry riverbed about three hundred yards from the house. I noted that the river, when it was flowing, passed under the road. I checked my watch. It was just after five-thirty.

I left the truck concealed among the trees and under-growth, pulled on my rucksack, grabbed a couple of essentials, and ran to the dark, damp tunnel that formed the bridge over the riverbed. There I crawled to the end and settled down to wait for the sun to set and for the Sanchez family to settle down for dinner. I had two and a half hours.

My view from the tunnel was not great. All I could see was a couple of guys with rifles standing by the balustrades and one guy on top of the tower. So I had no choice but to trust that they would all abide, more or less, by the pattern of behavior they had displayed the day before. It was an optimistic hope, but like I said, I didn't have enough time to confirm what I had observed. Sometimes you just have to go with your gut.

By seven p.m., dusk was fading fast into evening, and up on the terrace, lights started coming on, and they lit the torches that were fastened along the balustrade. At that point, I took a risk and crawled out of the tunnel and up a slope to a clump of undergrowth, where I was able to sit unseen. From here, I had a better view of the terrace, though in the growing dark, it was hard to see much more than a few silhouettes moving against the lights on the terrace.

At seven-thirty, with the help of my binoculars, I saw the guys in white jackets setting the table for dinner. I could hear music. It sounded like reggaeton. It's a music I can't stomach, but I was glad to hear it then, because any buzz from the drone would be drowned out by the music.

By eight-fifteen, judging from what little I could see and what had happened the night before, I figured they were all gathering around the table and settling down for dinner. I switched on the drone and the remote control, and it took off vertically to its ceiling of ten thousand feet. From up there, all its cameras could show me were tiny, glimmering lights, but I could figure which ones were the ranch, and I moved south a hundred yards and then steadily west until I was a little over two hundred and fifty yards from the house. Then I began to drop.

At about fifty feet, I began to make out details on the ground, and ahead, the camera showed me the silhouette of the house and the tower with the glow from the pool and the terrace showing as a glowing halo around the building. I began to accelerate, rising in an arc over the gabled roof. To the right, I glimpsed the guard in the tower. All I saw was a slight movement. Then I was looking down on the illuminated table, where nine faces were staring up at me. Jesus was not there. The chair at the head of the table was empty.

I swore violently. I was committed, and not to go in for the attack now would be to give away my presence without gaining any benefit at all.

The thought flashed through my mind in a fraction of a second, and I hurled the drone into a dive and buzzed the table. It was an instinctual response, but it worked. The women rose screaming and ran for the house. The guys got to their feet, drawing their weapons. Even a couple of the nearest guards came running. I dropped the drone on the middle of the table and pressed the detonator.

Fifteen pounds of C4 makes one hell of an explosion. It tore through the four lieutenants and the two guards who had run to their aid. It hurled burning, mangled tables and chairs across the terrace and rained bits of Sinaloan drug dealers into the pool and all around Sanchez's fortress home. But it didn't kill Sanchez.

I was going to have to do that myself.

I pulled the crossbow from the rucksack and took off at a sprint toward the house. The guard who had been nearest in the terrace was now raining down from on high, and the guard on the tower was in shock gaping down on the terrace. That allowed me to make the hundred and fifty yard dash across the open ground without being seen. I was focusing hard on the ground and on not tripping or falling, but I glanced up once and saw a tall column of smoke rising into sky, touched by starlight. There were inarticulate cries and groans. It was impossible to tell if they were men or women.

After what seemed like a long while, when I was finally sprinting up the drive toward the gate, I began to hear shouts, questions, and despair, but nothing that sounded like instructions.

When I reached the parked vehicles, I clambered onto the hood of the Land Rover and then onto the roof. I could see the guy on the tower, who was still staring down at the terrace and the pool, shouting something. I put the bow to my shoulder and sighted him. I reckoned he was less than fifty yards away and it was a safe shot. I pulled the trigger. There was a soft clatter and a whisper. The guy went quiet and sank out of sight behind the parapet.

I didn't wait. It was a six-foot jump to the wall, but that was topped with broken glass, so I jumped to the ground, pulled out the Smith and Wesson 29, and blew the lock off the gate. I holstered the cannon and heaved the gate back a couple of feet. Then I reached for the crossbow and slipped through the gap.

I was on a paved terrace that extended the length of the house and beyond, as part of that terrace that surrounded the house. I had expected to be faced with at least one of the guards who had been standing at the balustrades. But it looked like they had run to assist at the explosion by the pool. Instead I was faced with a barefoot guy in shorts standing wide-eyed in the front door of the house, staring at me, maybe fifteen feet away.

The reaction was instinctive. I reached out my arm like I was pointing at him and pulled the trigger. There was the slight rattle and whisper, and instantly there was a solid thud. The butt of the bolt was stuck solid in his forehead. His eyes crossed, and he fell sideways, twitching.

I moved fast and stepped through the door. I was in a large room, easily as big as a medium-sized apartment. Over on my left was a broad sitting area with scattered armchairs, sofas, and coffee tables. In the center of the floor was a copper fireplace probably six foot square, where huge logs were burning, to my right was a long dining table with ten or twelve chairs around it, and beyond that was a broad staircase.

I took this in in less than a second, and across the room, thirty or forty feet away, I saw a huge set of sliding glass doors that were open onto the vast patio where the pool was. In the spotlights, I could see the water still rippling and bobbing, and the broken chairs, a table, and bits of body floating in it.

I could see also men with rifles standing and moving around, still stunned from what had happened. I could make out seven of them: the two who had survived the blast and the five who were on call. I had killed one of those who'd been sleeping, at the door. His pals would be down in seconds.

Out on the terrace, I could also see another man, a man who stood at the center of the chaos with his hands on his head, turning in circles, shouting and screaming.

It took me less than a second to register all of that. Then, without thinking, I crossed the room at a run and started climbing the stairs. I could hear voices and confusion upstairs, doors slamming. I swapped the crossbow for the Sig Sauer P226 and moved along the landing with the weapon held out in front of me, calculating in my head: two killed in the blast, one killed on the tower, and one killed in the door left eleven. Seven were downstairs, so that left four upstairs.

And they came running around the corner, buckling their belts and cocking their weapons. I double-tapped, and the first guy went down with his hands on his buckle, making the three guys behind him stumble. I double-tapped again and shot the guy cocking his Glock through the eye and the nose. Of the other two, one pulled off a round, waving his gun wildly at me and hitting the ceiling. I shot him twice in the chest while his friend ducked back behind the corner where he'd come from.

There was one big difference between that guy and me, a difference that cost him his life. That difference was that he wanted desperately to live, and I didn't care. I didn't break my stride. I turned the corner with the Sig held out in front off me and pulled off two rounds into his chest and another one into his head.

These guys were carrying sidearms, which told me the assault rifles were stored below. I walked to the banisters and looked down. There were eight men down there, and they were just beginning to respond to the situation they had on their hands. Four of them had run to the front door and found the guy with the bolt in his head and the gate open. And just as the meaning of those two facts dawned on them, they had heard the nine shots upstairs. Now they were swarming back into the huge living room, while Jesus and the other three guys came storming in from the terrace.

I shot one of them before they knew I was there and ducked back behind the cover of the wall as a volley of shots split the banisters and tore plaster from the wall and the ceiling. I dropped to one knee as the hollering and shouting started and the eight men stormed the stairs, some with pistols, other with assault rifles. In that moment, I knew with absolute certainty that I was at the gates of hell. Though I vowed to take as many of them as I could with me, I knew I was going to die. And that brought me a terrible sadness because I realized that I had failed to save Ernestina, as I had promised to do. I felt the smoldering of frustrated rage in my belly and braced myself for death.

TWENTY-FOUR

DEATH DOESN'T ALWAYS COME WHEN WE EXPECT it to.

As they came over the top steps, I opened up and charged forward in a berserker frenzy. I was going through those fiery gates, but those bastards were coming with me. Everything seemed to go in slow motion. I wasn't aiming, but I wasn't missing either. I saw one set of startled eyes as a black and red Mohican erupted from the top of his head. I saw one guy cringe and writhe away as a fountain of blood sprayed out of his back. I saw another guy yelling as he tried to aim between the guys in front of him. I slammed my boot into one guy's face and shot another in the throat.

Then a body wrapped itself around my leg, and I crashed to the floor. A heavy boot stamped on my hand. Somebody sat on me. I smashed my fist into his balls, and somebody kicked me in the head.

I emerged from a nightmare into a world of pain. Something cold and hard was pressing into my face, and as I opened my eyes, I saw it was a stone floor. I tried to stand, but my arms and my legs seemed to be paralyzed. For a moment, panic burned in my belly. I thrashed my body and discovered cold iron biting into my wrists and ankles. I wasn't paralyzed, I was chained. I looked around me. I was in some kind of cellar with stone floors and a high, arched ceiling.

Craning my neck, I saw Jesus Sanchez sitting on a bentwood chair beside a stone staircase. His face should have been expressionless, but somehow you could see in the eyes that it was full of hate. Standing around him were four men, and behind them were three girls and a woman. The girls looked nervous and uncomfortable. The woman had the same look in her eyes as her husband.

"There are five of you," I snarled, "but this is the only way you're going to stop me, Sanchez, by chaining me."

For a moment, he just stared at me, then he spat the word, "Seven!" and he jerked his head toward my feet.

I looked down along my body and saw there was a chain looped around my ankles and secured with a hook. It rose up toward the ceiling where it looped through a pull and then traveled down across the room toward a mechanical winch. Two men were standing there. One was large, with dark olive skin and long black hair pulled into a ponytail. The other was short and wiry with pale skin and red hair.

"Which one of you is Sicario?" I asked.

The big Indian just looked at me and blinked. The little redhead smiled. "I am Sicario."

"I am going to kill you last," I told him. "Just before I kill your boss."

His eyebrows rose up his forehead, and he looked

genuinely surprised. He gave one short laugh, looked across the room at Sanchez and then everybody was laughing among nightmarish echoes in that stone cellar.

I twisted my head around again to look at Jesus. He wasn't laughing.

"You got cojones, gringo. Hijo puta, you got cojones!" He was nodding slowly. Everybody stopped laughing. "I been counting," he said. "You killed more than twenty of my men. You started with Ochoa, and I guess you enjoy killing, eh? Because you don' fockin' stop. One after another. And what is worse is you screwed up my operation in New York and Los Angeles." His face suddenly flushed, and he was crazy, shouting and stabbing his finger at me. "*I have to leave LA and come back to Mexico because of one miserable maricón!*"

The moment of rage passed, and a slow smile spread over his face as he leaned forward. "But I tell you, gringo, your wrists is tied with wire, like for hangin' your shirt. When you pull, you gonna tear all your skin off your hands. You tell me something, gringo. You comin' all the way to Mexico for me or for somebody else, eh?"

I knew what he was driving at. I also knew that what little chance Ernestina had of surviving lay in Jesus believing I didn't give a damn about her. It was a forlorn hope, but it was all I had. I curled my lip.

"I came here to kill you with my bare hands, Sanchez, and if you had any cojones, you'd fight me man to man."

He smiled. "I don't got nothin' to prove, gringo. I just want one thing. I want to see you weeping like a baby, like a little child, beggin' for me to kill you. I'm gonna see that tonight, cabrón." He pointed back at the girls and at the woman. "And they gonna see it too. They gonna see how Daddy deals with cabrones who try to hurt his family. But first, we gonna play a little game."

He nodded at one of his men, and two of them left the cellar, ran up the stairs, and disappeared. They came back five minutes later with Ernestina. She had her hands tied behind her back, and her eyes were puffy and red from where she'd been crying. Our eyes locked. Her lower lip curled in, but she bit back the tears.

Another one of the thugs grabbed a chair and placed it behind Ernestina, and they shoved her into it.

"You don't need to do this," I said. "She has nothing to do with this. This is between you and me, Sanchez. Leave her alone. Let her go."

He smiled. "I know you care about her, Gringo. This is gonna hurt you a lot."

They bound her ankles to the chair legs and her wrists to the back of the chair so she was completely immobilized. Then he jerked his chin at Sicario, and the metal winch began to clang as it drew in the chain and I felt my ankles being drawn slowly up and my body dragged along the floor.

Sanchez stood and walked over to me. The loathing in his face was profound. My body was hoisted up until finally my hair and the top of my head were just brushing the floor. Then the winch stopped. Sanchez hunkered down, looking into my upside-down face as he reached out his left hand toward his boys.

"Now I am going to tell you what I am gonna do." One of his men came over, laughing, and handed Sanchez a tub. My belly was on fire, and it was hard not to give in to panic. He showed me the tub. "This is a thing we make special. Is like a putrid pâté. Nobody can eat this. It makes you real sick. But the rats? The rats love it. And that's why we make it, for the rats. It makes them *crazy!* They fight, they scream, they bite, they claw at each other. Is crazy." He looked away, smiling, holding the tub near my face. "So I am gonna spread this stuff all over your face, then we gonna turn out the lights. We gonna keep on one light over there"—he pointed toward the stairs—"so we can see what is happening. We don't wanna miss that! They gonna tear your face off, gringo. They gonna eat your eyes and your mouth."

He stood and walked away toward where Ernestina was sitting biting her lips with her eyes screwed tight, fighting the tears.

Sanchez turned and spoke very loudly.

"But you can stop this from happenin' at any moment you want, gringo. All you gotta do is scream out, 'Kill her instead!'" He pointed at Sicario, who was standing behind her. "And we will put on the lights, shoot the rats, and let you down so you can see how Sicario cuts her throat."

He came over to where I was hanging, leaned down, and screamed into my face. His own face twisted and crimson with rage. *"You think you can come to me, kill my men, threaten my daughters and my wife, and then just walk away? Hijo de la gran puta! Maricón! Cabrón!"*

He kicked savagely at my shoulders, my chest, and my back. The pain was excruciating, but I swallowed it and didn't make a noise. Just a few feet away, I could hear Ernestina fighting back her own cries of fear.

Next thing, somebody had grabbed me to stop me spinning. I heard the lid of the tub clatter on the stone floor and Sanchez was spreading a vile brown paste on me. The smell was repulsive and made me retch, though fortunately my stomach was empty and I had nothing to bring up.

When he was done, he turned to his daughters and gestured them toward the stairs, telling them to go up because the rats were coming. "Suban! Suban! Que vienen las ratas!"

They giggled and screamed and hurried up the stairs behind their mother. The men gathered at the bottom, all but Sicario, who stood behind Ernestina with his wicked blade resting against her slim, white throat.

I called out, my heart pounding, frantic to delay him even a few seconds. "Don't you want to know who I work for?"

He turned, smiling. I was pulling, twisting my wrists, feeling the warm blood trickle down my arm.

"Who you work for, gringo?"

"You haven't put the pieces together yet, Sanchez?"

"Tell me."

"There's a contract out on you. That much should be obvious."

I twisted, but the pain was unendurable as the wire bit deep into my flesh and my tendons.

"So tell me, gringo. Who do you work for?"

"Let the girl go. We can negotiate. There is a lot I can tell you."

He threw back his head and laughed loudly. Then he shook it and narrowed his eyes at me. "No, gringo. I know who you are. I recognize you. You are not workin' for nobody. You want to kill me yourself."

He turned and walked away to the stairs. My heart was wild. I tried pulling my hands again, but the pain was too much. It would tear my hands down to the bone. I thrashed, biting back the shouts of agony.

And then the lights went out. One brilliant spot from the stairs blinded me, illuminating a circle around me on the floor. Then the scuffling and shuffling started. I heard Ernestina try to stifle a scream. The scrabbling grew closer, and I started to hear small, shrill screeches. I looked wildly, searching the blackness. Panic was taking hold of me. My heart was racing, and my lungs were bursting to scream and yell. And then they were surging out of the shadows with their sharp teeth and their small eyes. Something furry hit my face, and sharp teeth bit into my cheek. My wrists were screaming in agony. My whole body was screaming in agony. I could taste blood in my mouth, and my face was covered in a writhing, clawing, biting mass. I thrashed and lashed and twisted, clawing at my face with my bloody hands. Somehow, in the wild, screaming panic, I bent double, wrenched the hook from the chain, and fell to the floor.

Then I screamed. I screamed and roared and lunged as the lights came on and flooded the room. Sicario was staring at me, with his blade still on Ernestina's throat. His eyes went wide, and he thrust the blade at me as Ernestina stared and screamed in horror. She shied away, and her chair fell. Her screaming became hysterical as the rats scattered in all directions.

I ignored Sicario's blade as it cut into my shoulder. I kicked him hard between the legs and was still screaming and roaring as he went down. I jumped over Ernestina thrashing in her chair and charged the six men standing staring at the foot of the stairs.

Suddenly four guns roared as Indio lunged at me with a

huge hunting knife. The noise was deafening. And I half-heard Sanchez shouting, "No disparen!"

The blade gashed my other arm, but the rage in my head and in my chest was so crazy I didn't feel it. I lashed out with my foot and smashed my heel into his kneecap. As I felt it crunch, I clawed his eyes and his face with my right hand and smashed my right fist into the side of his head. It took all of half a second.

I stamped on his neck as I reached for the guy behind him. I saw they were all hunched and cowering. The searing whining and singing in the air told me there were at least a dozen slugs ricocheting around the cellar, but I didn't give a damn. I broke the guy's neck and took his piece as he went down. I shoved the weapon into the belly of the guy next to him and pulled the trigger. Above me, one of the girls had pulled open the door, and they were all screaming and running. Behind them was Sanchez and his second-to-last man. I shot that man in the back of the head, and his brains sprayed all over Sanchez's tailored chinos. The next round went into Sanchez's right calf. He cried out in pain, and I saw his wife come back for him.

I let them go and went back to Sicario, who was clutching his groin and weeping. I hunkered down beside him, and he looked up into my face. "No quiero morir," he sobbed. He didn't want to die.

"Do you know where you are, Sicario?" He didn't answer. He just pleaded with his face. "You are where all Sicarios are: You are at the gates of hell. You had a thousand chances to walk away, but you didn't do it. Now it's time to go through."

I took his knife from his fingers and drove the blade into

the side of his neck, cutting the vein and the artery. I gave his heart a couple of seconds to stop beating. Then I withdrew the blade and went and cut Ernestina's bonds. She scrambled away from me on her ass, staring at me in horror.

I turned away from her and went up the stairs.

I found myself in a courtyard at the side of the house. I was in the doorway of what, from the outside, looked like a small shed. Over on the left, about sixty yards away, was the pool, with all its blood and devastation still illuminated by the spotlights from the terrace.

Halfway across the courtyard, maybe fifteen or twenty feet away, was Sanchez's wife, holding her husband. He was hunched and limping, sobbing. As they hobbled, she looked over her shoulder at me. She could see me, but they kept going.

I started walking after them. I followed them as far as the gate to the driveway, where all the vehicles were. There they stopped, and his wife turned to face me. She had in her hand a semi-automatic she had taken from under Sanchez's arm.

"Now," she said to me, "you son of a bitch, you gonna die!"

TWENTY-FIVE

By the time Special Agents Elroy Jones and Cathy Newton arrived at Jesus Sanchez's house in Beverly Hills, the bodies had already been removed by the ME and taken for autopsy, but the crime scene guys were still there. Their work was painstaking, and on this case, they would be seeking microscopic clues for days to come. Detective Fokes had gone too but messaged them with the basic facts and told them he'd forward his full report to them at the Wilshire Boulevard Field Office.

They took their time going over the house, noting the location of each body and the blood spatter patterns. Then they walked outside into the evening air and sat on the hood of Newton's car, where she drew up a roughly accurate picture of the sequence of events.

"The son of a bitch rang at the door. Do you ever wish you smoked?"

Jones shook his head. "No. Uh...sometimes."

"Right now I could just use a Camel. It helps you focus.

He rang the bell, and the schmuck opened the door. Didn't they know he was coming? Wasn't that exactly why Sanchez left?"

"We don't know that. We just assume it."

"Did you have a Zippo when you smoked? My dad gave me an old brass Zippo. You poke a Camel in your mouth, flip the Zippo, and lean into the flame. Badass."

"Cathy?"

"Assume my ass, Jones. He saw the three horsemen of the Apocalypse coming, all in the shape of Clint Eastwood, and he hightailed it out of there. And they were so stupid, when he knocked on the door, that schmuck opened it, and Clint gave him the do-you-feel-lucky treatment. Then he worked his way through them systematically. Two in the living room, bam, bam. The two come in from the pool, he kills one, interrogates the other, bam, bam. You notice the one he shoots in the back of the head is the one known to be Sanchez's right-hand man. He was interrogating him. When he was done, he shot him in the back of the head. This guy is good. Stone cold but good."

"You sound like you admire him."

"I do. So do you."

Jones didn't reply, but after a while, he said, "I used disposable lighters. You know the ones that come in different colors?"

She shook her head. "Those things are bad for your health, man."

"I want to talk to Dave."

She raised an absent eyebrow at the streetlamp outside the open gate. "Dave the accountant?"

"He's a good man. He's smart, and he has good values."

She turned and studied his face a moment, more curious about him than what he was saying. "What d'you want to see him about?"

Jones shrugged. "I don't know, exactly. Gut feeling. I think he knows more about this guy than he's letting on. I don't like this guy, this vigilante." He eyed her a moment. "I think he gets inside people, and they start believing in him like he's some kind of good guy."

"Hey, take it easy, Jones."

"He's a stone cold killer, Newton. Maybe he takes out the trash and kills only the bad guys, like in the movies. But that is still murder, and when he does it, it is particularly brutal murder."

"I know that, Jones. Don't lecture me."

"All right. I just hope Dave knows it too."

He pulled his cell from his pocket, dialed, and put it on speaker.

"Yeah, Elroy, how you doing?"

"Tired. Where are you?"

"Yeah, I love you too, man. I'm at my office, about to head home, why?"

"Stay there for ten minutes, will you? I want to talk to you."

Dave groaned audibly. "Can it wait? I'm really—"

"No, Dave, it can't wait. I want to go home too, but I can't. I won't keep you long, but I need to ask you a couple of questions."

"Okay, I'll be here. But be quick, will you?"

Twenty minutes later, they parked the Charger beside a dark BMW. It was the only car in the lot. Newton took the first two steps up toward the office but stopped and turned, aware that Jones was not following her. He had walked to the back of the BMW and was checking the plates. He looked at her and pointed at the car.

"It's one of the cars missing from the house."

"Sanchez's?"

He nodded and passed her on the stairs, going up. He rang the bell and rapped on the door. Dave opened it after a couple of minutes. Jones didn't smile. He said, "Can I come in?"

"That's a stupid question, Elroy. Hi, Cathy."

"Dave."

"Go on through. Are you on duty or will you have a drink?"

They didn't answer. As Dave closed the door and made for his desk, Cathy sat on the sofa and Jones stood in the middle of the floor. Dave took his glass of whiskey and stood frowning at Elroy.

"What the hell's the matter with you?"

"You asked me if I'm on duty, Dave. The answer is, I don't know. I came here to ask you some questions, maybe off the record. We're friends, right?"

Dave was still frowning. "Of course."

"Jesus Sanchez has gone missing from his house. But five of his men, including Mateo Guzman, his right-hand man, were found in his house murdered." Dave sighed, aware that Newton was watching him closely. Jones went on, "But that's not all, Dave. There were two cars missing from his house: an Audi sedan and a BMW."

The two men stared at each other for a moment. Dave sat behind his desk and rubbed his face.

"It's the one downstairs, isn't it?"

"Yes."

Sudden irritation contracted Dave's face. "Sit down, for Christ's sake, will you, Elroy! And get yourselves a drink, for crying out loud!" He sagged back in his chair. "What do you want to know?"

Jones stood staring at him a moment. He didn't look happy. Newton got up, found a couple of glasses in a corner cabinet, and poured two generous shots from the bottle of whiskey on Dave's desk. As she handed a glass to Jones, she said, "Sit down, will you?"

He sat in an armchair, and Dave came around and took the other.

Jones said, "How'd the car get there, Dave?"

"I don't know. I guess he brought it and left it there."

"Where is he?"

Dave pinched the bridge of his nose and closed his eyes. "I don't know where he is, Elroy. You're asking the wrong questions."

"Yeah? What should I be asking you, Dave, how are your wife and kids? Don't bullshit me!"

Newton cut in before Dave could answer. "When did you last see him?"

"Yesterday, mid-morning, noon. Thereabouts."

Jones spread his hands. "What is this, twenty questions?"

Newton ignored him. "Where was that?"

"The last time I saw him was in Mexico, at the airport in Puerto Peñasco."

Jones sat forward with his elbows on his knees, his eyebrows high on his forehead. "*What? Are you kidding* me?"

Dave's face flushed. "Elroy, are you going to start asking questions I can actually answer sometime soon? What? That's your question? What? You want me to repeat everything I just told Cathy? Because I think she got it! Am I kidding you? That's your other question? No. I am not kidding you, Elroy. Now I am going to ask you a question. Have your questions moved us forward much?"

Jones sighed and sagged back in his chair. He made a helpless gesture at Cathy, then turned to Dave. "So let me see if I can get a handle on this. Did you drive this character, Clint Eastwood, the man with no name, to Mexico?"

"Yes."

He turned to Newton with the helpless gesture again. "So he walked into the Sanchez house, killed everyone there, took the BMW, and drove here"—he turned to Dave—"to ask you to drive him to Mexico."

Newton pulled her cell and made the call for the Crime Scene Unit to come and collect the car.

Meanwhile, Dave was saying, "I assume that is more or less what happened, but he called me first, from Ridgecrest. He said Jesus Sanchez had abducted a girl and killed her mother and brother at the Quality Inn. He said he'd reported it to the Ridgeway PD."

Newton was shaking her head and frowning. "Why would Jesus Sanchez want to abduct this girl?"

"He said Sanchez had the idea this girl was a way of getting to him. And by the looks of it, he was right. Sanchez was after the girl, so Rogue—"

"Who?" It was both of them at the same time.

"That's what he calls himself."

Jones said, "Rogue? As in rogue cop?"

"He calls himself Rogue. That's all I know. He took the girl, her mother, and her brother to Ridgecrest. So last night, when he went to check on them, the girl was gone, and the mother and the brother were dead."

"How do you know he didn't kill them?"

Dave raised two fingers in the victory sign. "Two reasons. One, he kills bad guys. Specifically, he kills people who traffic in drugs and women."

Jones turned to Newton. "See? What did I tell you?"

Dave ignored him. "And two, he told me he was, and I quote, 'otherwise occupied in Beverly Hills.' From what I hear on the news, I am inclined to believe he was telling the truth. Besides, this guy's MO is to turn up, walk in, and kill a bunch of pushers. Why the hell would he take a family of innocent people to a motel out in the Kern County desert and kill them? And if he did that, where's the daughter? It doesn't make sense."

Newton asked him, "So he came to you and said the girl had been abducted and he wanted to go and get her?"

Jones snorted, "Sir-fuckin'-Galahad!"

"Yes. He said he thought the son had been in touch with a gang he was involved with, and word had reached Sanchez's men." He gave a slow shrug and sighed. "If Jesus was seeing this guy taking out all his men, getting closer to him each day, it kind of makes sense. If he was sweet on this girl, and Jesus knew it—"

Newton narrowed her eyes. "How would he know that?"

"I don't know. I don't know anything about him except he had a *big* problem with drug dealers and sex traffickers. Obviously, he and Jesus Sanchez have some kind of history.

Sanchez probably knows more about him than any of us do." He paused, looking down at his drink. "He offered me two hundred and fifty grand to help him across the border, and another two hundred and fifty grand once he was across."

Jones frowned. "You took the money?"

"I told him I didn't want his damned money. I wanted him to get that girl home—what was left of her home—and I only regretted I couldn't help him."

"God dammit, Dave! What am I going to do now? You know you broke—I don't know how many laws!"

"What are you going to do now? Your duty. You inform the DA and ask her if she thinks it's worth wasting taxpayers' money on a prosecution. Ask her if she thinks it likely that a California jury would convict a private detective for helping a man cross into Mexico to rescue a young Mexican girl from the Sinaloa cartel. What do you think, Elroy?"

Cathy sniggered, cleared her throat, and asked, "So where is he now?"

"I don't know. He took my car and left me at Puerto Peñasco. My assumption was that he was driving south to Sinaloa. If memory serves, Jesus Sanchez's home was down around Guamúchil, about two hundred miles south of Ciudad Obregon. If they abducted her and didn't kill her, I guess that's where they'd take her. So that's where he would go looking for her." He raised his shoulders. "You're asking me where he is? I'd say he is probably dead by now, somewhere in Sinaloa."

Newton smiled. "You think there's anyone left in Sinaloa to kill him?"

Jones scowled. "That's not funny, Cathy."

Dave grinned at her. "Yeah, it is. And who knows, you may be right." He turned to Jones. "Elroy, I have to confess to you that at first I thought the guy was dangerously insane. But the more I got to know him, the more I came to believe those sons of bitches did something bad to him, and he came back fighting." He paused a moment. "We have the right to do that in the United States."

Jones arched an eyebrow at him. "You going to lecture me on constitutional law now?"

"Only if I have to."

"So you figure he's dead."

Dave gave a small laugh. "It's hard enough for a guy without papers or any kind of official identity to survive here in the States. How long do you think he'll survive in Mexico —in *Sinaloa*—going after El Mayo's probable successor? He's facing not only the virtually unlimited army of Sinaloa men they can recruit by snapping their fingers; he is also facing the army and the cops who work for Sinaloa. Even this guy can't survive that."

"Okay."

Newton raised her eyebrows at him. "So what? We close the case?"

He gave a small shrug. "Probably, but before I do, I want to make some inquiries at Federal Plaza in New York, and then I guess we should talk to Mexico, as a courtesy."

"You're assuming he's an American."

Jones' eyes became hooded, and he turned to Dave. "Now you're going to tell me he had a Swedish accent?"

"No, Elroy, he didn't have a Swedish accent. But with no official identity, I don't know that it is your responsibility to inform the Mexican authorities of this man's presence or his intentions. If the wrong people talk to the wrong people, it could cost this guy his life. Assuming he's not dead already."

Jones drained his glass and set it on the small coffee table. He smacked his lips and made to stand.

"How to get yourself a fan club in the United States in one easy lesson. Get yourself a gun and go shoot a bunch of Mexican drug dealers." He levered himself to his feet. "Who cares if you're breaking the law?"

Newton stood and, diminutive by his side, punched his shoulder. "I'm guessing, if Rogue Clint were here, he might tell you if law enforcement was doing its job and keeping these bastards off the streets, there wouldn't be any dealers for him to go out and kill." He drew breath, and she wagged her finger at him. "Don't give me that bullshit about it not being a civilian's job. In the first place, he ain't no civilian, no sir! And in the second place, if I pay you to protect my kids, and you fail in that job, I am going to protect them myself."

Jones rolled his eyes and turned to Dave. "If you hear from him, give me a call, will you?"

Dave nodded. "I will."

Outside, Jones paused to smell the night air. Cathy stood by his side with her hands in her pockets.

"I am hungry and thirsty, and it's your fault. The least you can do is buy me a pizza and a beer."

He sighed and sagged his shoulders. "Fine." But as he followed her down the stairs, he was wearing a secret, private smile.

TWENTY-SIX

HER HAND WASN'T TREMBLING. NOT FOR THE FIRST time that day, I had the certainty I was going to die. There was a throbbing, nauseating pain in my face that was sending tendrils into my brain, and my whole body ached. On some level, I was half-hoping she would pull the trigger and put me out of my damned misery, but the rest of me was not going to let that happen unless I took Sanchez with me.

He turned slowly to look at me. His wife spat. "You not going to go and kill and rape my daughters? Hijo de puta!"

I snarled at her, "I leave that kind of stuff to your boys." I pointed at Sanchez. "I want an answer from you."

She reached out her arm, aiming the pistol at my head. "I give you the answer!"

He laid his hand gently on her wrist. "What answer you want, gringo?"

"Who am I?"

I could see his eyes glazing from time to time with the pain that was throbbing in his leg, but he smiled through the pain and shook his head. "Who you are?" He backed up a step and leaned against the Land Rover. "What question is this? Who you are?"

I took a step closer, and she waved the gun in my face. "You stay away! You stay away from him! He is mine! I will kill you!"

He spoke softly. "Carmen. Tranquila. I am curious." And to me, half-laughing, "You are making a spiritual journey? You should go to India. People go to India to find themselves. Or in your case, maybe you should go to hell. I am sure Satanás can help you find your real self."

I felt a tear trickle down my face, through the slime he had spread on it.

"The night I killed Ochoa, Gavilan, Peralta and Borja—"

He became serious. "So it *was* you."

"Yes, it was me. I had followed them from New York. I went into the house, I went from room to room, killing them, one after another—"

"And Peter and his men."

"Yes."

"And Steve."

"Yes, and the sons of bitches you left behind in your house. I killed them too. But after I had killed them, Ochoa and Gavilan and Peralta and Borja, my memory went blank. I remember nothing."

He narrowed his eyes at me. It was like he had filed the pain away so he could see me more clearly. "Nothing?"

"I don't know who I am. I don't know why I killed your men or why I continued to kill them. I don't know why I am hunting you, why I want to kill you."

His smile deepened. "You want me to tell you who you are."

"Yes, who am I?"

He spread his hands and shook his head. "And if I tell you, what do I get?"

"I won't kill your wife or your daughters."

He threw back his head and laughed out loud. Gesturing to his wife, he said, "I think you forget who is holding the gun here. You gotta do better than that, gringo—"

"You keep calling me gringo. You don't know my name."

He didn't falter. He nodded. "I know your name. I know who you are. I remember you. But you gotta give me something. I give you your life, I give you your identity, what do I get in return?"

"Tell me who I am."

He nodded, winced, and seemed for a moment to flag. "I tell you this. I tell you what you already suspect. You are a professional killer. You are a hit man for Oscar Malherbe." He stared at me for a moment, like he was waiting to see if that registered. "The Gulf Cartel. You are a paid assassin, workin' for the Gulf Cartel." He waved his finger around near his temple. "But you went crazy, you know? You lost your mind. Something happened to you in New York, and you went crazy. Start killing everybody, like a crazy man."

"What happened to me? Why did I go crazy?"

"Aaaah, amigo!" He laughed and waved his finger at me. "I am in a lot of pain. I need a doctor." He pointed at me. "You too. So we gotta reach some agreement. I tell you what happen to you, I tell you who you are, you do something for me."

"What do you want?"

"Really?" He smiled. "You don't know?"

"You want me to kill Oscar Malherbe."

"Good, see, you're smart. Now—"

"No. I'll tell you what the deal is, Sanchez. You tell me what you know about me, and I will spare your wife and your daughters, and I'll make your death quick and painless."

He stared at me for a long count of three. His face was rigid, mixed with rage and disbelief. In my peripheral vision, I saw his wife raise the gun, her face twisted with rage. She shrieked, "Hijo de puta!" and the air was filled with the explosive crack of the pistol.

I stared at her, waiting for death, welcoming the peace it would bring. Instead I noticed the small black hole in her chest. She looked down at it and frowned, and the pistol dropped from her hand. Then she fell sideways, like a felled tree, and hit the ground with a thud. Sanchez gave a strange shriek and lunged for his wife's body but stumbled and fell. I stepped over to her where she lay, took the weapon, decocked it, and slipped it in my belt. I looked behind me and saw Ernestina standing, trembling, holding a gun in both hands. I moved to her and took the weapon from her hands. I pointed to the Audi and said, "Get in the passenger seat. I'll take you home in a minute."

She stared at me for a moment with crazy eyes, but she went to the car and got in. The door slammed, and I went and hunkered down by Sanchez, where he was weeping on the ground.

"Is the Audi yours?" He stared into my face like it was the craziest question he had ever heard. He nodded. "Do you have the fob? The key?"

He reached in his pocket and pulled it out with trembling hands. "Take it! Take it! I can give you money. I have lots of money! In the house, five millions of dollars. It's for you. Go. Just go away."

I took the fob. "I don't want your money, Jesus. Tell me who I am and I will let you live."

"You are Fletcher, John Fletcher. From New York. You were special forces, Delta. You resign and work as hit man. Oscar Malherbe paid you lots of money to kill me when he discovered I was in New York." He gripped my sleeve, trembling. "We are fighting with the Gulf Cartel. They are trying to control distribution in the States. They have good distribution, through Texas. But I want to make better distribution, and we were fighting. So he employed you to kill me."

"You're lying."

"No! No! Is truth."

"I hate you. I hate you and your organization. Why? Why do I hate you so much?"

"No." He was shaking his head and weeping. "No, gringo, I don't want to die."

"You said you remembered me. What do you remember?"

"No." He shook his head. "No..."

A rage that was hard to describe welled up, burning in my belly and through my chest, making my heart pound and my breath come short, and surged into my head. I stood and pulled the Glock from my belt, cocked it, and fired four rounds into his belly. His eyes went wide with terror, then pain. He stared up at me, and his face twisted with hatred. His voice came with the venomous hiss of a snake. "Hijo de puta," he rasped. "Your puta wife, we killed her, your puta wife, and you cried in the street like a woman, cabrón."

I shot him one more time in the head and walked to the car.

Then I turned and ran back onto the terrace, among the carnage, in through the sliding glass doors and up the stairs. I ran from bedroom to bedroom, each more excessive and over the top than the last. They were all empty. Until I came to a passage at the back of the house with one door at the end. There I could hear sobbing. There I went, blew out the lock, and kicked the door in.

Two of the girls were huddled in the corner, clinging to each other and crying. The third was on her feet with a pair of scissors in her hand. She screamed and ran at me. I fired the Glock at her feet, and she stopped dead, her face pale and waxy, her eyes staring.

"You speak English?" She nodded. "Where are my things —my rucksack, my possessions? Where did your father put them?"

"His office, upstairs."

"Show me."

"Will you kill us?"

"If you show me, you can leave. All of you. Move!"

They led me back the way I'd come. The house was like a maze. They led me down a passage and up a spiral iron stair-case into a large attic space. It was paneled in wood. At the far end was a large, Castilian oak desk with a huge, black leather chair. At the near end, there was a calico sofa and a nest of chairs. There were bookcases and world maps on the walls but no windows. And in the far, right hand corner there was a large, steel safe. Beside it I could see my rucksack.

I turned to the girls. "You listen to me, and you listen good. In the last week, I have killed over thirty men working for the Sinaloa Cartel. That includes your father, the heir to El Mayo. You go now, you take a car, and you go. If you talk about what happened here tonight, I will come and look for you, and I will kill all three of you. Do you understand?"

They all nodded. There was real terror in their eyes, and I felt bad. But I needed to get Ernestina out of there. The logical thing would have been to kill them. But I knew in that moment that I did not kill women.

I did not kill the innocent.

"Take the Land Rover. Go. Never speak about what you saw tonight."

They ran, and I went to the rucksack. I had five pounds of C4 left in it. I shaped it and placed it over the lock on the safe, stuffed in a detonator, and went out to the staircase, taking my rucksack with me.

The standard quantity of C4 for destroying a vehicle is one and a quarter pounds. I had four times that on the safe, and it tore Sanchez's den to pieces, blew the door off the safe, and made a hole in his gabled, wooden ceiling.

I picked my way through the rubble and peered into the safe through the smoke. There was a very large stash of money, all US dollars, a laptop with a couple of external drives, and a stack of notebooks. I dumped the crossbow, put the Smith and Wesson 29 under my arms and the Sig Sauer in my waistband. Then I managed to stuff all the cash in the rucksack along with the laptop, the external drives, and the notebooks. The .357 went on top with the Fairbairn and Sykes knife, and I ran down the stairs, praying silently that Ernestina would still be there when I arrived.

I crossed the terrace, trying to ignore the throbbing pain in my face and head and made it to the Audi. I threw the rucksack on the back seat and got behind the wheel. Ernestina was staring at me.

"The girls," she said.

"What about them?"

I pressed the starter and the engine roared.

"They escaped."

"I let them go."

I moved down the track toward the road, keeping my headlights switched off.

"They took the Land Rover. They'll go to Sanchez's Family. They will organize a hunt all over Sinaloa. They control the police, the army..."

"I know. We'll manage somehow."

"You should have killed them."

"I don't kill women."

She was silent till we reached the road. There I turned north and west onto Highway 15. I drove fast for maybe five minutes until I came to a gas station on my left which I had seen when I arrived. Beside it there was a mechanic. At this time of night, both were closed, but there was a handful of cars outside which the guy was working on. I pulled into the gas station, swung out of the car and, using the Fairbairn and Sykes, I removed the plates from the Audi.

I carried them over to the garage and removed the plates from the nearest truck, replaced them with the Audi's plates, and put the truck's plates on the Audi. That would give us at least a few hours, maybe more.

Ernestina joined me where I was hunkered down, fixing

the front plate. As I stood, she said, "Have you seen your face?"

"No."

"Your face is more of a liability than the plates. You need to wash it and treat the bites. You could get gangrene."

"How do you suggest I do that?"

She pointed at the gas station door. "It's a shop. They'll have soap, water, maybe tequila."

She followed me to the door. There I rammed the blade of the knife into the lock, gave it a good thump, and it opened. Inside we found a small bathroom where she washed my face with soap and water. Then we found some bleach for the bites, which hurt like hell, and some Band-Aids.

She studied my face a moment and sighed. "You look more or less human. It will get us to the border, anyway. What we do then we'll have to work out." She gestured at me. "You a crazy guy with no papers, and me a Mexican claiming to be a US citizen."

I nodded. "We'll cross that bridge when we get to it. First we need to get away from Sinaloa. Pretty soon they'll be hunting for us high and low."

She held out her hand. "Give me the keys. They are looking for you. If they see a beat-up gringo in an Audi they'll stop you. They won't be looking for a girl alone."

It made sense. I handed her the keys and stretched out on the back seat. She got behind the wheel and pulled back onto Highway 15.

I closed my eyes and tried to ignore the pain of the bites and the bleach and the bruises all over my body where Sanchez had been kicking me. Until now, the adrenaline had kept me going, but now, lying there as we moved along the dark highway, pain seemed to seep in from all sides.

"When we get to Guamúchil, turn left for a few miles. We want to take the secondary routes, at least until we reach Sonora."

"Okay," she said. "I got it."

We drove on in silence, but after a while, I began to hear the rush and hiss of cars racing past, headed south and east. Some sounded like sports sedans, others like trucks. I heard her say, "It's started."

I pulled the Smith and Wesson from under my arm. We wouldn't go down easy.

TWENTY-SEVEN

As it was, we reached Guamúchil without incident. My guess was there was chaos and pandemonium going on back at the ranch with people trying to work out what the hell had happened, and all the pretenders who had been standing in line behind Sanchez suddenly going crazy to take his place. Either way, nobody seemed all that interested in an Audi being driven north by a Mexican girl, if they even noticed it.

At Guamúchil, she turned left as far as Angostura and then drove the next two hundred miles threading along narrow, desolate country roads, among ranches and tiny villages, heading steadily north. At some point, it may have been two or three in the morning, it started to rain, and the wipers took up a steady rhythm of squeak and thud.

After a time, she said, "Are we even still in Sinaloa?"

She sounded strained, close to breaking. I sat up and asked her, "What was the last village we passed through?"

"It had that crazy name, just before that really big river.

Bolsa de Tosalibampo Uno. It was just after the other village that had the same crazy name, but it was dos instead of uno. You remember?"

I made an "Mm-hmm" noise, checking my cell phone. After a moment, I told her, "Bolsa de Tosalibampo one and two are both in Sinaloa, but here's the good news. You just keep heading north along these roads, and in twenty miles, we'll cross the border from Sinaloa into Sonora. We're not out of the woods, but we are out of the jungle. You stop outside La Planchita, and I'll take the wheel while you get some sleep. From La Planchita, we can get back on Highway 15, and it's four hundred miles to Nogales. We should be there in six hours, in time for a late breakfast."

And that was what we did. We didn't see another living soul until we had crossed into Sonora and rejoined the highway. Then I swapped with Ernestina, and she lay down on the back seat and cried herself to sleep while I broke the speed limit, hurtling north at a hundred miles per hour. I figured at this time of the morning, the traffic cops would either be asleep at home or asleep in some brothel. One place they wouldn't be was out in the rain watching for speeding gringos.

We bypassed Ciudad Obregon at about five in the morning, and as we passed Guymas, just two miles from the Gulf of California, the sun began to rise over the Sonora Mountains. We were halfway to Nogales, and I began to feel the first tenuous shoots of hope.

As we passed Hermosillo, I took out my cell and called Dave. He answered on the second ring. He sounded cautious.

"Yes...?"

"Don't worry. It's me."

"Where are you?"

"I just passed Hermosillo, headed north. I figure I'll reach Nogales by ten or ten-thirty."

There was a silence of maybe four seconds that felt a lot longer. Then, "What about the girl?"

"She's with me."

"Jesus Christ!"

"He wasn't there. I had to do it myself."

"But..."

"Dave, listen to me. Get some coffee, then call your pal at the Bureau. My name is John Rogue. Me and my girlfriend were on holiday in Mexico, visiting Nogales, and we were mugged. They took all our money, my wallet, her purse, everything. I need you to get us out of here. If your pal tells you it's not his problem, tell him I have Sanchez's personal laptop—the one he kept in his safe at the ranch."

"You have *what?*"

"Go have coffee, Dave. We'll talk in a couple of hours, on the other side."

Two and a quarter hours later, in Nogales, less than half a mile from the border, I pulled into a taco bar opposite a gas station. I locked the car, and we found a table on the terrace. Ernestina ordered coffee and pancakes for us and sat in silence while I telephoned Dave. He was less than enthusiastic when he answered.

"Hey."

"That doesn't sound like welcome home."

"It's a little complicated."

"No shit, Sherlock. Where are you?"

"We're here in Nogales."

"Which side?"

"Arizona."

"So what happens now?"

"The Feds are making representations to the Mexican authorities in Nogales, but the Mexican authorities are not being very cooperative."

"Why not?"

"They say they had a major terrorist attack last night, and they are watching the border like hawks for a man and a young girl."

"A terrorist attack? The only people who carry out acts of terror in Mexico are their own cartel members."

"Yeah, well, that's the situation."

"You need to get an emergency passport for Ernestina and get her out of here. I'll go over the border tonight. I'll tell you where, and you have somebody meet me."

"Keep your hair on, Rogue. Even an emergency passport with a rush put on it is going to take hours. Just be patient and let us sort it out. Where are you?"

"At the Tacos la Frontera."

"Did you bring my truck?"

"I'll buy you another, bigger one."

"Great, I was fond of that truck. What are you driving?"

"A dark Audi."

"Okay, hang on."

A moment later, another voice came on the phone. "This is Special Agent Elroy Jones. I understand you have a laptop computer that might be of interest to the DEA."

"Yeah, but you'll have to shoot me to get it off me before I cross the border. And if you do, you won't know if I have it on me or if I left it somewhere."

"We have no intention of shooting you, and we have every intention of getting you both across the border. In a moment, a Federal agent will present herself to you. Please do everything she says."

With that, he hung up, and as he did, a Jeep with Arizona plates pulled up on the road beside where we were sitting. Three men and a very slim, very pale woman climbed out. She approached me and showed me her badge.

"I am Special Agent Catherine Newton, and these are Agents Hernandez, Brown, and Gunther. Are you the man known as Rogue?"

I thought about telling her to go to hell, but the possibility I might end up there myself made me say, "Yeah."

"Are you Ernestina Lopez?"

Ernestina looked at me. She looked scared. "Yes."

"Is that your car?" She pointed at the Audi. I hesitated, and she gave me a look that might have castrated the statue of David. "Save us all a lot of trouble, sir, and just say yes."

"Yeah. It is."

She nodded at Hernandez and Brown. Hernandez stepped over to me and held out his hand. "Key?"

My choices were kill them and escape back into Mexico or give him the key. So I gave him the key. They both climbed in the vehicle and drove toward the border control. Newton jerked her thumb toward the Jeep.

"Get in. Let's go. We haven't got all day."

We climbed in the back, and I noticed the windows were tinted. Newton got behind the wheel, and Gunther sat passively by her side. Next thing, we were surging up the road toward the border. Before we reached the checkpoints, she took a side road, flashed her badge at a border guard, and suddenly we were in the States. I took a deep breath and felt myself relax. Beside me, I heard Ernestina begin to sob. I placed my hand on her shoulder, and she winced and pulled away.

"Don't." She said it quietly, but I saw Newton glance in the mirror.

A couple of minutes later, we pulled up outside a long, low red brick building with a gabled roof and red steel doors. She and Gunther climbed out and opened the back doors for us. We were shown in through the red steel door into a sparsely furnished room with a beige carpet and blue chairs against the walls. There was also a table beside a window. Newton pointed to the table and said, "Sit," and they both left the room.

Ten minutes later, a big, black guy in a well cut suit and very tired eyes came in and sat at the table. He pulled out his badge and showed it to us.

"I am Special Agent Elroy Jones of the FBI. We spoke a while ago on the telephone. Now let me explain the situation to you. The Mexican authorities are looking for you, or for a couple very like you, whom they suspect of having killed Jesus Sanchez."

When he said that, he looked me straight in the eye. I held his gaze and didn't waver.

"How long have you been in Mexico?"

"A couple of days."

"Where have you been, besides Nogales?"

"A friend of mine, Dave Marshall, lent me his truck, and we drove down to Puerto Peñasco, where Ernestina lived as a kid. We stayed the night, and early this morning, we were mugged by four guys who took all our money, our papers, and Mike's truck."

He narrowed his eyes at me. "I am very interested in how you are going to answer this next question, Mr...."

"Rogue. John Rogue."

"When Special Agent Newton picked you up at Tacos de la Frontera, you told her that a dark Audi that was parked there was yours."

"That is correct. Fortunately, I had a few thousand dollars in the back pocket of my jeans. It's a precaution I always take when I am abroad in countries with high levels of crime. If you give a mugger what is in your wallet, the chances are they won't check your back pocket. So I bought that secondhand Audi from a guy who was selling it. He had a sign taped to the window, it said something like *se vende*. Ernestina told me that meant it was for sale. So I bought it cash for two thousand bucks."

He nodded thoughtfully. "And what will I find if I look in the trunk, Mr. Rogue?"

"Well, I'm not sure. You see, I have had problems with my memory recently. I am seeing a psychiatrist, Dr. Elizabeth Grant, who will vouch for that if you ask her. Not that I see any reason why you should need to. We are, after all, the victims of crime, not the perpetrators."

He turned and studied Ernestina's face for a long moment.

"You understand," he said to her, "that aiding and abetting somebody who commits a serious crime like homicide is, in the eyes of the law, the same as committing that homicide yourself?"

She glanced at me, and I could see real fear in her eyes.

Not just fear of what could happen to her, but fear of who she had discovered I was. I smiled at her, held her eye, and nodded. "Tell them the truth," I said to her.

She turned to Jones, squared her shoulders, and looked him square in the eye. "John and I have become lovers. I know my mother would disapprove, but we care for each other, and we ran away to Mexico. Then this horrible thing happened, probably a punishment from God. But I don't care."

He nodded some more and stood.

"Will you both come with me, please?"

He led us through another red steel door, down a passage, and out into a parking lot. The Audi was there, and Gunther was sitting on the hood. He handed me the fob, Jones nodded at him, and he went inside. When he was gone, Jones said, "Would you please open the trunk, Mr. Rogue?"

I opened it, and we all three stood looking at my rucksack. Inside it I knew was at least a million bucks, most of my weapons, and Jesus Sanchez's files, laptop, and external drives.

"Is that your rucksack, Mr. Rogue?"

I nodded. "But you know what? Did you say your name was Special Agent Elroy Jones?"

"I did."

I turned to Ernestina. "Do you remember, honey, this morning, that guy who came up to us? He looked like he'd been in a fight or something. He looked in bad shape. He asked us if we were Americans. I told him we were, and he said something pretty crazy. What was it?"

Ernestina cut in. "He said he had just driven all night

from Sinaloa and there were men after him. He gave us a bundle of stuff, a laptop, some files and some external drives, and said, 'Make sure this stuff gets to the FBI.'"

I nodded. "That's right, exactly right. And he used your name. He said, 'make sure it gets to Special Agent Elroy Jones.' And then he ran. I hope the poor guy is okay."

I smiled and reached in the trunk. I pulled out the laptop and handed it to him along with the files and the drives.

I heard a door open behind me, and Agent Newton stepped out. I looked at them both in turn and said, "Is there anything else, Agents? We are both keen to get home, and I need to see my therapist so we can start the process of recovering my identity." I smiled at Ernestina. "And we have a lot to discuss. It's been a pretty harrowing experience."

Newton stepped up close to me and pressed her finger into the middle of my chest. Her eyes narrowed and tried hard to bore into mine.

"We all know, Rogue, what has gone down these past few days. You're a lucky man, and your lack of identity has helped you. We can't prove a damned thing. It's all circumstantial, and there's not a judge in Cali who wouldn't throw it out of court. But we all know. So from here on in, Mr. Rogue, you keep your nose clean and you tread the straight and narrow. You read me?"

I shook my head. "I have no idea what you're talking about, Agent Newton. I think you have me confused with somebody else." I looked at Jones. "Probably that man in Puerto Peñasco. Can we go now?"

He nodded. "You can go now."

"Thanks for getting us across the border." I pointed at the laptop and the files. "I hope they are useful."

I opened the car door, and Ernestina climbed in the passenger side. As I went to get in, Jones said, "Ever been to New York, Mr. Rogue?"

I paused, looked back, and smiled. "I have no idea."

We drove in silence for ten or fifteen minutes, following I-19 toward Tucson. Eventually I said, "A prosecution would have been complicated, and a good defense attorney might have gotten me off, but I think there was a certain reluctance to prosecute as well."

"Yeah. I guess you're right."

"Thanks for backing me up."

"You came and saved my life."

I shrugged. "I guess I got you into this mess too."

"No, you didn't. Agustin and Pete did. And Nelson with his stupid phone call."

I studied her sad, beautiful face a moment. "I am so sorry about that."

"Don't be. You came and got me. I don't know anybody else who would have done that."

"What will you do now?"

"I don't know, but I think maybe it's best..." She trailed off, then started again. "Maybe it's best if we take a break. I think I need to come to terms with everything that has happened."

"Sure."

"Don't be hurt."

"No."

At Tucson, we merged with I-10 and headed north. At

Red Rocks, I said to her, "I won't be hurt, but I want you to promise me something."

"What?"

"You will receive a monthly income from an anonymous benefactor. I want you to accept it, I want you to go to college, and I want you to make a life for yourself, far away from Sinaloa."

She wiped her eyes and her nose on her sleeve and said, "I promise. But what are you going to do?"

I was quiet for a while. Then I told her, "I am going to New York. I need to find out who I am."

Don't miss HELL'S FURY. The riveting sequel in the Rogue Thriller series.

Scan the QR code below to purchase HELL'S FURY.
Or go to: righthouse.com/hells-fury

(Or scan the QR code below.)

DON'T MISS ANYTHING!

If you want to stay up to date on all new releases in this series, with these authors, or with any of our new deals, you can do so by joining our newsletters below.

In addition, you will immediately gain access to our entire *Right House VIP Library*, which currently includes *SIX* riveting mysteries and thrillers.

righthouse.com/email

(Easy to unsubscribe. No spam. Ever.)

ALSO BY DAVID ARCHER

Up to date books can be found at:

www.righthouse.com/david-archer

ROGUE THRILLERS

Gates of Hell (Book 1)

Hell's Fury (Book 2)

PETER BLACK THRILLERS

Burden of the Assassin (Book 1)

The Man Without A Face (Book 2)

Unpunished Deeds (Book 3)

Hunter Killer (Book 4)

Silent Shadows (Book 5)

The Last Run (Book 6)

Dark Corners (Book 7)

Ghost Operative (Book 8)

ALEX MASON THRILLERS

Origins (Prequel - Free)

Odin (Book 1)

Ice Cold Spy (Book 2)

Mason's Law (Book 3)

Assets and Liabilities (Book 4)

Russian Roulette (Book 5)

Executive Order (Book 6)

Dead Man Talking (Book 7)

All The King's Men (Book 8)

Flashpoint (Book 9)

Brotherhood of the Goat (Book 10)

Dead Hot (Book 11)

Blood on Megiddo (Book 12)

Son of Hell (Book 13)

NOAH WOLF THRILLERS

Way of the Wolf (Prequel - Free)

Code Name Camelot (Book 1)

Lone Wolf (Book 2)

In Sheep's Clothing (Book 3)

Hit for Hire (Book 4)

The Wolf's Bite (Book 5)

Black Sheep (Book 6)

Balance of Power (Book 7)

Time to Hunt (Book 8)

Red Square (Book 9)

Highest Order (Book 10)

Edge of Anarchy (Book 11)

Unknown Evil (Book 12)

Black Harvest (Book 13)

World Order (Book 14)

Caged Animal (Book 15)

Deep Allegiance (Book 16)

Pack Leader (Book 17)

High Treason (Book 18)

A Wolf Among Men (Book 19)

Rogue Intelligence (Book 20)

Alpha (Book 21)

Rogue Wolf (Book 22)

Shadows of Allegiance (Book 23)

In the Grip of Darkness (Book 24)

SAM PRICHARD MYSTERIES

Fallback (Prequel - Free)

The Grave Man (Book 1)

Death Sung Softly (Book 2)

Love and War (Book 3)

Framed (Book 4)

The Kill List (Book 5)

Drifter: Part One (Book 6)

Drifter: Part Two (Book 7)

Drifter: Part Three (Book 8)

The Last Song (Book 9)

Ghost (Book 10)

Hidden Agenda (Book 11)

SAM AND INDIE MYSTERIES

Aces and Eights (Book 1)

Fact or Fiction (Book 2)

Close to Home (Book 3)

Brave New World (Book 4)

Innocent Conspiracy (Book 5)

Unfinished Business (Book 6)

Live Bait (Book 7)

Alter Ego (Book 8)

More Than It Seems (Book 9)

Moving On (Book 10)

Worst Nightmare (Book 11)

Chasing Ghosts (Book 12)

Serial Superstition (Book 13)

CHANCE REDDICK THRILLERS

Innocent Injustice (Book 1)

Angel of Justice (Book 2)

High Stakes Hunting (Book 3)

Personal Asset (Book 4)

CASSIE MCGRAW MYSTERIES

What Lies Beneath (Book 1)

Can't Fight Fate (Book 2)

One Last Game (Book 3)

Never Really Gone (Book 4)

ALSO BY BLAKE BANNER

ALSO BY BLAKE BANNER

Up to date books can be found at:

www.righthouse.com/blake-banner

ROGUE THRILLERS

Gates of Hell (Book 1)

Hell's Fury (Book 2)

ALEX MASON THRILLERS

Odin (Book 1)

Ice Cold Spy (Book 2)

Mason's Law (Book 3)

Assets and Liabilities (Book 4)

Russian Roulette (Book 5)

Executive Order (Book 6)

Dead Man Talking (Book 7)

All The King's Men (Book 8)

Flashpoint (Book 9)

Brotherhood of the Goat (Book 10)

Dead Hot (Book 11)

Blood on Megiddo (Book 12)

Son of Hell (Book 13)

HARRY BAUER THRILLER SERIES

Dead of Night (Book 1)

Dying Breath (Book 2)

The Einstaat Brief (Book 3)

Quantum Kill (Book 4)

Immortal Hate (Book 5)

The Silent Blade (Book 6)

LA: Wild Justice (Book 7)

Breath of Hell (Book 8)

Invisible Evil (Book 9)

The Shadow of Ukupacha (Book 10)

Sweet Razor Cut (Book 11)

Blood of the Innocent (Book 12)

Blood on Balthazar (Book 13)

Simple Kill (Book 14)

Riding The Devil (Book 15)

The Unavenged (Book 16)

The Devil's Vengeance (Book 17)

Bloody Retribution (Book 18)

Rogue Kill (Book 19)

Blood for Blood (Book 20)

DEAD COLD MYSTERY SERIES

An Ace and a Pair (Book 1)

Two Bare Arms (Book 2)

Along Came A Spider (Book 28)

Cold Blood (Book 29)

Curtain Call (Book 30)

THE OMEGA SERIES

Dawn of the Hunter (Book 1)

Double Edged Blade (Book 2)

The Storm (Book 3)

The Hand of War (Book 4)

A Harvest of Blood (Book 5)

To Rule in Hell (Book 6)

Kill: One (Book 7)

Powder Burn (Book 8)

Kill: Two (Book 9)

Unleashed (Book 10)

The Omicron Kill (Book 11)

9mm Justice (Book 12)

Kill: Four (Book 13)

Death In Freedom (Book 14)

Endgame (Book 15)

ABOUT US

Right House is an independent publisher created by authors for readers. We specialize in Action, Thriller, Mystery, and Crime novels.

If you enjoyed this novel, then there is a good chance you will like what else we have to offer! Please stay up to date by using any of the links below.

Join our mailing lists to stay up to date -->
righthouse.com/email
Visit our website --> righthouse.com
Contact us --> contact@righthouse.com

facebook.com/righthousebooks
x.com/righthousebooks
instagram.com/righthousebooks

Made in the USA
Middletown, DE
11 December 2024

66698100R00172